KEEP YOUR FRIENDS CLOSE

Taylor was a TV promotions writer and producer for many before turning to writing plays and fiction. She was runner-up in the 2011 *Times*/Chicken House Children's Fiction Competition with Young Adult novel *Lovely me, Lovely You*. *Keep Your Friends Close* is her second psychological thriller for adults. June is active in the Yorkshire writing scene, including serving on the board of Script Yorkshire and taking part in Leeds Big Weekend.

🐦 @joonLT
www.junetaylor.co.uk

Th
sta
re

Also by June Taylor

Losing Juliet

KEEP YOUR FRIENDS CLOSE

JUNE TAYLOR

KILLER
READS

KillerReads
an imprint of HarperCollins*Publishers* Ltd
1 London Bridge Street
London SE1 9GF

www.harpercollins.co.uk

First published by HarperCollins*Publishers* 2018

A catalogue record for this book is available from the British Library

ISBN: 978-0-00-831811-6 (PB)

Set in Minion by Palimpsest Book Production Limited, Falkirk, Stirlingshire

Printed and bound in the UK by CPI Group (UK) Ltd, Croydon CR0 4YY

MIX
Paper from
responsible sources
FSC™ C007454

This book is produced from independently certified FSC™ paper
to ensure responsible forest management.

For more information visit: www.harpercollins.co.uk/green

for Juice and Lemon

1

Karin

Red hair, red dress.

Karin looked at the image of herself in the mirror. She liked the clash of red against red. A clashy confidence. It seemed appropriate today, her birthday. And not just any birthday; she had made it to twenty-two. At one point, she didn't think she would.

She wished her mother could see the woman she had grown into. Not just see, but know. The bundle of letters, tossed onto the bed earlier, reflected in the mirror. Still tied with the same string from five years ago. Her mother, Birgitta, had sent them all back, of course, and Karin wasn't sure why she was still hanging onto them. For several reasons, she ought to get rid. There had been no birthday card this morning. She had known there wouldn't be, there never was, but Karin had still searched through the pile of post to check. Birgitta had no idea where in the world Karin was and didn't care. But the money had gone into her account, as promised. Karin had logged in at work to check. Always true to her word. That was the scariest thing of all about her mother.

Someone at work had asked if Karin was okay. *Wasn't she feeling well? Had she received some bad news?* She felt dizzy and the pain had come quickly after that. Scurrying down the corridor, avoiding her colleagues, she had burst into Will's room and quickly shut the door. It shocked Will; he was busy painting the

1

walls, but broke off from his task to sit with her. Because Will understood. He had read every word that she and Birgitta had ever written to each other, and Karin was grateful for this place of sanctuary.

She could feel it coming on again now as she stared at her reflection in the mirror, the cycle repeating itself, and the sight of those letters only added to her distress. It was as if a sharpened icicle was being pushed into her head, boring a hole between the eyes. That's how it always came, and she couldn't stop it no matter what she did. Hands over her head to form a tight-fitting lid, as she was doing now; or elbows at right angles, squeezing against her ears to shut out the screams. Sometimes she scrunched up into a tight ball on the floor.

All this so she can never forget.

Even with her eyes closed she is still able to see his legs swinging. Side to side. A human pendulum. She runs down the garden and finds him there. In her log cabin. The steps kicked over, lying on their side. Minutes later she hears Birgitta screaming. Karin has never heard her mother scream like that before. It wasn't what she did. Normally so cool and composed, this sound is primal and raw, yelling at Karin to help get him down.

But it's too late.

It was always too late.

The episode passed, gradually, and Karin was used to it now. She just had to let it work its way through and back out again. But it still happened as often, day or night. Night-time was the worst. Everything was worse in those hot, twisted sheets of insomnia.

She raised her head slowly, checking to see whether it really had passed this time, and caught sight of herself in the mirror again; different from a few moments ago. Her cheeks were flushed, as though they had been too near a fire, and she would have to reapply her make-up. Her painted fingernails danced across her face as she wiped the sweat off it, trying to reassure her that everything was going to be okay; she hadn't been gnawing on them quite so much lately.

How can you miss someone you really hate?

Perhaps that was why Karin had unlocked the box today. On this special day. Releasing cedar wood and iris, and something else, she didn't know quite what, from beneath the lid, filling the room with Birgitta's scent. Avocado. Lavender. And a whiff of her homemade Swedish *fläderblomssaft*. In one of those letters it said that if Karin was to contact her again, she would call the police.

Were there times when her mother felt this way too? Had Karin been on her mind at any point today? Did she wake up this morning remembering it was Karin's birthday? Probably not. Probably never gave it a second thought. Not when she had sent Karin away to boarding school by the time she was eight and barely seen her since.

She checked the time on her phone then sniffed the letters one last time. Still another forty minutes before she had to be ready. Her heart raced as she began to work quickly on the knot, setting her teeth onto it, and picked out a letter.

A few paragraphs were enough. Too much. That's why she had chosen never to return to them in all these years. So why was she keeping them? Really, she knew why.

Retying the knot as swiftly as she could, stuffing the letters back inside the box, Karin noticed in one corner was the tiny pebble from Louie. The letter *K* painted on it in bright yellow, a bobbing seahorse on the other side. She held it in her hand, running her fingers over the pebble's smooth curves, not quite prepared for the rush of memories that came flooding back with this object either. Strange to think she must have kept it in her pocket for all the time she was trying to hide from Louie. Having moved in here, feeling safe again, she had put it away with the letters.

Karin threw it back into the box and, with trembling fingers, managed to close the lid. She scrambled the numbers on the padlock, but then dropped the box on the floor. It made a loud thud, just missing her foot. She picked it up and returned it to the drawer, covering it with her T-shirts.

It really was time to get rid.

Karin was not that person any more.

2

Mel

The extractor fan made its toothless rattle, sucking out stir-fry fumes and taking some Radio 6 Music with it. Mel stood at the sink, distractedly running the washing-up brush over her plate and staring out of the window. She was thinking about Karin, what to do, what to say, whether to say anything, when a bruiser of a magpie came to land in the overgrown grass. She strained her neck to see if she could spot another flash of black and white anywhere. Not that she believed in that rubbish. She had been around long enough to know that you create your own luck in this life.

The patch of grass stretching out from the kitchen window ought to have been as neat and lush as the other lawns in this row of Headingley terraces, but instead it was long and floppy, much like a student's haircut, and Mel had lost count of the number of times she had caught next door's dog fouling in it. The fence was blown down on either side, a slap-in-the-face reminder that at her time of life she shouldn't still be living in a place like this.

But it was okay for now.

A loud thump came through the ceiling, giving her a jolt. Karin must have dropped something. Mel flicked off the extractor fan, listened to Karin coming downstairs, and began to prepare herself. Returning to the sink, she picked up the wok and dunked it into the soapy water. She did a half-turn as Karin hopped into the kitchen, one sandal clicking on the Yorkshire stone flags while she attempted to catch her foot in the other, almost toppling over. Steadying herself on the unit, Karin succeeded in getting her sandal on properly and grimaced at Mel, as if acknowledging that she needed to be more ladylike. She immediately forgot this, however, and began grabbing things off the unit – lipstick, keys, pen – firing them into her handbag like missiles.

Mel dried her hands on the towel and smiled at her housemate. She detected a new perfume on Karin. It smelt expensive. The stir-fry odour was beginning to wrap around it though, concocting a rather sickly scent once it hit the back of the throat.

'Is this a bit much?' Karin asked, standing up tall, pulling her dress over her curves. It was red, halterneck, with a diamond-shaped slash that accentuated her soft white cleavage against the rest of her lightly tanned body.

'Depends what you're after,' Mel replied, raising an eyebrow. 'It's very Marilyn.' But then she thought Karin might not know who that was. 'Monroe,' she added.

'I know who Marilyn Monroe is. But she was blonde.'

'Well you look a million dollars, even so.'

'Hm. More like £3.50 from the charity shop. Don't you dare tell Aaron, or he'll think I haven't made an effort.' She pointed a warning finger at Mel, and Mel did the same back in an attempt to relax her. Karin's jitteriness suggested she might actually know something. But then she said: 'He's making a massive deal of my birthday and I'm really not sure why.'

No wonder Aaron was in such a hurry. Karin was particularly striking when she was out of her work clothes, a pair of baggy dungarees usually, and tonight her shock of red hair was let loose down her back, instead of scrunched up messily on top of her head. Another style that suited her, of course; she was young and could get away with anything.

It was precisely this, her youth, that was Aaron's biggest fear.

Although he had never said as much, Mel knew he was afraid that, one day, sooner or later, Karin would wake up and realize he was too old for her. He was twice her age after all. When he had called round a few days ago to fix the dishwasher – without succeeding – Mel had immediately picked up on the fact that he was going to ask her opinion on something. It didn't take much to work out what it was concerning, but Mel wished she could have been better prepared.

Over the three and a half years she had been living here, they had reached the point of chatting comfortably over a cup of tea when Aaron came round to sort out anything in the house. He was good that way, usually acting promptly to address any problems she brought to his attention. Trivial matters they talked about mostly: holidays; places they would like to visit; new bars and restaurants opening in Leeds; a bit of work chit-chat now and then; and the on-going battle he had against the dishwasher, with his stubborn refusal to let it beat him. They had touched on his divorce once or twice but as a rule it was no more than small talk. So, being relatively at ease in one another's company, an unspoken confidence had evolved that perhaps they could rely on the other person in a crisis, or confide, if ever there was a need.

Therefore when Aaron had come round a few days ago and begun his sentence with: 'You and Karin are pretty close, aren't you?', Mel had known exactly what was coming. Instead of answering yes, she had asked him: 'why?' To which he'd replied: 'Well, what do you think Karin would say if …?'

'If?'

Mel didn't make it easy for him. Aaron had stuck his head in the dishwasher to hide his embarrassment. He had an old-fashioned way of doing things at times, and really Mel ought to have seen this coming much sooner. It was part of his charm, too, of course, and Mel could clearly see why Karin had fallen for him. But what was she supposed to say? Even if she thought Karin was seeking a father figure, it wasn't her place to tell him this.

'I'm taking her away somewhere for her birthday,' he continued, still talking to the dishwasher. 'Somewhere special. And I'm going to – I'm thinking of asking her to marry me.' When Mel didn't respond, he resurfaced again looking sheepish. 'So erm. So, what do you think?'

'Wow,' she replied, half-laughing. Taking a moment to swallow the news. 'It's a bit soon, isn't it? You've only known her a few months. Why so quick?'

'Sometimes you get a good feeling. Don't you?'

'What about your ex-wife?'

'I doubt she'll mind.' It was Aaron's turn to let out an uncomfortable laugh. 'Let's just say I ignored my bad feelings on that one. Look I know it's swift, but I only mean for us to get engaged for now.'

Mel began to speculate then; she couldn't help it. Was the age difference, and this fear of Karin being snapped up by someone else, his only reason for accelerating things? Or was there some other motivation?

The advice Mel had given him was that perhaps he should wait a little longer, at least a few more months, otherwise he might scare Karin away. She was only twenty-two. Aaron had thanked her for listening but, when his parting words had been: 'Life's too short,' Mel could only assume that he was going to go through with it.

Karin seemed to be waiting for some sort of response from Mel, and Mel realized she had become distracted. Her head was tilted to one side, and she was chewing her lip looking questioningly at Mel.

So now she found herself in this rather awkward position. On the one hand, Aaron, asking for her discretion. On the other, Karin, a vulnerable young woman who was likely to say yes.

Mel was concerned about the repercussions from all of this.

Despite her youth and an ever-growing confidence, Karin still had no sense of her own beauty, or if she did she wasn't quite at the stage of being totally at ease with it. Nonetheless she had come a long way since Mel had first discovered her, almost a year ago now, sitting in a forlorn heap under the Dark Arches of Leeds railway station. At first, she had thought that Karin was a skinny, pubescent teenager. Sixteen at most. Mel had been shocked to discover that she was in fact much older.

Karin had filled out a bit since then, her malnourished curves realizing their full potential. She had flourished in other ways too, doing well in her job at the charity. Despite all of this, Mel knew there were still insecurities that lurked beneath. Things which, even now, Karin was reluctant to talk about. When she had first moved into the house, Mel used to hear her sometimes at night, muffled screams and sobs coming through the walls, and she would go into her room and try to console her. Although Karin had confided to an extent, Mel knew there was still something she wasn't telling her and without that insight it was difficult to guide her. Or Aaron for that matter. Not that he had taken much notice so far.

'Have you any idea where he's taking you?' Mel asked her.

Although she had enquired at the time, Aaron hadn't been prepared to share that part of his plan with Mel, other than to hint that it would be done in style, as one might expect of him, and with enough flare and fanfare to increase his chances of a positive outcome.

'I've no idea,' Karin replied. 'He just said pack an overnight bag for the weekend and you don't need a passport.' Karin stopped what she was doing, detecting there was something in the way Mel was looking at her. 'You know, don't you?'

Mel let out a sigh of responsibility. 'All I can tell you is, well, it's about more than just your birthday. Put it that way.'

'What do you mean?'

'I'm just warning you. So you can think about your answer.'

'Answer to what?' Karin gasped. Eyes opening wide, her body stiffening. 'You think he's going to propose to me?'

'Have something prepared just in case.'

Karin immediately bristled, pinning her shoulders back. 'What, like *no* you mean?'

'I didn't say that.'

Mel followed the strong outline of Karin's shoulders all the way down her arms. Shoulders that were no longer bony, arms now toned and bronzed from the many hours she spent working outdoors lately. Her skin had a body-lotion shimmer to it tonight. Mel had never known Karin to take such care over her appearance. Nail varnish too. Even toenails.

'It's your call, Karin. I'm just giving you a heads-up. It's a big decision and easy to get carried away. Don't let him hurry you.'

Karin held onto the unit to steady herself, as though she might expire if she didn't. Her face lit up by a ripening glow; it made Mel anxious to witness it.

'I love the way he makes me feel,' Karin said, giving Mel an almost pleading look.

'Oh, Karin, I know you do.' She spoke softly this time, realizing her tone maybe sounded harsh before. She moved closer to Karin, cupping her cheek gently. 'But you're twenty-two years old, and who do you have for comparison? Hm?'

Karin pulled back, although Mel still didn't let her escape, holding onto her shoulders. When Karin refused to meet her gaze, Mel lifted up her chin. 'Look,' she said, 'if Aaron loves you, he'll wait until you're ready. Five months is no time at all to get to know someone. I mean why *wouldn't* he want to marry you? Look at you, you're gorgeous. He wants to snap you up before anyone else can.'

Karin mused on that for a moment, ran her fingers through the freshly blow-dried waves that she had just created. When she realized she was undoing all her effort, she allowed her hand to flop onto the unit, trying to read Mel's thoughts. 'So *do* you know where we're going?'

'Of course I don't. He told me in strictest confidence that he was thinking of proposing when he came round to fix the dishwasher, and that's all I know. You have a bright future ahead of you, Karin. You still have to work out who you are and what you want, before you rush into anything like this.'

Karin pulled away again. 'If you're referring to—'

The back door was suddenly flung open, giving them both a start.

3

Mel

Mel looked at Karin, zipping up her mouth as Will's greasy mop of hair presented itself in the kitchen, followed by his decorating overalls and paint-splattered boots.

'Hi, Will,' said Karin, giving him an exaggerated double thumbs-up. 'Good work today. Soon be in.'

Will nodded, signing something back to Karin which Mel couldn't understand. He brushed against Mel's shoulder as he reached over to the bread bin and slung a piece of on-the-turn white bread into the toaster. Mel waved her hand in front of his face and said, 'Hi, Will.'

Will nodded, then blustered out into the hallway.

'Could you see that he eats something decent this weekend while I'm away?' asked Karin, screwing up her nose in that way of hers when she wanted something. 'It's just he never eats at work and—'

'Sure.'

It was falling to Mel to do that anyway, but she resisted mentioning it. Mel glanced out of the window, not intentionally, but Karin took that to mean she must be wondering about the garden because it prompted her to say something. 'He can't tackle that yet, Mel. He's working long hours at Ashby Road.'

'It's fine,' she replied. 'I'll see that he eats. I'll make him some pasta later.'

'Look, I've said I'll chip in a bit extra with my rent, now that I can, and Aaron says it's not a problem, Will still being here, so—'

'Read – my – lips – Karin. It's fine. He's kipping on the floor in a holey sleeping bag for God's sake.'

Karin smiled, lightly embracing her. 'Thank you,' she said. She looked embarrassed and they both knew why.

'Oh, don't go setting the two of us off,' said Mel, seeing Karin's eyes were starting to gloss. She pulled Karin into her, making the hug tighter. 'I'm so proud of you. Getting from where you were to where you are now, you've done amazing. And I'm only saying all these things because you have no one else to say them to you. As your surrogate big sister, it's my job.' Hearing a tearful snigger, Mel released her again. 'That's more like it.'

Karin had given her the title of surrogate big sister. It was a role Mel was more than happy to fulfil, especially as Karin had nowhere else to go for advice, but it was by no means easy. They came from two very different worlds.

Karin managed to sniff away any further tears, dabbing a finger under each eye to clear up the mascara runs.

'It's okay, you still look gorgeous,' said Mel. 'But just let me say one more thing and then I promise I'll shut up. Can I?' Finally she got a nod from Karin. 'Okay. So if you're going to go through with it, then get a pre-nup.' Karin began to protest. Mel caught her hands, imploring her to listen. 'I know – I know that sounds terrible and unromantic, but Aaron went through a very messy divorce.'

'What are you saying?'

'That money you got from your mother for your birthday, well it's not exactly a tenner shoved in an envelope, is it? You really should protect yourself. That's what I'm saying.'

Karin frowned, pulling her mouth to one side like a petulant teenager. 'He doesn't even know about that. I wasn't sure I'd get the money, was I? Might as well be dead to my mother.' Her words made Mel think about her own mother, sad to reflect on how much she missed her.

Karin leant back and thumped against the unit.

'Well that's good then,' said Mel. She realized Karin was staring at her. 'Not about your mother, obviously. It shows Aaron loves you for just being you. Well. I guess it does.' She paused. 'There is one thing though.'

'What? Tell me, Mel.'

'He's bloody useless at fixing kitchen appliances.'

This had become something of a joke between them. Karin took a playful swipe, and Mel put up her hands as a shield. Then Karin stopped fooling around, folding her arms like the petulant teenager again. 'Someone might want to snap him up too, you know, Mel.'

'Of course they might. I can totally see why you've fallen for him. He's charming, funny, handsome. But don't rush it, okay? That's all I'm saying. Just do what you think is right for you. You deserve to be happy.'

Karin sank her teeth into her bottom lip as a loud rapping, on the front door this time, broke into their conversation.

'Shit,' said Karin, straightening her dress nervously.

Aaron came into the kitchen dangling his keys. 'Hope you don't mind,' he said, referring to the fact he had let himself in.

Mel shrugged. 'You're the landlord.'

He hovered for a second, waiting until it was safe to give Mel a secret wink. When she refused to participate he seemed disappointed, and maybe a little embarrassed. 'You going out tonight, Mel?' he asked.

'Me? No, I have some work to catch up on. But I'll be thinking of you both on your lovely *birthday* weekend.'

'Well erm, my suitcase is in the hallway,' said Karin.

'Great. I'll load it into the car,' Aaron replied, rubbing his hands with renewed excitement. 'See you later then, Mel.'

'Don't do anything I wouldn't do,' she shouted as he disappeared again. 'And don't you either,' she added, pointing her finger at Karin who was still hovering awkwardly.

'Really appreciate you telling me, Mel,' she whispered.

'Let me know how you get on. Okay? And just remember what I've said.'

Karin nodded.

Despite her underlying vulnerability, Mel knew that Karin could also be headstrong when she wanted to be. But at least she had given her something to think about.

Karin pushed her handbag onto her shoulder, emitting a kind of schoolgirl squeal as she ran her nails across her teeth to show both her fear and excitement. 'Wish me luck,' she said.

Mel thought she had gone, but then Karin rushed back in again to say: 'Forgot to mention it, Mel. I've transferred five thousand pounds into your account today. To cover rent, bills, all my arrears. Plus a little bit extra to say thank you.'

'Aw, Karin. That's very generous of you.'

'I know it's more than I owe, but it's the least I can do.'

'You didn't have to do that. But thank you.' Mel gave her a kiss on the cheek. 'Now off you go.'

Karin smiled, blowing her a kiss in return.

'And remember to enjoy yourself,' Mel shouted.

She waited to hear the front door close then poured herself a large glass of wine. Not long after sitting down to relax, she heard Will padding about in the kitchen, probably snacking on toast and jam. Thinking of her promise to Karin, she returned to the kitchen and offered him some wine, remembering that he didn't drink, and told him that she would make pasta in a little while.

Will gave her one of his looks that shivered down her spine then went back upstairs.

4

Karin

The Friday night queues out of Leeds had died down, although there was still a weekend frenzy about the way cars jerked and swerved across the baking tarmac. It was 7.15, the evening warm and sultry. Even the buildings looked too hot, the bricks of the older ones as well as the glassier newer ones straining to stand up tall.

Crossing the city always prompted memories of when she had first arrived here. Back then all she was interested in was huddling in shop doorways and under bridges down by the canal or the River Aire. That secret part of her life, which Aaron hadn't known anything about. Not at first. He was under the impression that Karin had answered an advert for a room to rent. Mel had preserved her secret, thankfully, knowing how ashamed Karin was about this aspect of her life. But in the end, Karin had told Aaron herself because there were so many other things she would never be able to share with him and this was one thing she could.

He didn't even know about Louie.

Karin shifted in the passenger seat as her temperature began to rise. Yet at the same time a chill dug into her skin as the rawness of that winter, after she had run away, returned. A pop-up tent and warm sleeping bag were all that she had wished for on a daily basis. That or some money for a hostel. Apart from her phone, the bundle of letters and the clothes she was wearing,

16

her only possessions had been a hairbrush and a worn-out toothbrush. Karin had left in a hurry, not wanting to make it look like she was leaving at all.

Afraid to go. Afraid of what might happen if she stayed.

It was her dad who always said that her hair was her best feature, so even on the streets she didn't want it to go into matted dreadlocks, because she knew her dad wouldn't like that. He was already dead by then, but it still mattered. Brushing her hair obsessively nine or ten times a day would often attract attention. Karin made sure she was drunk and past caring, in case the attention wasn't the best kind, but she had Will as her protector and he kept her safe.

Whether her mother had realized it or not – more likely an oversight on her part – she had still been paying for Karin's phone contract back then. However, unless Karin could get into a hostel to charge it up, it had been of limited use and she'd had to guard it with her life. Staring out of the car window at the passing trees, Aaron by her side at the wheel, she could, even now, remember the excitement of seeing all those messages appearing, and how quickly it would turn to guilt.

Always Louie:

Where have you gone? Please come back, let's talk.

Never anything from her mother.

Karin had carried the bundle of letters stuffed into the waist-band of her knickers. She knew it was risky hanging onto them, because they could do real damage in the wrong hands, but without them she had nothing.

She was no one.

Despite having Will, trusted friend and loyal companion, those days on the streets were the loneliest of all. She often wondered, had Birgitta been aware of her living rough, might she have given her the lump sum sooner, instead of making her wait until she turned twenty-two? Unlikely though, knowing her mother. Because the deal was that if Karin didn't finish her schooling and go to university, the money would be stopped, with no more until today. What little Karin had left from her hotel earnings, she had given to Louie, leaving herself with just enough for the train fare to Leeds, plus a small amount besides until she found her feet again. But Karin had got drunk on the train on the way over, and then she was robbed.

Karin was pretty sure it wouldn't have made the slightest bit of difference if she had known. Birgitta was a Swedish torpedo. That's what her dad used to call her. He said that no one could ever stop her or change her direction. He certainly couldn't, and Karin couldn't either. Even as a child, Karin wondered why her parents were together; her dad was always hovering and quivering in the background. Without doubt, this sharp-pointed focus was the reason for her mother's success as a world-class designer, but it torpedoed through everything else. Every*one* else.

Karin knew it had been a mistake to start looking at those letters before setting off this evening. She had managed to ignore them until today, despite clinging to them all this time. Her own letters were wound up in that bundle too, of course. It was the bereavement counsellor's suggestion that they write to each other after her dad died. On paper, and with stamps. So they could think about what they wanted to say to each other, before sending. Safer that way. Better than any text or email fired off in the heat of the moment. Karin had still managed to fire off, even so. And then one day all the letters were returned to her in a bulging jiffy bag, along with the words:

'Karin,
    *I suggest you read back over these. I hope you have a good
    life, but I no longer want to be a part of it, nor you a part of
    mine.*
    Mamma (no longer).

Remember, if you come anywhere near me again, try to contact me in any way, I shall go straight to the police. Your accusation has ruined my life.

scribbled on a Svendsen business card.

Karin could recall sitting on her bed in her room at school, putting the letters in date order. '*From Karin*'. '*From Mamma*'. The word 'love' never came into it. Then she had tied them up and hidden them away. Since then only two people had read them.

First Louie. And then Will.

No one else ever would. Not even Mel.

Definitely not Aaron.

Throw them away, Karin.

She had bought the box when she moved in with Mel, using the date of her dad's death as the security code. Another option would have been to use the date of her stepdad's death, as a sort of prompt for why she shouldn't look inside, but she decided the box alone was enough of a reminder. One of the letters was missing; she had set fire to it at school. It went up in an orange angry fireball. At a time when Karin most needed her mother's support, she got nothing but criticism and a whole heap of deceit.

Karin didn't blame herself for what happened. She might be sorry, but it wasn't *all* her fault.

'You okay?'

She felt Aaron's hand on her thigh. It pulled her back to the present and she managed a thin smile. Sweat was beading on her forehead. She lowered the window for a blast of 30-mile-an-hour air. It was enough to cool her. Aaron gave her a look; he preferred the air-con. But his expression also said that he was making allowances for her birthday.

Then he seemed worried. 'Is it a headache coming on, Karin? Do you want me to pull over?'

'No. No, I'm fine,' she replied, smiling at his kindness. 'Just hot, that's all.'

They slowed for the next set of traffic lights. Aaron began to get agitated as they waited, his hands turning white from gripping the steering wheel so tightly. Karin wasn't sure why, at first, until she realized that three young lads in their souped-up Ford Focus were making gestures at him. Intent on getting a reaction, they began shouting: 'Come on, old fella. Give it some metal. Wouldn't mind a ride of your daughter.'

'Idiots,' said Karin as their car sped away with a blast of exhaust. She could sense a part of Aaron wanted to take them on, checking his mirrors for a way through, but she managed to distract him by putting on his 'Music To Drive For' compilation, fast-forwarding through Travis and Coldplay. Karin patted him on the leg, because this was worse than not using the air-con, but it forced another smile out of him. It had taken her a long while to feel brave enough to do this kind of thing. Desperate to be his contemporary and not some alien from another generation, initially she felt obliged to like whatever he liked. Now that she knew him better she could relax and be herself, most of the time.

'So where are we going?' she asked as they approached signs for both the M62 and M1 up ahead. Aaron wouldn't say, but when they turned onto the M621 she thought she might have an idea. 'So is it Manchester? Chester? Oh God, if it's the Lakes I didn't pack any outdoorsy stuff.'

'It's not the Lakes,' he said, grinning.

'You tease-ball. I hate you.'

Aaron smiled. 'You'll love it,' he said.

He was always so keen to please and surprise. But what she liked most about him was that he didn't make her feel like she was on a runaway train, about to crash. This was a proper romance, not a teenage train wreck. Karin began to contemplate him with an intensity neither one of them would have felt comfortable with had Aaron not been driving. Either that or he was pretending not to notice. Aaron was sweet like that.

What if Mel was right about this weekend? At this precise

moment she was feeling somewhere between terrified and ecstatic at the prospect of someone asking to marry her. Not just anyone. Aaron. Marriage was not something she expected would ever happen to her. Not something she had even considered for herself, something other people did. And Mel was right about it being sudden. Whirlwind. Wasn't that the term? They had only been together a few months. So did she really need to make that final commitment yet? Karin was in no doubt that she loved Aaron, but weren't they doing fine as they were? She had only just got her life back together.

Having abandoned her education, Karin was now doing far better than she ever imagined, with a level of responsibility she probably ought to have a string of qualifications for. The pay was poor in the charity sector, but the cause was certainly worth fighting for, and for the first time, she felt valued and needed. That wasn't even about money. It was about hard work and a self-belief she had never had in all the years of being crushed by her mother, feeling, always, the inadequacy of her existence; the burden of living in Birgitta's frozen shadow. It was a cruel irony that the one inferior product her mother had designed should be the one she gave birth to. Karin was never allowed to forget that, but now the real Karin had emerged. Thanks to Mel. And also to Louie. She couldn't forget the part that Louie had played in her recovery. But it was Mel who, in the end, had got Louie off her back and she could never forget that either.

The money she had received today from her mother's accountant would certainly change things. Almost a million pounds was going to make a huge difference to her life. It meant that she no longer had to scrounge off Mel for one thing, and she could pay her own way with Aaron too. At the moment, he picked up the tab for practically everything, but this enormous sum of money would set them on equal terms. No longer feeling like she had something to prove just because of her age. Plus Aaron had a tendency to spoil her. Take this birthday treat for instance, whatever it was, it wasn't necessary. Karin had grown up with wealth and status and found it loveless and cold. Not that she wasn't grateful. Scraping away at the very bottom of human existence had taught her what it was really like to be hungry and afraid. So she could fully appreciate this lifeline that she had been thrown. And to think that she had once been homeless, yet could now afford to buy a place of her own, was mind-blowing.

Karin actually wanted to tell Birgitta these things, to say thank you, but she knew that wouldn't be possible. Her life would be over just as soon as she made contact again.

Pushing aside this regret, but with a giddiness in her stomach, Karin looked out at the dramatic Pennine sky and the outline of Manchester beginning to take shape in the distance. She thought she understood now what Mel was trying to say. This was a pivotal moment, a chance for an even better Karin to flourish, to be totally independent and self-sufficient.

A golden opportunity, and Karin did not intend to squander it.

After a few more moments of reflection, she was convinced that she had found the perfect solution. Turning to Aaron again she began to study him with the same intensity as before. What was to stop her from having her independence, but with Aaron as her husband? They could buy a place together, build a joint future, while still pursuing their own individual goals. Isn't that what people did?

Don't rush, take your time, don't let him hurry you.

If she said 'no' or 'not just yet', she might lose him. And she loved him. Because Aaron didn't make her feel like she was on that runaway train.

Even if she still was.

5

Karin

The lanes of traffic filed past and slowed down on the M62, the same cars repeating the same pattern in the roadworks. Karin's phone was resting on her lap. Its sudden ping brought her out of her reverie. When she saw what Mel had sent her, she laughed. A photo of Will tucking into a plate of pasta, and a message:

> *BOTH OKAY.*
> *HOPE YOU ARE TOO.*
> *LOVE MEL & WILL*
> *XX*

If Mel had chosen to walk by that night after tripping over her outstretched legs, as she sat in her usual spot under the damp stone ceiling of the Dark Arches, Karin might not even be here now. She knew she looked and smelt like rotting garbage, a stinking heap cluttering up the pavement, yet something in Mel had made her stop. She had bent down to ask her name, wrapped a scarf around her neck and given her gloves to put over her freezing fingers, white and numb at the ends. Then she began asking questions: *Why was Karin in such a state? How had it come to this?*

Some people bothered to do that.

When Mel reached her limit, Karin watched her go, calling,

'You have a nice night.' That's what happened: she was used to it. So twenty minutes later, to see her returning with piping hot coffee and a cheeseburger, seemed like a miracle. Mel also gave her money for a hostel, making Karin promise that she would be sure to find one. Karin didn't let on that it was too late for that night, but she did use the money for the following one.

'Is this where I can find you?' she enquired before abandoning her to the cold again. Karin remembered that question had made her laugh, sitting in this gloomy Victorian tunnel under the railway station, full of shadows, and thunderous noises from above.

'Yes, this is my current address,' she replied. 'The Dark Arches, Leeds.'

A couple of days later Mel came back to see her, took her to lunch in a greasy-spoon, where Karin ate like an abandoned dog. They chatted for a while and when she had finished eating, Mel offered her the spare room in the house that she was renting. 'It's in Headingley,' she said, as if Karin might actually care. 'Look I can't bear to see a young girl like you out here on the streets. It's not right.'

Mel's kindness stretched beyond the initial trial period of a couple of nights. If Karin could find herself a job, then she was welcome to stay. In the meantime, she let her off paying rent and Karin did some volunteering with the homeless charity, helping out with the *Love an Empty* scheme. Eventually they asked her to manage the project on Ashby Road. It paid next to nothing and she still couldn't contribute very much, but Karin always promised to repay Mel.

'In a year's time, I should be back on my feet. When I turn twenty-two.'

Mel always said it didn't matter about paying her back, just to contribute as soon as she was able. That's why today had felt particularly special. Although Karin did consider giving her more than five thousand pounds, she appreciated that Mel would probably be insulted if she did. However, it bothered Karin that she hadn't been a terribly good housemate in return, spending most of her time at Aaron's place rather than in Headingley. So Karin had decided to make it up to her with flowers, meals out, extravagant presents instead; more Mel's style in any case. Starting next week, she would take her to the new Swank restaurant that had opened down on The Calls. Mel said the other day how much she would love to go there, but could never afford it.

A few months after moving in, she was introduced to Aaron and they had started going out together. It still gave Karin a flutter in her stomach thinking about that, even now. He had come round to fix a temperamental dishwasher – the very same – and an instant spark had fired up between them. Mel teased Karin relentlessly, but without holding back on her concerns over his age. She clearly believed it would fizzle out soon enough. It hadn't though, which left Karin feeling somewhat guilty.

'You don't know anyone who'd be suitable for Mel, do you?' she asked, twirling her hair round her finger. Aaron's laughter surprised her, but then she realized the question had come from nowhere. 'No, I'm serious though. You must know some decent men out of all your work contacts, surely. It's not like she's unattractive.' He gave her a rather noncommittal half-shrug. 'It's just I feel bad sometimes about her sitting in the house on her own, when I'm out all the time with you. Hardly see her these days and she's been so kind to me.' Aaron gave her another shrug, implying that wasn't Karin's problem. 'You know what she did for me, Aaron.'

'I'll have a think.'

She leaned over to kiss him on the cheek.

'Can't promise anything, mind,' he added.

'No, I know. But she deserves someone nice, that's all.'

Perhaps Mel's problem was that she was too good-natured, and people took advantage. Karin was aware that Mel dabbled in internet dating from time to time, but without any success as far as she could make out, and Mel had hinted at some difficult scenarios, people in it for the wrong reasons.

Aaron accelerated and at last they were moving again. Karin turned to him and smiled, sinking her head into the headrest with thoughts of how much she had come to love him these past months and how fortunate she was to have found him.

He was wearing well for a man in his mid-forties, a full head of brown hair, and a pretty good physique through playing squash and sessions at the gym. Not handsome as such, but he had a face that got more interesting with age and to Karin that was preferable to handsome. It wasn't the crazy, wild passion she had once known, but she associated that with the past in any case, and her adolescence was thankfully behind her now. Louie had been a big part of her initial healing process, and without Louie she would never have survived, but the wild, experimental journey they went on together wasn't really who she was. It had left an emotional scar, on both sides she didn't doubt, and she hoped that Louie had also met someone else by now. She closed her eyes to squeeze out the memory, wanting only Aaron to be in her head and to imagine what it might be like waking up to his face every morning for the rest of her life.

She swallowed, telling herself to slow down.

Aaron glanced over. 'You seem deep in thought,' he said, giving her hair a stroke.

Karin flushed. The likelihood of him proposing in any case was pretty remote.

Mel had got it wrong.

A sharp pain suddenly jabbed her forehead and she tried to massage it away. If she ever did get married, would she write and tell her mother the news? *After* the event, obviously. Like Birgitta had done to her. But Karin knew that any letter she sent would only come back in the post unopened. Or perhaps her mother would even go so far as to get the police to return it to her, so they could arrest her at the same time. As her dad used to say, Birgitta's decisions were set in ice.

'You sure you're okay?'

The sound of Aaron's voice snapped her back into the moment, and Karin realized she had become unbearably hot. Her dress was clinging to her and her scalp felt prickly. 'Yeah, sorry,' she said. She lowered the window and stuck her head out, not bothering about what it might do to her hair at this speed. 'I was just thinking about where we might be going.'

'You'll soon see,' said Aaron, holding her hair down until she came back in again and put the window up. 'You look amazing tonight, by the way.'

'Thanks. You don't look too bad yourself.'

The sharp blast of air seemed to work, and Karin visualized them making plans for the future, getting their first place together. A house with a garden where children could play. A log cabin, and plenty of long grass to run around in and be wild. She would be a good mother. Stay home and spend time with her kids. There would be more than one; an only child was a miserable child. She would wrap them in love and laughter, never abandon or ignore them and definitely never send them away.

And Aaron would make a great father.

But what if he ever *did* find out? What then? Aaron didn't deserve to be hurt, not again. His marriage had ended badly. Infidelity, not on his part, followed by a messy divorce.

Karin's heart began to thump against her chest. She wrapped her fingers round her wrist, something the bereavement counsellor had taught her to do at school to force the positive thoughts through. It was the bereavement counsellor who had explained about the post-traumatic stress headaches too. She said Karin had been through a lot. The strained relationship with her mother. Losing her father. Her stepdad's suicide. She asked if there might be one incident in particular which could be behind such violent

27

headaches. Karin never told her. Apart from her mother, there were only two people who knew the truth.

Will and Louie.

She trusted Will with her life.

Louie, she was never going to see again.

Karin closed her eyes, trying to hang onto these positives. When she opened them again she registered they were heading north up the M6, the sign for Morecambe having fleetingly caught her eye. 'Erm. Are we going to the coast?' she asked, turning quickly to look at the sign even though she knew it would have disappeared by now.

Aaron didn't pick up on the panic in her voice. 'We might be,' he said, a boyish grin spreading across his face.

But the signs repeatedly said Morecambe. And after a while there it was. Marine Road West. She could see it up ahead, a building of elegant white curves. Of all the places to bring her. Why here? It was her birthday, a simple meal in Leeds would have been perfect. Couldn't they just go back to Leeds? Couldn't she suggest that? Was it too late to turn round?

They swung into the car park of The Midland hotel, gleaming white in all its restored Art Deco glory, and Karin felt herself shaking. As beautiful and magnificent as it was, she never intended coming back here.

Not ever.

It stood before her now like a defiant ghost, keeper of memories she didn't want to revive. Karin held onto her wrist so tightly her fingers turned white. She thought she had left all this behind.

6

Mel

Mel had heard Will come down for a second time, boil the kettle then go back upstairs. That was nearly an hour ago. Now she was in the kitchen chopping up ingredients for a simple pasta dish.

They had taken Will in on the *Room for a Night* scheme, another initiative of the charity Karin worked for, but he had been here for nearly eight weeks now 'as a friend', which wasn't really how Mel had understood it would be. She didn't mind as such, not really. The Ashby Road project was very near its completion, so he would be gone soon enough. It was just that, as Karin was hardly around, the responsibility for Will was falling mostly on her shoulders.

Mel took the same precautions with Will as she had done with Karin in those early stages: stowing her handbag and papers away, changing passwords on her computer and locking it in her desk whenever she went out. Mel was in the habit of such measures in any case, given the nature of her job, handling complaints at the call centre. But taking a total stranger off the street and into the house was a risk. She was also aware of the scare stories surrounding such types, suddenly turning on those who showed them kindness, repaying them with violence. And worse. It had been a gamble taking Karin in, of course, but Karin was different.

Most of the time Will stayed in his room reading, curled up in his sleeping bag on the floor with a mug of tea. All Mel really

29

knew about him was what Karin had told her: that he was born deaf, rejected by his parents, let down badly by the system and ended up living on the streets, which was where he and Karin had become friends. Allies too, apparently. However, Karin's track record on being able to judge a person's character was not exactly reliable. Not if Louie was anything to go by.

Will could be any age from twenty-five to forty; his long Russian beard and dark eyes gave away few clues and Mel found his Rasputin stare most unnerving. He seldom smiled. She had begun to feel the tiniest flicker of unease in his presence. Perhaps it was his silence. It definitely wasn't the same as with Karin. Mel hadn't wanted to leave her festering on the streets of Leeds, falling prey to anyone who came across her. At the same time, she certainly didn't want to make a habit of feeding and housing all of Leeds' waifs and strays. That would be a lifetime's work. Besides, Mel had her own sob story. Growing up with a sick mother and not much money was far from easy. Her education suffered, as did her youth, both seeming to slip away from her at an alarming rate.

Mel tapped lightly on Will's door. She knew this wasn't necessary, but she did it anyway, pushing the door open slowly so as not to startle him. Will was leaning against the radiator, his head bowed into a book. His sleeping bag was in a heap next to a small, tatty rucksack blotted with greasy patches; a few old newspapers were piled on the pillow. His decorating overalls had landed on top of his work boots. They were shabby too, a hand-out, like everything else he owned. His elbow was resting on a tower of books stacked up by his side. Will seemed to be acquiring more and more, perhaps for the first time having somewhere to store them. The ironing board, laundry basket and other household paraphernalia had been pushed into the corner so that Will wouldn't feel quite so cramped. That was Karin's doing. The room smelt mouldy, due more to the leaky roof than to Will, to be fair. It was a matter Aaron hadn't got around to addressing, although he said it was on his list.

Mel waved her arms to get Will's attention. He looked up and she began a ridiculous mime of shovelling food into her mouth with an imaginary knife and fork. Will closed his book and stood up, following her downstairs.

'If you want to wash your hands,' she suggested when they got to the kitchen; once again performing a stupid hand-washing action pointing to the sink. Will never seemed to scrub up clean, and Mel longed to cut off his hair and get rid of that beard. Aaron had donated some of his clothes, which Will had changed into, but even then he just looked like a dirty homeless man in a smart man's shirt and trousers.

After giving his hands a cursory rinse, Will continued eyeing her as she dished out the pasta.

'I take it you still don't want any,' she said, pointing to her wine glass.

Will shook his head.

She handed him his plate and some cutlery, indicating it was fine for him to eat in the lounge. He hung back, waiting for Mel to lead the way and then sat down cross-legged on the floor, propped against the other sofa.

Mel was glad of the distance he put between them, but still said: 'You don't have to sit there, you know.' He was looking the other way, so probably didn't even realize she had spoken. She handed him the remote, thinking he might need the subtitles.

The clock on the TV box said 7.40. Still no news from Karin as yet and Mel had been keeping a close eye on her phone. Had he proposed yet? If so, what had she said?

She realized Will was staring.

'Good?' she asked, putting her thumb up.

He gave a solemn bow of his head, continuing to eat.

'Actually, do you mind if I take a photo to send to Karin? She likes to know you're eating properly.'

Will shrugged, acknowledging the fact that he probably didn't have any choice.

'She worries about you, you know,' she added, getting him to lift his plate in the air and give a thumbs-up. A smile was out of the question, it seemed, even for Karin.

'Thanks,' she said, feeling the need to excuse herself. 'I have to go and do some work now. But feel free to stay and watch TV.'

Mel went into the kitchen and drank a glass of water, taking another with her upstairs. When she got to her room she thought again about Will's cold watchful stare. How he moved silently about the house. Suddenly it began to bother her that she had left him downstairs on his own. She liked to monitor his movements, just in case. There had been one or two issues of late.

7

Karin

The girl on reception gave her a glossy smile while Aaron was busy signing the checking-in form in his illegible sprawl. Karin didn't recognize the girl.

She looked around nervously; her mouth had gone dry. Might Louie still work here? What if Louie discovered that she was living in Leeds and that she had lied about going to the States? Aaron's details were in the system now; it would be easy to track her down properly this time. Could she *never* escape?

Karin felt her whole life unravelling.

Please let Louie not be here any more.

When Aaron was done with the paperwork he put his arm across Karin's shoulders and kissed the top of her head. Their suitcases were instantly swept away as someone else escorted them to the lift. It was strange to be back here. As far as Karin was concerned the past had no place in the present. The only fragments of time she actually wanted to keep were pieced together in the scrapbook of her dad. Not a real scrapbook, the one she carried in her head. Everything else could go.

Memories are pebbles. Pebbles on a beach. Pick up the ones you want and put them in your pocket. Throw the rest into the sea.

It was something else the bereavement counsellor had taught her. But at the time, Karin had only been able to do the pebble thing in her imagination. Her school was a long way from the

33

sea. This was another reason for heading to Morecambe, so she could see those pebbles exploding into the waves.

Karin taught Louie to do the same. They would stand on the beach side by side and throw their 'bad shit' into the water together. Sometimes a pebble might wash back up onto the shore; the counsellor warned this might happen. 'Throw it away again, Karin. That's if you still don't want to keep it. Although, you might find that you do. It happens.'

She never did. She would never want to keep any of them, especially the most persistent one of all which drifted back in on every tide. Her stepdad swinging from the beam. That one would never go. Nor would Birgitta. But then Louie became one of those pebbles too. So what on earth was she doing back here in Morecambe at The Midland hotel? After everything she had done to get away. As if leaving Louie hadn't been agonizing enough.

Karin scanned the foyer. It was magnificent, but she felt exposed. She looked beyond the brilliance of the architecture, the white curvature of the walls; instead, taking note of each member of staff who happened to glide past. With any luck, by now the entire workforce had changed. Working at The Midland had been a lifeline to her, at least for a while. It had given her a focus, a purpose, after she had bailed out of sixth form, trying to get as far away from school as possible. It was Louie who had thrown her this lifeline, putting in a good word when the hotel needed seasonal staff.

As they stepped into the lift, her heart was pounding so hard she feared it would give her away, that Aaron would be able to hear it above the lift's murmuring as they ascended. She felt him staring, desperate to please her and no doubt trying to gauge her reaction. Although she wanted to make him feel at ease, it was impossible to meet his gaze or give him any sense of reassurance. Not yet. Not until she knew it was safe.

Their bodies jolted to a standstill. Aaron hung back for Karin to step out of the lift first. He had booked them into a luxury roof-top suite. Karin was able to picture it before the door was even opened: the quirky furniture, rotating chairs, the sea view extending the full length of the balcony with its Art Deco curve. The red cushions. Decadent bathroom. Sadly, all she wanted to do was lock herself away in the cleaning cupboard along the corridor.

Why on earth hadn't he asked her?

'You okay?' said Aaron.

'Yes,' she replied, suffocating under the pressure. 'It's just a bit strange to be back here, that's all.'

'In a good way I hope?'

She let the question drift.

'You always said how wonderful this place is, and I thought—'

'Of course in a good way.' Karin leaned into him to show her appreciation. 'It *is* amazing. I-I suppose I just never imagined I'd return here again. Not as a guest. Well not as anything really. And it costs a fortune to stay in one of these suites in peak season.'

'Well you're worth it, aren't you?' Aaron replied, squeezing her shoulders together as he opened the door with his other hand. 'I know you hate extravagance, but I can assure you I negotiated a very good rate in exchange for putting some corporate events their way.' He tapped his nose, adding, 'It's all about connections.'

Once they were inside with the door closed, Karin began to feel a sense of relief. Able to process things without such trepidation racing through her mind, and she told herself that she would soon get over the shock. It was unlikely that Louie still worked here; had probably moved away by now.

'Well, you weren't wrong,' Aaron remarked, flinging himself onto the bed, hands behind his head, lapping up his surroundings. He beckoned Karin over, so she went and perched beside him, sinking into the luxury of the mattress. Aaron may have noticed that she was clutching her stomach, but didn't say anything if he did. She could feel the tension knotting like seaweed inside it. A knock at the door saved her from having to explain, although she still sprung off the bed and prepared to dart into the bathroom. On seeing that it was one of the older members of staff, who didn't seem to register her presence, she could relax again.

He set their suitcases down by the bed and gave Aaron a nod after a tip was pushed into his fist on his way out. Aaron closed the door, his hand lingering on the handle. He took another moment or two to consider Karin, then crossed over to the window.

The panoramic view of Morecambe Bay was stunning. But it unnerved her. Nevertheless she made an effort to see it through Aaron's eyes and went to join him. Aaron seemed grateful for this and draped his arms around her neck.

Karin shuddered at the memories circling out there beneath the darkening sky: *throwing her pebbles into the sea; two figures grappling on the wet sands.*

'Not too shabby a view. Is it?' said Aaron.

She couldn't allow him to see the swell of tears gathering behind her eyes and turned away from him.

He was distracted though, luckily, checking the time on his phone. 'I think we should go and get some supper,' he said. 'Are you okay to go straight down? It's getting late.'

Karin sniffed. She had somehow managed not to let a single tear fall and was fanning her arms down her dress. '*Come ready*, you said.' It did occur to her at that point to suggest room service, but she knew this wasn't really an option. And what if Louie was on duty and brought it to their room? She tried to rid herself of that thought before it expanded any further. Besides, Aaron had already said how much he was looking forward to dining in the Sun Terrace and what a stunning location it was. Karin didn't want to disappoint him. He had gone to such lengths. All for her.

He guided her out into the corridor in a gentlemanly fashion. She liked those old school touches, the way he held doors open for her, the small gifts he presented her with and the way he sometimes took her in his arms and glided her round the room in a slow dance. She welcomed his calmness too. With Louie it was always fast and intense, driven by the brashness and daring of youth. A rough-and-ready sort of love which spun out of control. Karin should have ended it far sooner than she did.

Closing her eyes, she drew in a deep breath and made herself smile. Louie no longer worked here. She was absolutely certain of it.

'Oh. But we ought to take the stairs,' she said, immediately thrown into turmoil when Aaron started heading back down the corridor to get the lift. 'They're really something. You need to see them.'

The staircase was indeed a stunning feature of this hotel, but it was a delaying tactic on her part. To chance upon Louie directly out of the lift would be like stepping in front of that train. At least the slow, downward twist of the stairs would give her more time to think, and Aaron seemed pleased that she was at last entering into the spirit of this special place.

Karin forced him to linger at the top of the Art Deco stairway, the red carpet spiralling all the way down in an elegant shell shape to the entrance hall below. 'Wait though,' she said, still not permitting him to set off until he had also looked up to admire the fresco on the ceiling.

The curved handrail offered itself to her like an old friend. Smooth and solid, it seemed to want to take away some of her stress as her hand wrapped tightly around it. Karin closed her eyes again, feeling for the first step with her toes. These were stairs not to be rushed, like red piano keys unfurling underfoot; a stairway to be seen on, to savour, evoking a bygone era but with a modern-day twist. Karin turned to Aaron and smiled. She was about to remark on some of these things but stopped herself when all the other memories came crashing against her chest;

feeling like she was being crushed; causing her to stumble. Aaron was there to catch her, insisting on holding her arm the rest of the way down. Karin couldn't help thinking that every step she took was delivering her that bit closer to Louie.

8

Louie

Louie woke up that morning with the same thing on her mind as every other morning. Her hand reached out across the bed.

But she wasn't there.

Louie pulled back the curtain, flinging the window upwards to fill her lungs from the salty mists of sea air floating past, using the broken broom handle to prop the window open once the frame had stopped rattling. Even before filling the kettle, she felt her nostalgia settling in once again, knowing it would tighten its grip as the day wore on.

Today was Karin's birthday.

Breakfast in bed, small gift to open. Later on, they would take a stroll on the beach. A few hours painting and lovemaking, then maybe popcorn and a film in the evening when they had finished their shift. Karin wouldn't want to go out; she rarely did after work, and certainly not with anyone else. She liked to have Louie all to herself.

Louie moved the mannequin into the corner on her way to the bathroom, having to dodge the various canvases as she went. Some propped against walls, pieces of furniture, some already bubble-wrapped and others still waiting to be framed. The whole place looked more like an artist's studio these days. When Karin was around she had forced Louie to confine the art to one area of the room with a screen round it, as a way of keeping the living space separate. Now it was allowed to spill everywhere. Strange artefacts occupied many of the surfaces, things washed up by the sea. They had collected most of it together. Shells. Bits of wood, all shapes and sizes. Lengths of rope and faded fishing nets. Glass bottles, of interest because of their shape or colour. Broken toys, back from unexpected voyages, nibbled by sharks and other weird-looking sea creatures. Rusted chains. A selection of worn-out coins. A pile of pebbles. Large and small.

The kettle fizzed into a frenzy and switched itself off. Louie slopped a generous amount of milk into her mug but left the teabag in the other to brew a bit longer, the way Karin liked it. After a few seconds of staring at Karin's mug, she tipped it away and flung it into the sink, breaking the handle.

This room was full of reminders.

The mannequin had on one of Karin's old T-shirts and a pair of cut-off denim shorts which she had also left behind. Louie rubbed the ends of the T-shirt between her fingers, releasing a tiny bit of her into the air, because it still held a faint trace of Karin's scent. Something caught her eye on the shelf. A previous birthday offering, a flick-book of the sea that she had made for Karin's twentieth. As she fanned the pages, a mini-breeze wafted into her face and a tiny seahorse bobbed up and down on the watercolour waves in the bottom corner of each page.

'Don't you like it?' she had asked, because Karin hadn't said anything at first. Then she realized she was crying, said it was the best birthday present she had ever been given and kissed Louie on the lips.

Louie tried desperately to recreate that, how it felt to have Karin's lips pressing warm against hers. As time went on she could feel it less and less. Karin had left a void in her life the size of Morecambe Bay. Equally unpredictable, the swirling tide pulling her down when she least expected it. For a long time afterwards, Louie tried to find her. In the note that Karin had left, she said she had gone to the States, although Louie didn't necessarily believe that. She phoned and messaged her constantly in the hope that Karin would let slip where she had really gone. Was she okay? Why had she left in such a hurry? Did Louie do something wrong? Wasn't she happy? Had something happened? Why wouldn't she speak to her? Then the voice of an American girl had finally convinced her, but it had wounded Louie more than anything to think that Karin might have found someone else so quickly. Not long after that, she must have changed her number because Louie couldn't get hold of her any more.

Despite this, she viewed the separation as a temporary thing. Karin would come back to her one day because they were linked by an inexplicable force, connecting them through life, death, and forever. Meanwhile, Louie found a certain amount of peace in her painting. Her obsession had become her therapy. Although it was as bitter as it was sweet, because Karin was the one who had always encouraged her, and Louie found she was at her most productive in the vacuum Karin left behind. Where this might lead, she wasn't entirely sure. Selling paintings was a tough way to scratch out a living and, even when the odd commission came her way, she could only afford to treat herself to new canvases and more paint with the proceeds. Karin had left a small amount of money in their joint account to cover a few months' rent on the bedsit. Louie had blown that in one go, drinking and smoking it away as a kind of protest.

She continued with her shifts at The Midland, arranging for her wages to be paid into her business account instead of the joint one. Of course, she hoped Karin had enough money to live on and that she had found another job, wherever she was, but Louie didn't want to be subsidizing her relationship with someone else, if that was what was going on.

On her days off, Louie didn't eat or sleep properly. She just painted, took walks on the beach and thought of Karin.

The invitation to exhibit had given her a new and much-needed focus. It had come out of the blue. Someone had seen her display of portraits on the walls of the Royal Lancaster Infirmary and subsequently got in touch. So at least she now had something to aim for while waiting for Karin to come home. As the exhibition date got closer it became increasingly difficult to move around the bedsit without banging into something. The paintings had taken up enough space as canvases, but in their bulky frames that she made herself from driftwood found on local beaches, they took up even more.

The thought that Karin would not see the exhibition, however, made her achievement seem empty.

She was everywhere.

Only yesterday Louie had come across another of her hairs. It was hanging from the light fitting in the bathroom of all places. Long, twisting and red. She didn't think there would be any more. Not now. But there it was, glinting in the sunshine streaming through the window. Louie put it with the others.

Her shift at The Midland started at three thirty on a Friday. When Louie stepped out of her block onto the street, in her black trousers and one of Karin's long-sleeved white shirts, she immediately broke into a sweat. Walking down Albert Road the seagulls laughed mockingly from above. The smell of fish and chips and last night's beer slops filled her lungs as she turned onto Marine Road West. They had walked this route together many times and Karin was everywhere on the outside too.

Louie thought she could hear her voice. A burst of laughter carried along by the wind. She was even in the cracks in the pavement. They had once spent hours searching for an earring because it was a special gift from her dad. Louie could still identify which crack it had slipped down, and picture the smile on Karin's face when she said she had found it.

A coach was pulling in up ahead, the next batch of hens and stags arriving into town. Coming towards her was a procession of old cars, tooting their horns as they passed the sign for 'Vintage Evening of Tunes from a Bygone Era' at the Winter Gardens.

Morecambe was a curious mix of the best and worst of English seaside; like many other resorts, in pursuit of its former glory. Apart from the resplendent Midland hotel and the continuing restoration of the Winter Gardens it was still waiting for the rest of the town to catch up.

But Morecambe was in Louie's blood. She was born, bred and bullied here and had a fondness for it which she had never been able to shake off, nor did she want to. From a young age she had found her own way of coping with the physical pain others chose to inflict on her – for whatever reason; they must have had one – simply by inflicting greater pain on herself. Burning, cutting, striking, jumping, falling, kicking. Thereby raising her tolerance to pain in general.

The first painting she ever did was in her own blood taken from the wounds given to her by her tormentors. It was of a young girl walking across the waves. The girl was red, the waves were red, the sky was red; everything was red and bloody. It gave Louie back control.

9

Karin

Karin paused to look out of the window on their way to the restaurant. The beach, the pier, the sea, they all brought back a rawness in her and made her feel panicky again. She blamed her mother for the way things turned out. If it wasn't for her total failure at being a mother then she would have stayed on at school, finished her studies, maybe even gone to university. Instead she unravelled, finding herself washed up on the beach in Morecambe, a wreckage of a human being with no one in the world she could to turn to.

Until Louie showed up.

Whether or not her mother had deliberately set out to hurt Karin, the pain still cut deep, even now. Losing her dad was bad enough, but then for her to remarry just a few weeks after he died was truly unforgiveable. How did she expect Karin to feel? The way she had done it, too, in secret, and to someone Karin had never even met. It was cruel and disrespectful, an insult to her dad's memory.

Nothing was ever Karin's business. Not the small stuff, not the big stuff. She was even the last to know that her father had died. What mother does that? Waits four days to tell her daughter that her dad has passed away? *Four days.* 'It was better to wait until after your exams, Karin. Those are important.'

What?

44

More important than her dad dying?

Karin was sixteen, nearly seventeen. So perhaps she should have been used to it by then, built up some resilience having been wrenched from the family home at the age of eight and packed off to boarding school. Despite complaining repeatedly of being miserable and homesick, her feelings were never taken into account. She was always out of sight, out of mind. No wonder she lost control.

On those occasions when she was allowed home, Karin began to pick up on a strange atmosphere between her parents, something in the way they interacted. And something that made her keen to know why her mother had remarried so soon after he died. She refused to tell Karin of course. But Karin did get her answer. In many ways she was relieved to be rid of her mother. If Birgitta felt that Karin had ruined her life, then she totally deserved it. In that case they had ruined each other's. But still, there was a gaping hole where her mother ought to have been. That was the hole that Louie had filled.

If Louie still worked here, she was likely to be in the Rotunda Bar. Karin kept her head bowed, just in case, as they were being led through to the restaurant.

'Is this okay for you, sir?' the waitress asked, showing them to a sea-view table.

'Perfect,' Aaron replied.

Karin felt the waitress studying her, hovering with the menus as she waited for them to sit down. She looped her bag over the chair, avoiding eye contact even when she was handed the menu.

'You look familiar,' said the waitress.

'Erm. Yes, I used to work here,' Karin replied, having no option then but to look up. 'I left about a year and a half ago.'

'Thought so. Think I'd just started then. You were front of house, weren't you?'

'A bit of everything actually. It was only temporary.'

'So where are you now?'

45

'I work for a charity.'

'Oh. Still round here though?'

'No. I moved away.'

The waitress nodded, picking up the vibe. She smiled and said she would leave them to decide and someone would be over shortly to get their drinks order.

'Very enigmatic answers,' Aaron commented.

It was in those nervous glances which followed – first at Aaron, trying to reassure him all was well, and then at the waitress as she walked away – that Karin caught a glimpse. Her blood ran cold, yet she could feel herself overheating again. If it was Louie then her hair was longer, in a messy topknot, and she was carrying a tray of empty glasses. Karin saw her look back, as if something or someone had caught her eye, and then Karin panicked, shielding her face with the menu.

'Are you sure you're okay?' Aaron asked. 'Tell me, is this all wrong?'

'No. No, 'course not.' She put down the menu and grabbed his hand. 'I just need a moment, that's all. We were straight up to the room and now suddenly in the restaurant. There're a lot of memories here for me.'

One way or the other though, Karin had to be certain. If it was Louie, then yes, this was all wrong. She pushed back her chair and walked round to the back of Aaron's, resting her hands on his shoulders and massaging gently, the way he liked it, trying to keep her hands steady. Dropping her fingers down his chest she leant over to kiss him. 'It's a lovely thing, Aaron,' she whispered. 'But do you mind if I go to the Ladies before we order?'

'Aren't you feeling well?' he called as their hands trailed apart.

'I'm fine. Back in a minute.'

She walked briskly, her eyes scanning every direction, her heart racing.

Passing through the central bar area.

46

Clear.

Adjusting quickly to the purple lighting and pinky hue of the booths in the Rotunda Bar.

It was bustling. The weekends were always like that.

Some people stared back at her, wondering what she was all about, but Karin was on a mission and she didn't apologize for her intrusion. Because if it was Louie that she had seen, they needed to get out of here. Fast. Tell Aaron that she really was ill and return to the room immediately. Leave first thing in the morning. Maybe even tonight.

She swallowed. She could not have Louie back in her life.

Maybe it wasn't her after all. As Karin's heartbeat slowed to a more regular pace, she told herself that she must have imagined it and quickened her step towards the Ladies. Feeling Louie's presence around this place was perfectly normal, her memory playing tricks trying to convince her that Louie was still here. Almost at the Ladies, Karin sensed someone rushing her way, and froze, unable to look. She felt someone brush against her. It was the receptionist returning to the desk. Karin let out a sigh of relief and reached for the door.

'I knew it was you.'

'My god!'

Louie had stepped into her face. From nowhere.

'Louie.'

'I knew you'd come back. Happy birthday.'

'No. I-I'm just staying here.' She still tried to open the door, but Louie was blocking her.

'What, so that's it? Seriously? You never even said goodbye to me, Karin.'

'I know and I'm sorry. I thought that would be the best thing for both of us.'

Karin moved her aside, enough to be able to push on the door with her shoulder, but bashing into it so hard a pain shot down her arm to her elbow. In the same instant, Louie was behind her, jostling her inside.

'Lou, what the hell are you doing?'

She bundled Karin into the toilet cubicle, the one with the 'Out of Order' sign.

'You owe me an explanation at least,' she said. Her voice was low but forceful. 'Why did you just disappear like that?'

Louie was staring at her. Sea-blue eyes. Perfectly sculptured cheekbones. Karin wanted to tell her that longer hair suited her. She was thinner. Perhaps. But she had forgotten how tall Louie was, much taller than she was even in her heels. She smelt of paint and the sea. Karin saw the damage in those eyes, along with her own reflecting back at her, and a dangerous wave of nostalgia swept over her again. It was a time of extremes when nothing else mattered. They were two broken bottles washed up on the beach. And they were young.

She reached her hand up to Louie's cheek.

It happened quickly. Louie's lips, firm and hot against hers. Their hands were grasping at each other's clothing with a sense of urgency. She didn't protest when Louie undid her dress, or when it fell to the floor, enjoying Louie's touch on her skin, over her breasts. Karin fumbled under Louie's apron to undo the zip on her trousers and pulled apart the studs on her shirt. They tried not to make too much noise beating against the partition.

It was over in minutes.

Karin pushed Louie away again. Her hands trembled as she tore off a length of toilet paper. 'Leave me alone, Louie.'

'Who're you with?'

'Please, Lou, just stay away from me. That won't ever happen again. I've moved on and so should you.'

The intensity of Louie's stare unnerved her.

Louie slapped her hand against the partition and left.

When Karin heard the door swish to a close, she could finally let some air escape from her lungs. She badly needed to pee. It came out hot and burning, the throbbing sensation a reminder of what she had just done. Louie's fingers inside her, they knew exactly where to push, where to press. She began to wipe herself down, trying to put herself back together inside and out. What *had* she just done? The man she loved was waiting out there, possibly going to propose. Karin was capable of many things, but this wasn't one of them.

When she exited the cubicle, she was relieved to find herself alone. Walking towards the gleaming array of sinks, she tried her best not to look in the long mirror above them, but couldn't avoid it. The person staring back was unrecognizable. The tell-tale signs: lipstick wrecked, cheeks flushed, hair totally deranged. She regretted coming in search of Louie now. Even the possibility that it was her should have been enough to take evasive action.

Tugging a tissue from the box on the ledge, getting angry when it didn't come out, Karin began to rub away at the red smears around her mouth and the one streaked across her cheek like some tribal marking. Maybe it wasn't so bad though. Get rid of the mascara smudges, rearrange the hair, and she might be able to get away with saying she had been sick. If only she could wipe away the last fifteen minutes of her life. If only she could undo many things.

Back at the table, Aaron was waiting anxiously. 'You've been gone ages,' he said, putting down his glass of water. 'I was getting worried.'

'I know, I'm sorry. I felt sick and-and then I was.'

'Oh no. Really? Here, drink some water.' He poured a glassful and pushed it towards her.

'Thanks,' she replied, gulping it down. 'I think I'll be okay now.'

'Well, should we go back up to the room? I mean—'

'I'll order something light and I'll be fine. Really, I will.'

The damage was done in any case, and her anger was rising.

49

Karin refused to let Louie ruin this for them, and why should they have to leave? But when the smell of sex wafted over her again, she almost changed her mind.

'Better?' asked Aaron.

'Getting there,' she said, forcing a smile. 'It's so hot in here.'

Aaron reached for her hand across the table as she drank some more water. Karin considered it for a moment, because she really didn't deserve his hand in hers. She didn't deserve Aaron. But she allowed him to stroke her fingers and heard herself apologizing to him again.

'No, don't be sorry,' he said, the kindness in his voice almost unbearable. 'You *sure* you're all right now?'

'I'll be fine.'

He gave her hand a squeeze but Karin was still too embarrassed to look him in the eye. Her hair fell forwards over her face and Aaron pushed it to one side. She raised her head, brave enough to meet his gaze. As she did so, she automatically touched her ear and realized she had lost an earring. The special one from her dad. Karin panicked, quickly pulling her hair forwards, coughing nervously. Luckily Aaron was trying to get someone's attention to come and take their order.

'Hey guys. What can I get you?'

Karin froze.

'So, what are we celebrating tonight?'

It was Louie.

Aaron didn't answer. He seemed to be leaving it to Karin to respond. 'Oh,' she said, fixing her eyes on Aaron. 'Erm. My birthday. It's my birthday. Today.' Karin had no choice but to look at Louie then. Becoming aware that she was using Aaron's hand as a stress ball, she immediately slackened off, giving him another apologetic smile.

'Well in that case, let me get you something suitable,' said Louie. 'I've been informed you used to work here, so it's with our compliments.'

50

'Very generous. Thank you,' Aaron replied, beaming at Karin. Then when Louie had gone, he asked: 'Do you know that girl?'

'I can't really remember. It's a while since I was here. Staff come and go all the time. Listen, do you think we could step outside for a bit of air?'

Aaron got up, coming round to Karin's side of the table. Covering her shoulders with her cardigan, he pulled out her chair and waited patiently for her to stand. On their way out, he caught someone's attention and had a quiet word to explain, pointing over to their abandoned table. It didn't seem to be a problem.

The evening was hanging on to its unusually warm air as they stepped onto the terrace, but Karin was grateful for the relative coolness. From here the sea was a glistening mass, breathing its dark silky waves, in and out. It made no sound, a silent predator awaiting its next victim. This was a dangerous stretch of beach.

'It's beautiful,' said Aaron, putting his arm around Karin's waist to steady her down the steps.

'Yes. I did love it here,' she replied, her eyes drawn to the pier. She pulled on Aaron's arm to go in the other direction, away from the pier, and they began to stroll along the promenade towards Heysham, holding hands.

They'd celebrated her twentieth birthday on the end of that pier. Louie had suddenly produced a cheap bottle of wine and they each took a drink saying: 'Meet me at the edge'. Karin wasn't even sure what she meant by it, it was just a feeling back then, but it was always there. She remembered the sea beating against the pilings beneath them as they hung their heads over the side, dangling their arms into the inky-black waves, daring one another to let go.

'Should we head back?' said Aaron, coming to a standstill. 'We've probably walked far enough. You feeling any better?'

'Sure,' she replied, allowing him to turn her round. She would carry on to Blackpool if she could, all twenty-eight miles of it in her heels. Karin was surprised to learn they had already been walking for over ten minutes.

'Must have been great to live by the sea,' Aaron said, as they strolled back in again. 'I'd love to do that, one day.'

'Yes,' said Karin, shuddering at the memories she had left here. Then she felt Aaron's arm across her shoulders and wondered if he meant the two of them together. 'Oh. Well I'd really like that too,' she added, looking into his eyes. He gave her a half-grin and Karin realized that, yet again, she sounded foolish.

Walking with her head down the rest of the way, the fear of running into Louie returned.

The champagne was waiting for them when they arrived at their table, sitting in a bucket of ice ready to be popped and poured into flutes. Louie was hovering nearby, but held off for a moment, giving them time to get settled. As Karin saw her approaching, she was also aware of Aaron rummaging in the inside of his jacket.

'What are you doing?' she asked, keeping a close eye on Louie.

He pulled out a box. Black velvet, expensive-looking.

Did he have to do this now?

She didn't dare check on Louie again. She must have seen what was happening though, and maintained a professional distance. All Karin could think about as Aaron placed the box down in front of her was Louie's pain. How much this would hurt her.

'Happy birthday, Karin,' he said, nudging the box towards her. 'Open it.'

Her fingers were trembling; she could barely lift up the lid. Karin let out a gasp, no longer pretending to be surprised. It was a cross-over design, white gold set with tiny diamonds. A label was looped through the ring which said:

Marry me, Karin xx

'Oh Aaron, it's beautiful.'

'Well?'

She hesitated.

52

'Yes! Of course, yes.'

Plunging the ring down her finger she clasped both her hands round Aaron's, until she was aware of Louie coming over and quickly released them again.

When Louie reached their table, her face was set. She pulled the cooling bucket in nearer. A droplet of water dripped onto the tablecloth as she lifted out the bottle. She gave it a wipe before opening it and began to pour.

'Happy birthday,' she said, handing Karin a glass.

Then one for Aaron.

The sound of the bottle crashing back into the ice sliced through Karin's nerves, leaving her conscience in shreds. But she had to be strong. She had come a long way since Morecambe.

'Actually, it's more than just a birthday,' she heard Aaron say, feeling her fingers being flaunted under Louie's nose. Karin almost shouted, *No, don't do that*. It was too cruel, but Aaron wasn't to know. In any case it was too late.

Louie flinched.

Karin recovered her hand as soon as it felt appropriate to do so. Her betrayal was pulling both ways; she felt as though she might snap in two. Aaron picked up his glass and Karin did the same; the jubilant tap of crystal, bubbles fizzing up her nose. The only way Karin could cope with this was by pretending that Louie wasn't there at all.

'In that case it's double congratulations,' said Louie, somewhere in the background.

Karin felt her whole body collapse as Louie walked away. But then saw her spin round again, as if she had remembered something. Karin let out a gasp, seeing her return to their table. She tightened her fingers round her wrist in her lap, trying to make the moment end quickly.

'Someone saw you drop this over by the toilets,' said Louie, placing an earring in front of Karin. 'Looks like one you really wouldn't want to lose.'

10

Mel

A dog was barking outside. Mel rushed to the window, banging on it as loudly as she dared, fearing it might break if she did it too hard. Next door's dog was squatting down in their poor overgrown excuse of a lawn and wasn't taking a bit of notice. Even when the neighbour came to retrieve it, he wasn't going to clean up its mess either, not until Mel banged on the window again. He put up his hand as if to say sorry, but probably wasn't.

Mel slumped back into her chair and sighed. Not only was she fretting about Karin, she was also distracted by the number of adverts on her computer suggesting she should jet off somewhere, instead of sitting here on a Friday night in a shabby rented house, all alone except for some weird homeless man watching TV downstairs. Mel would like nothing more than to retire to some sunny part of the world. Who wouldn't? But daydreaming was certainly not going to get her there and she needed to get back to work.

In the end she couldn't resist sending a text to find out how Karin was getting on:

WELL? HAS HE POPPED THE QUESTION YET?
MEL XXX

It was late, nearly eleven, and she didn't expect to hear back, slightly regretting now that she hadn't followed up with another message sooner, but she didn't want to get in the way and become a distraction. When the screen flashed up *message sent*, Mel imagined herself shooting off into the digital tangle along with it. She stood up again, this time to take in the view across the rooftops of Leeds.

She had moved to this city to make a fresh start when her mother eventually passed away. Glasgow had too many sad and difficult memories and she needed to figure out what to do next. Leeds seemed as good a place as any. Beyond the immediate streets was an ever-changing skyline, cranes dangling like gallows as more development took place. The darker area of woodland fought hard to retain its position between the bricks and concrete that were continually sprouting around it, but at least this city still had plenty of green space in which to breathe. Hyde Park was on their doorstep, with its fine trees and a vast expanse of grass to stroll along or sit on for an hour or two. It was the place Mel generally went to do her thinking.

She pictured the Friday night revelry going off in Headingley, students in fancy dress doing the Otley Run, tattooed white flesh bulging out of tight-fitting clothes, tumbling through sweaty bars and clubs. This whole era had passed her by and Mel couldn't afford the more sophisticated scene that Leeds had to offer, even if she had anyone to share it with. In the far distance she could make out the silhouetted Lego-like blocks that had been put up quickly and cheaply during the boom time. Supposedly high-end offices and apartments but few could pay the inflated rents that went with them. A smile spread across Mel's face when she thought of Karin's naivety, once she had learned that many of these were still empty and had begun to badger Aaron into getting his contacts to consider them for the *Room for a Night* scheme. Aaron had let her down gently: Who would want to move into a prestigious office or apartment after a bunch of homeless people had been living there?

Karin's youthful passion on this subject was probably the

reason why the charity had taken her on in the first place: to convince people, with her limitless enthusiasm, that they should support and give generously to the cause. Perhaps she was a reminder of an idealism they had lost as they consumed more and more *stuff*. 'Capitalism with a conscience is what we need to work towards,' Karin would say to anyone who would listen. 'There are so many of these buildings just doing nothing. Never been occupied since the day they were finished. It's criminal to think of the hundreds of people with nowhere to live in our towns and cities when there's all this empty space.'

She did have a point. But although Karin had lived on the streets, she still had much to learn about the real world. Mel thought Aaron might have grown weary of this by now, and she found herself questioning his motives again. Whether he truly loved Karin remained to be seen. Mel rapped her fingers on the desk, wondering if his plan was working: birthday treat, element of surprise.

Then her phone pinged.

K: YES HE PROPOSED!

M: AND?

K: I SAID YES. BUT HE'S BROUGHT US TO THE MIDLAND HOTEL WHERE I USED TO WORK. CAN'T BELIEVE IT. AND LOUIE IS HERE!!

M: OH GOD, NO! THAT'S NOT WHAT YOU NEED. STAY OUT OF HER WAY. YOU DON'T WANT ALL THAT STALKING TO START UP AGAIN.

K: I'M TRYING TO.

M: KEEP IN TOUCH. MAYBE YOU SHOULD JUST GET OUT OF THERE.

56

Mel couldn't quite believe Aaron's mistake. Morecambe was the last place on earth he should have taken Karin to this weekend, or any weekend. She could have told him that, if only he had allowed her to advise him on that too. *Why would Karin want to return to somewhere she used to work?* That's all she would have needed to say, without letting anything slip.

Despite encouraging her to be honest with Aaron on this matter, it was Karin's big fear that Aaron's 'conventional thinking' would not allow him to accept that she once had a girlfriend. It wasn't just some lesbian dalliance from her youth either; they had been in a relationship and lived together for at least a couple of years.

Mel needed another glass of wine to help her think.

Later on in the evening, the TV was still blaring in the lounge. Mel could hear it through the door. But when she returned upstairs she noticed that the light was on in Karin's room. Resting her glass on the banister, she crept the rest of the way.

A noise from inside Karin's room stopped her from going any further. Mel reached for her mobile, tucked it into her pocket, just in case.

A figure appeared in the doorway.

'Will. My god! What on earth are you doing in there? That's not your room.'

He signed something back to her, but Mel had no idea what he was trying to say. He had in his hand some jewellery, belonging to Karin, and seemed to be implying that he had come across it on the landing. Walking his fingers towards Karin's room possibly meant that he was intending to return it.

Mel met his stare. He dumped the jewellery into her hand, making her arm give way with the force, but she managed to keep hold of it. With a disapproving shake of her head, she moved Will to one side and marched into Karin's room, placing the jewellery back on her bed.

Turned off the light and shut the door.

Will hadn't moved, still out on the landing. He stared at Mel, long and hard, pushing past her to get to his own room and slammed the door in her face.

'Will. Will,' she shouted. 'We should talk about this.'

But he couldn't hear her, and it was pointless knocking. She left it a few seconds before turning the handle, opening his door just enough to make herself visible.

Will was in his usual position leaning against the radiator. His eyes, almost black, penetrated hers. Mel would have thought them beautiful, if they weren't so unnerving. He began to pull on greasy lengths of hair either side of his face, moving on to his beard.

'Will.'

She realized he couldn't lip-read from where she was standing and went in a bit further, as near as she dared, exaggerating her words as she tried again. 'I think we need another little chat, Will. Don't you?'

She waited. Nothing came back.

'I need to remind you that this is our home and you have to respect that.'

After a few moments he began to sign something. Angrily. Fingers slapping together, arms flapping. His facial expression never altered.

'Look, I have no idea what you're saying to me,' said Mel, 'and it doesn't sound very pleasant. Are you able to write it down? We might understand each other better that way.' Mel pretended to scribble something in the air, but Will shook his head. She had asked him to do this before and he always refused.

She decided to take a different approach. Pushing his books to one side, she sat on the floor, an attempt to make this less confrontational. She just had to hope that he wouldn't lash out. 'Look, Will, I take it that you do still want this chance Karin is giving you? It'd be such a waste if you mess up now, after all the hard work you're putting in. Don't you agree?'

Silence.

58

'So have you anything more to say, or do we understand one another?'

He stood up, towering over her.

11

Louie

Louie was waiting for her moment to come again, watching their table discreetly in between preparing drinks orders at the bar. Karin looked sensational in that dress. How easily it had slipped off. Louie observed her pushing food around her plate. Occasionally a miniscule forkful would end up in her mouth as she smiled at the old fart she had just agreed to marry.

As soon as the waitress began clearing away their plates, Louie was ready to make her move. She held off for a few more moments until they were handed the dessert menus. On her approach, armed with a carafe of water, the old fart took hold of Karin's hand across the table.

'I'm so sorry,' said Louie, placing the carafe between them with a thud, forcing them apart. 'I don't mean to interrupt, but I think I recognize you now. You used to work here, right? Left about a year or so ago, maybe. Was it?'

'Yes,' Karin replied, snapping the menu shut, her face turning pale. 'That's right.'

Louie registered the anxious smile that Karin gave to the old fart, and then she continued. 'Is it erm, Karin? Karin—?' She genuinely did wonder what Karin would be calling herself these days, doubting very much that she would have gone back to using Svendsen because of the association with her mother.

'It's Rhodes,' she replied. There was a strain in her voice.

'Of course,' said Louie.

At least that was something then. So this man, who had blatantly just proposed to *her* girlfriend, probably didn't know who Karin's mother was. But did he know the significance of her twenty-second birthday?

Karin began twisting her newly acquired ring round her finger. 'Maybe I do remember you. Vaguely,' she said. 'Oh erm. This is Aaron. My fiancé.' She might as well have fired the words out of a gun. Likewise when she said, 'Aaron, this is – I'm sorry, I don't remember your name.'

'Louie. *Some* people call me Lou.'

Aaron offered his hand. Louie shook it, even though it disgusted her.

Then, pointing an accusing finger at Karin, as if the thought had only just occurred to her, Louie said: 'You once caught me sketching seahorses when I was meant to be working, didn't you? And promised you wouldn't tell.'

'What?' said Karin, laughing to cover up her discomfort. 'Oh. Yes, I do remember that.'

Louie hoped the memory was digging into her heart, picturing Louie with her sketchpad and pencil. Karin would be recalling how much she loved her then, how perfect they were together and how much she still loved her now. But to give Karin some time for these things to sink in, Louie turned her attention to Aaron, giving him the tourist spiel about the two Eric Gill seahorses carved into the exterior of the hotel, plus the other forty-seven that had been added to the interior. 'Have a look in the shower grate in your room,' she added, 'before you put the anti-slip mat down. Even *young* people find it a bit slippery in there.'

'I certainly will,' said Aaron, not taking issue with her last comment. He leant in to Karin and kissed her hand. 'So. Did you tell?'

Karin swallowed, her cheeks as red as her hair. 'No. I would never do that.' She looked up at Louie, dabbing her mouth with her napkin. All of a sudden, she fired back her chair and stood up. 'Sorry. I really need to go to the Ladies again.'

Louie watched her go. 'Is she okay, do you think?'

'She'll be fine. Her stomach's playing up.'

'Shouldn't you go after her?'

'I can hardly follow her into the Ladies, can I?' Aaron took a large gulp of wine, holding it in his mouth before swallowing, fixing his gaze on Louie. 'So, are you an artist?'

'Of sorts, yes.'

'Are you any good?'

'Not for me to say really.'

'I'm always on the lookout for artwork.'

Louie lifted up her apron and fumbled about in her back pocket. 'Not sure where you're based, but if it's anywhere near Leeds, I have a show on next Thursday. Here's a flyer.' She managed to retrieve one and handed it over. 'It's a pretty small exhibition.'

'Hm,' said Aaron. 'We live in Leeds.'

'Really?'

Louie's professionalism deserted her at that point. She had to sit down. Aaron poured her a glass of water, but she didn't drink it. He thought she wanted to discuss art.

So near? Had Karin been in Leeds all this time? A short hop over the Pennines, less than two hours away by car. How could she be that cruel? Karin told her she had gone to the States.

12

Karin

Karin stepped out of the shower and reached for the towel. She had been desperate to wash away Louie, but the cleansing process hadn't worked. Could still feel her touch on her skin, still feel her fingers inside her. No amount of soaping and scrubbing was going to erase that. She dried herself and put on the bathrobe, not quite ready to go out there yet. Sitting on the side of the bath, she wondered if she could ever face Aaron again. She deeply regretted her actions. To some degree, was still in shock.

It had all happened so fast.

The only reason she had chosen to come to Morecambe in the first instance was because it was her dad's birthplace. For that reason alone, it had been perfect; she had to take her own life somewhere. It was Louie who had found her on the beach, sinking deeper into her cold, muddy grave. The sea nearly claimed them both that night, spreading its watery tentacles around them, shutting off any means of escape.

Karin hadn't wanted to die. Not really. She just didn't think she deserved a future.

There was no doubt that Louie had brought her back to life in every possible way. She managed to get her a job at The Midland and they found a place together, a cosy bedsit off Albert Road. Gradually Karin discovered a happiness she didn't think possible for herself, and their shared sense of recklessness was like a drug.

Karin also loved the fact that Louie was an artist, embracing all the quirks and peculiarities that came with that, and she would sit for her whenever she asked.

Louie had opened her eyes, her mind, made Karin look at things and really see them. But there was a need, a dependency, which wasn't healthy. Karin realized too late what was happening. No one was allowed into their world. The possessiveness became suffocating and isolating, and Karin was losing all sense of herself.

The way she handled the break-up was not something she was proud of. The lie that she had found a job in the States seemed as cruel then as it did now. She had simply handed in her notice at the hotel and vanished. At the time, this was the right thing to do, the only thing to do. Close the door on Louie quickly, limit the pain and break the connection. Louie would never accept it was over otherwise.

Karin shuddered, pulling the bathrobe around herself. She couldn't hide in here all night. When she finally emerged, Aaron was lying on his front on the bed, scrolling down his phone. He threw it to one side and shuffled over to make some room, leaning on one elbow. He had been kind enough not to ask her a single difficult question over dinner and Karin was grateful for that because he must have had plenty buzzing round his head. Her behaviour had been strange from the moment they pulled into the car park.

This was meant to be a happy occasion, yet there had been no more talk of a wedding since his proposal. When she hadn't returned to the table, Aaron had had to come up to the room to find her.

Poor Aaron. She had ruined their perfect moment.

'Is that better?' he asked, pulling Karin into him.

She nodded, feeling safe again in his arms. 'Thank you,' she whispered.

'For what?' Aaron laughed, kissing her neck. 'Asking you to be my wife?'

'Well yes. And all this, I don't deserve it.'

He pulled away and sat up. 'You having second thoughts already?'

'No. Anything but. I swear.'

As that squalid act with Louie was working its way out of her body, Karin was even more convinced about her feelings for Aaron. No one else. She didn't want anyone else.

'Have *you* changed your mind though?' she asked, tentatively.

Aaron pulled the bathrobe down over her shoulders and moved his body into hers. She really didn't want to do this right now, it was too close to the time with Louie, but she owed it to Aaron as proof of her commitment. She loved him too much to allow Louie to destroy their future together. But she couldn't deny that she was scared. She had escaped from Louie once. Now it seemed she might have to do it all over again.

Karin felt her body going through the motions while her mind raked over the broken fragments of her past: conversations, accusations, Louie, her mother, father, so-called stepfather. And before she could do anything about it, an icy blast of pain shot through her head and she knew what was coming next.

Birgitta's screams. Legs swinging side to side. A human pendulum. The sound of the rope grating against the beam, the smell of sweat hanging in the air.

The steps lying on their side.

Karin tried tossing pebbles into the sea one by one in her mind but as fast as she threw them they came right back, refusing to disappear. She just wanted tonight to be over as soon as possible. Her cries and moans sounded like a convincing orgasm, despite where they really came from.

This special night. The night Aaron proposed to her.

13

Karin

The next morning unravelled itself slowly, creeping out of the darkness between short bursts of sleep. Karin had inherited Birgitta's sleepless gene. The difference was that her mother claimed it was a waste of time anyway: 'For losers, Karin,' she would say. Sometimes, when ghosts and monsters got the better of Karin, she would creep into her parents' room, distressed and frightened. 'Silly child,' was her mother's only comfort. 'Either go back to bed, or else get up and do something useful.' So Karin would return to bed, muffling her cries until the morning made her feel safe again.

The only way to get Karin to be more independent was to send her away to boarding school, where she would develop the powers of 'thinking for herself'. Karin was never officially told this was the reason, just snippets of conversations wafting upstairs or through doors left slightly ajar. But once Karin did develop the powers of 'thinking for herself', she worked out that there must be other factors involved in this decision. Birgitta's career was beginning to take off. Furniture design and quirky household products. Later, log cabins and trendy alternative living spaces. Her work was revered the world over, in magazines and trade press. But the name Svendsen was a curse as far as Karin was concerned. She got rid of it as soon as she could.

There was also the oddness to her parents' relationship. Karin couldn't remember what age she was when she detected it. Perhaps it had always been there, but this must surely have been a factor too, to get rid of Karin so she wouldn't see what was really going on. In some perverse way, maybe her mother was trying to be kind. But Karin ended up resenting being robbed of so many years that could have been spent with her dad. He never wanted Karin to go away any more than Karin did, but had no say in the matter.

She suddenly became aware of someone touching her hair.

'Had one of your restless nights again,' Aaron whispered, kissing her forehead. 'Get some more sleep.' He must have gone in the shower after that, because the noise of the water carried her away to the beach.

Drowning, sinking. In mud, heavy and bulbous. Water pouring into her nostrils.

When she opened her eyes she noticed a cup of tea by her bedside. It had gone tepid and undrinkable. She remembered managing a grunt of thanks when Aaron had placed it there. Now he was calling to her from the bathroom. His words were unclear, and at first she thought something was wrong, until he appeared with a toothbrush in his mouth and white-coated lips.

'*I said*, she has an exhibition in Leeds next Thursday.'

'Who does?'

'That waitress we were talking to last night. She's invited us to her launch. You'd disappeared by then, but we got chatting – until I realized you weren't coming back.'

'Oh.' Karin sat up. Her chest felt tight. 'In Leeds?'

'Yeah. I said we'd go along. That's okay isn't it?'

Aaron disappeared again, returning a few moments later wiping his face in a towel.

'Erm. I suppose.'

'Well it's just some pop-up place in the Victoria Quarter, but

I said we'd swing by, and we can always go for a meal afterwards, make a night of it.'

'Not with her!'

Karin even startled herself at such an abrupt response. She immediately tried to soften it with: 'I mean it's not like we know her or anything.' Pulling the duvet up to her chin, she waited for his response.

Aaron clambered on top of her and covered her face with kisses, saying, 'Of course I just meant us.'

'Okay, that sounds nice,' she said, pressing her lips to his.

Wasn't this her moment to tell him about Louie? Not about last night, but she could say they were once good friends who fell out or something. Although, wouldn't that contradict her reaction last night of 'only vaguely recognizing' her? And saying just now that she didn't really know her at all? That would make it seem like she had something to hide. And what about her strange absences, returning from the toilet dishevelled minus an earring?

'The stuff on her website looks pretty good,' said Aaron, but Karin could only hear him in the background of her thoughts.

'Does it?' she said, realizing there must have been a long gap. All she could think of was that Louie must now know she was living in Leeds.

'I might even have some work for her, if she's interested,' Aaron continued. 'Bars, restaurants, big corporates, they all want new artwork at a good price. I could do with branching out a bit.' Karin was still only half-listening. 'That's what comes of being taken to the cleaners by the ex-wife.'

'Oh.' His last remark, any mention of his ex-wife, was enough to get her attention. But it suddenly struck her what the consequences would be if he ever found out about Louie. How could Aaron possibly forgive her when his ex-wife had cheated on him? Karin had no intention of telling him of last night's indiscretion, but what if Louie did? And what else might Louie say? She risked losing far more than a fiancé at this rate. Louie had the power to destroy her life completely.

Did she really have it in her to do that?

They took a walk on the beach in the late afternoon sunshine. The bay looked stunning, miles and miles of shiny, flat water and it was bright enough to see the Lake District on the other side. Despite the sun's presence, every now and then a cool breeze blew in from the sea sending Karin's hair in every direction and she had to tie a loose knot in her silk scarf to hold it down. She was clinging to Aaron's arm as they picked their way over the pebbles.

Karin had known how treacherous parts of this bay were, how easy it was to get caught by the tide, swallowed up by the sands. She had heard on the news about the Chinese cockle pickers drowned in 2004, trapped by waters coming in from both front and behind faster than any man could run away from them. And fishermen getting trapped in rising tides.

She had done her research.

'I nearly drowned on this beach once,' she blurted.

Aaron stopped.

'What? Really?'

'It's easy to get caught out, and I did. It was foggy, I lost my bearings.'

'My god, Karin. So what happened?'

'Well, luckily someone saw me – not sure how – and managed to pull me back before it was too late.'

'Who was it?'

'Just some bloke.'

She gulped a breath of salty air, knowing she had to leave it at that, but felt better for having got that bit out in the open at least. There was no way she could tell Aaron that it was Louie who had saved her. The same as Aaron could never know that she hadn't wanted to be saved, that she had deliberately chosen that foggy night to walk out onto the mudflats and wait for the sea to swirl around her feet, creep up to her knees, thighs, waist, swallowing her further and deeper into the quicksand until she was no more.

'You know you *can* tell me stuff, don't you?' He took hold of her hand and kissed it. 'You've had a rough time, Karin, I know that. I just want to look after you.'

'Thank you, Aaron. Honestly, I appreciate it.'

He knew about her dad dying, her stepdad committing suicide, but no way did Karin want him to know that she had once been a suicide case herself, even if she was a teenager at the time. It wasn't that long ago, that's what he would think. It seemed so unfair when she had made real progress since then.

She only wanted Aaron to see the person she was now, a mature, competent young woman. She had seen photos of his ex-wife, well-groomed and in her forties, still attractive enough to get herself a younger man apparently. From the little Aaron was prepared to say about her, Karin knew she must be a strong person, and the fact that Karin was only twenty-two played to her insecurities as it was. Sometimes Aaron laughed when she didn't understand his jokes because they contained references from before she was even born, actors she had never heard of, musicians, TV programmes, films. He found it charming, but it made Karin feel foolish.

As they were heading back to the hotel she thought she could see someone watching them from the promenade. The outline was familiar, tall, slender, and something sinister about it in silhouette.

Was the stalking beginning all over again?

Karin felt a chill run the length of her spine, but after a few more steps she came to an abrupt halt, bending down to pick up a pebble. She threw it with such force it almost put her shoulder out.

'Don't think that'll quite make it,' said Aaron, laughing at her for even attempting it. 'The sea's a mile off.'

Karin pulled Aaron towards her and kissed him. 'I do love you, Aaron. We'll be so happy together.'

'We are happy together. And I love you too.'

Aaron rubbed her shoulders, smiling. They carried on walking, holding hands again. As they got closer to the promenade, Karin glanced up and spotted Louie disappearing up the curved steps leading into the bar of The Midland.

Her body tensed.

'You okay?' Aaron asked.

She gave him a look of contentment, but fear gnawed at her insides.

How could she make Louie go away for good this time?

14

Louie

Louie positioned herself at the top of the steps, dropping down onto the promenade so she could lean against the railings. Her phone was on full zoom, framing an image she had to hold steady: Karin, her hair rolling across one shoulder, a flimsy scarf trying to free itself with the help of the sea breeze. She took a photo just as Karin turned her face. The motion blur would be good to capture when she came to paint her later.

Louie was aware that she had been spotted, but she had seen enough in any case. This nauseating display – kissing, holding hands with someone old enough to be her father – didn't fool Louie for a second. She knew exactly why Karin had returned to Morecambe. It was because she was still in love with *her*. Karin had come back to remind herself of what she had walked away from, before she made the biggest mistake of her life.

Louie always knew she would return.

When she saw they were coming inside, she disappeared into the bar area. There was something about that old fart she didn't like. Not solely because Karin was supposedly marrying him either, more of a vibe he gave off. She had chatted to him briefly last night after Karin disappeared. He had a sort of shifty arrogance about him. Louie couldn't quite decide whether it was just his age, or that was really a part of his character. Even if he could find outlets for her artwork, tempting though that was, did Louie really want his help?

She worried about Karin. Louie didn't want either of them to owe this guy anything when they eventually got back together. Why was she even with him in the first place? He looked like he might have money, although appearances could be deceptive and he could easily be one of those *all flash no cash* sort of guys. Louie saw enough of that type at The Midland. But Karin didn't even need his money, not if her mother had been true to her word yesterday on her birthday.

The way he looked at her made her skin crawl.

Louie cleared some more glasses off the tables, returning them to the bar while still keeping an eye on things outside. A few of the guests were braving the terrace in their summer dresses and shirt sleeves, but the breeze was driving most people indoors now. There was no sign of Karin, and for a moment Louie wondered if they had gone round to the front entrance, but when they finally appeared she retreated behind the bar to serve a customer.

Karin's arm was linked through his, like he had glued it there. She saw Karin take a quick scan of the room. Panic swept over her face the moment her eyes landed on Louie. Louie smiled back, giving her a nonchalant wave. Karin must have said something to him after that, like she was feeling the chill, because the old fart began rubbing her shoulders and folded her up in his big, hairy arms. He gave her a peck on the shoulder, moving the neckline of her shirt to one side.

Karin moved her body round to face him, turning it into a full kiss, and Louie had to clench her fists inside the pocket of her apron, digging her nails into her palms to distract from doing anything foolish. As soon as their display had ended, Karin looked across to gauge Louie's reaction. But what she hadn't anticipated was the round of applause they received for such a public performance. It took Karin by surprise, and Louie knew she wouldn't have wanted all that fuss.

'It's okay, everyone. They're almost newlyweds!' That was Janine shouting, their waitress from last night. 'They've got engaged.' Her comments prompted wolf whistles, cheers and more applause. The old bastard said something to Karin, clearly embarrassed, and he escorted her under a bridge of hands and grinning faces.

Louie was desperate to rescue her from this circus. As soon as she had finished serving the next customer, she hurried out into reception, where she found Karin fleeing upstairs and Aaron making his way to the desk. Her heart said to follow Karin, but the front desk was unattended.

'Hi. Someone will be along in a minute,' she said, hurrying over to him.

'Oh. Hello again.' Aaron greeted her with a smile, his face like a deflated balloon, all lines and wrinkles.

'Anything I can help you with?' she asked. She was trying to imagine what he would look like in another ten years. Dead probably. He was *so* old.

'Yes, maybe you can. My fiancée – Karin – lost her scarf while we were out walking on the beach. She's only just realized. It was a present, so if anyone should hand it in—'

'Of course.'

Fiancée. What an arse.

'Em, do you have a pen?' he asked, looking round for one.

Louie took the pen from behind her ear and slapped it onto the notepad. When she realized that Aaron was scribbling down an address, she was about to tell him that it wasn't necessary, it would be on their database. Giving her the perfect excuse to look for it, of course. However, as if he had been reading her thoughts, he glanced up and said, 'The post is terrible at my place. Better send it to her. That's if you do find it.'

'No problem,' she replied, delighted at how easy he was making this for her.

He carried on scribbling and Louie noticed his hair was showing the first signs of thinning on top. 'How was your night?' she asked. 'Did you sleep okay?'

'Very well, thank you.'

He tore off the sheet of paper and handed it to Louie. She was tempted to ask if he needed any more Viagra. 'Well, I do apologize for that scene in the bar,' she said instead, 'if it embarrassed you. I'll have a word with my colleague.'

At that moment, her other colleague was scurrying back to the desk. 'Sorry about that,' she said, flustered. 'What can I do for you?'

'I'd like to sort out a few things for this evening,' Louie heard him say as she slowly edged away. She could still hear their voices as she waited for the lift, followed by polite laughter. The lift took far too long; she held her finger in the button to hurry it along.

When she stepped out onto the top floor, Karin was only just heading down the corridor. She must have been taking her time on the staircase, waylaid by nostalgia, overcome by all the reminders of Louie and their time together.

Louie was about to call out to her but, as Karin hadn't registered that she was even there, she decided to surprise her instead. Just as Karin was going to unlock the door, she pounced.

'You're not seriously marrying that guy, are you?' said Louie, pressing her hand over her mouth, twisting her arm up her back. She pulled Karin out of sight, round the corner at the end of the corridor, and only then removing her hand.

'Louie, what the hell are you doing?' Karin spoke in an angry whisper, wiping her mouth as if having Louie's fingers across it was in some way disagreeable. Louie still wasn't fooled. Nor by Karin's rubbing of her wrist. She used to beg Louie to grab her like that, take her by surprise. Last night was proof that she still wanted it that way. She grabbed her again, attempting to kiss her, but Karin backed off.

'Don't tell me you prefer plain old boring now,' said Louie, slapping her hand against the wall. 'Shit, Karin. He could be your dad.'

'Well he isn't. And stop spying on me. I could get you sacked.'

Louie gave her a look as if to say *I could do far worse to you.* 'So come on then, how old is he? Forty?'

'He's forty-four actually.'

'Seriously? Forty-four. Jeez, Karin. It's not like you need a sugar daddy. Not if your Swedish mamma—'

'It's none of your business,' she snapped. Then she sighed, softening her tone. 'Look I'm sorry, Lou. It was an insane time for both of us. I'm just not that person any more.'

'You were last night.'

'Please don't say anything,' said Karin. 'I mean he doesn't even know we were together.'

'Oh really? I'd never have guessed that. Okay, so when you're fifty, he'll be what? Let's do the maths, shall we? Seventy-two. In a bath chair sipping hot chocolate out of a feeder cup, waiting for you to wipe his arse and empty his colostomy bag.'

Louie gave the wall another slap as she delivered her last remark.

Karin went back down the corridor, but Louie got there first. She put her hand over the card reader as Karin tried to unlock the door.

'So what was last night all about if you don't still feel anything for me? Answer me that one.'

'I told you, it was a mistake,' Karin replied.

'"Meet me at the edge". Remember that?'

'Look. In the end, you and me—'

'We're the same, Karin.'

They were disturbed by the pinging of the lift. The doors swished open. Then someone whistling 'Flowers in the Window', by Travis, coming down the corridor.

Tragic.

'Right. So if there's anything else you need,' said Louie in a suitably loud voice, 'you just shout up. Okay?'

'Y-yes, I will,' Karin replied. 'Thank you. That's very good of you. I appreciate it.'

Aaron turned the corner, clutching a huge bouquet of flowers.

'Here's the lucky man,' said Louie. 'I just came to make sure you have everything you need.'

'We do indeed,' he replied, with an unbearable smugness. 'Just been to sort out dinner in our room for this evening.'

'Don't blame you,' said Louie. 'Well, you know where we are if you need anything. I'm going off shift now, but see you both in Leeds next Thursday.'

'We'll be there,' said Aaron.

'Great.' Louie set off up the corridor then spun round on her heel. 'Ooh. Tell you what though. Might be a good idea if you give me your number. These things can change at the last minute. There was talk about moving the preview to a different night. Wouldn't want you trailing down to the gallery unnecessarily.'

'Sure,' said Aaron. 'Why don't you give her yours, Karin? Got my hands rather full, but there's a pen in my top pocket. Actually it's your pen.' He nodded at Louie. 'Think I stole it from you earlier.'

'No worries,' said Louie. Tempted to say that wasn't all he had stolen from her. She handed Karin a piece of paper, suppressing a smile at seeing her hand shaking as she scribbled down a number. Louie snatched it from her and read it back. 'Zero, seven, seven … two, seven, eight, four.'

'Eight, seven, three, four,' Aaron corrected.

'It's my writing,' said Karin, weakly.

Aaron was struggling to get his key card to work; the flowers were hindering him. 'Not sure why I'm still holding onto these,' he said, laughing as he offered them to Karin. He gave her a peck on the cheek and went inside the room, leaving the door open.

'Have a good night,' Louie shouted. Then, lowering her voice down to a whisper, she pressed her face in to Karin's. 'I'm guessing he also doesn't know you've killed people, Karin.'

15

Mel

Mel shuffled into the kitchen, still in her pyjamas and slippers. A mug of tea in one hand, a bowl of muesli in the other, she slumped into a chair and released an animal-like yawn. Karin was already dressed, in her work dungarees, sitting at the table. She seemed distracted, chewing her nail, and didn't acknowledge Mel's presence. Mel hadn't seen her until late yesterday evening. She had been staying round at Aaron's since Sunday, when she had got back from Morecambe.

Had Mel waded in too heavily with her interrogation last night? She wondered what sort of mood she would find Karin in this morning, before coming downstairs.

Trying to make an assessment of what to say now.

Karin's hand was clamped around a mug of cold-looking coffee. There was an envelope resting on her plate and her other hand was covering her phone, also on the table.

'Oh. Has the post come already?' asked Mel in a cheery voice. She could see that the envelope, addressed to Karin, looked like it had been opened. 'Anything interesting?' Hesitating before reaching for the milk carton, Mel asked, 'You okay?', then poured some milk onto her muesli, noticing how pale Karin was. 'Hey look, Karin. I'm sorry if I was out of order last night. I was in shock that you'd said yes, that's all. And then – well I shouldn't have accused you of only saying yes because Louie was standing over you. You know I'm really, really—'

'Happy for me.' Karin forced a smile. 'You told me a hundred times already.' She gave Mel's hand a squeeze. 'Don't worry, you can still be my bridesmaid.' They both knew she had no one else to offer that job to, but Mel was relieved all the same. Not about being a bridesmaid, but because they still seemed to be friends. In any case Karin had given her assurances that it was *just an engagement* at this stage, so not like they were going to dash off tomorrow to get wed or anything. There was still time to think about this.

A noise out in the hallway caused them both to look in that direction. Karin got up, and Mel could soon hear Karin's voice drifting through into the kitchen. Exaggerated speech, followed by long pauses while she was signing.

'I'm sorry. I've not seen you in a while, Will,' she heard Karin say. 'I've been staying at Aaron's. Since I got back. And been working at the office. In town. But I'll be down at Ashby Road. Later today. We need to crack on. Don't we?'

There was an extra-long gap at that point, which made Mel feel uneasy.

'Are you okay, Will?' Karin asked. 'You seem a bit subdued.'

Mel supposed, in the next silence, that Will was signing something back to her, but it was difficult to follow these one-sided conversations.

'So. I'll see you at work then,' Karin continued. 'You *are* going in today? Aren't you? We need you, Will.'

Mel heard the front door close.

When Karin returned to the kitchen she looked puzzled. 'Has Will been okay? He seemed a bit odd just now.'

'Erm. Yes, as far as I'm ever able to tell. He hasn't been around much these last few days. But I did feed him when he was here. I sent you proof of that.'

'Thanks,' said Karin, but she was distracted.

After another mouthful of muesli, wiping the drips off her chin, Mel decided this was as good a time as any to confront

Karin about the next thing. She had found a flyer on the floor after Karin had gone to bed last night. Mel held it up and proceeded to read it out loud: '"Meet Me at the Edge. Seahorse Studio Art Show by Louie Fallon".'

Karin rubbed her face. If she rubbed any harder, she would erase all her features.

'In bloody Leeds, Karin?'

'I was hoping you might come, actually.'

Mel's spoon rattled against the side of the dish as she let go of it. 'Please tell me you are not seriously considering it.'

'Well, Aaron really wants to go. He's seen some of Lou's work and—'

'You still haven't told him, have you? My god, he's even met her now, how's that going to look? You can't have secrets like this, Karin, if you're marrying the guy.'

'I know, but Louie was just a moment in my life. She happened to be there when I needed someone.'

'So that's what you tell Aaron.'

Karin was still rubbing her face. Luckily she didn't wear make-up during the day. Her style was more tomboy than girlie as a rule, although Karin's beauty came through whatever, even as a wasted kid on the street. Despite herself, Mel felt a pang of jealousy. She began stroking Karin's arm.

'You just say it was a fling between you and Louie, a youthful experiment, and you don't want to encourage her again now.'

Karin sat back in the chair. 'I should have told him at the outset. You were right. Now it's just too complicated.'

As Mel studied her, she thought she saw a hot flush sweeping over Karin's face. 'Hey, nothing happened at the weekend, did it? With Louie? Mm?'

''Course it didn't.'

Mel sucked air through her cheeks.

'Okay, okay,' said Karin, wiping the sweat that had gathered above her top lip. 'She did try to kiss me, but I slapped her face.'

Mel held her gaze, waiting for a full confession if there was one.

All she said was: 'I don't want her back in my life, Mel. But now that she is, I just have to deal with it.'

'She's fucking crazy! Are you forgetting it was me who had to *rescue* you from her last time around? She was harassing you every minute of the day, you were in a right state.'

'That's why I need you there on Thursday,' Karin replied, looking pleadingly at her. 'I'll book us a table at Swank for afterwards. Aaron won't mind. Let's spend some time together, just you and me. I was going to ask you in any case. I know how much you want to go to that place and I'd love to treat you.'

'Why do you have to go to this stupid art exhibition though?'

'I told you, Aaron likes her work. And I also don't want Louie to think I'm being intimidated—' Karin's voice dropped as she was removing something from the envelope in front of her, '... by this.'

She offered the piece of paper to Mel.

'What the hell is this?' Mel pulled a face when she read it: '"I know everything Karin".' She couldn't help laughing. The clumsily stuck-on words were cut out of newspaper headlines. 'What's she playing at? Who on earth does this these days?' Then she turned serious again. 'Why the hell did you give her your address?'

'I told you, it was Aaron. I lost my scarf.'

Karin's expression reminded Mel of the vulnerable young woman she had found on the streets just over a year ago. A scared, raggedy heap huddled under a blanket, with a blaze of red hair when she pulled back her hood.

'You should really go to the police with this,' Mel said. 'Before it all starts up again. Or she just won't leave you alone.'

Karin was scraping nail varnish off, like it had no right to be there in the first place, working along her row of fingers.

'Why not? What is it she thinks she knows about you anyway? "I know everything Karin." What's that all about? Are you in trouble?'

Mel placed her arm round Karin's shoulder because she looked like she was about to cry.

'She's just trying to scare me. Punish me.'

'Clearly, someone is,' said Mel through an exasperated sigh.

Karin's frown was so deep for someone so young. 'Well who else might it be?' she asked. 'Who? Mel, tell me who you think it is.'

'Could be Will?'

'What?'

'Possibly.'

'Are you serious? Why do you even say that?'

Mel let out another sigh. 'I wasn't going to tell you this, but maybe I should.' She paused, because she knew how much it would impact on Karin. 'I caught Will snooping on Friday night.'

'What?'

'He was in your room, making some pretence of returning jewellery that he claimed to have found on the landing.'

'No. Well are you sure?' Karin considered it for a moment. 'There must have been some genuine reason why he was in my room.'

'Oh come on, Karin. Like what? Like he'd "heard" something.' Mel drew unsympathetic quotation marks around the word. 'He had your jewellery in his hand. I'm sorry, I just don't trust him now. I mean where does he go and what does he do when he's not here? What company does he keep? Have you any idea?'

Karin started on another fingernail, spitting out a flake of nail varnish. 'You're wrong about him, Mel.' She was getting more agitated. 'I've lived on the streets and I know when I can trust someone. It's like Will has another sense to make up for being deaf. He could always spot danger a mile off, long before I could. And he can read people too. He probably did "hear" something on Friday night.'

'Yeah right.'

'Will is the kindest soul. He's such a good person. I mean even

82

on the streets he never stole anything. A bread roll once from Sainsbury's when we were both starving, but that's it.'

Mel reached across for the envelope. She sniffed it, although wasn't quite sure why. There was possibly a hint of perfume, but mostly it smelt like paper. She ran her finger over the stamp, holding it up to the window. 'I'm not even sure if this really did come through the post,' she said, after a close examination.

Karin grabbed it back to scrutinize for herself. 'You think someone delivered it by hand then? So not Louie?'

'Well it's easy enough to get across to Leeds from Morecambe. Or from anywhere, for that matter. It might have been posted, I've no idea. I'm not bloody Sherlock Holmes, am I? All I know is that you should go to the police, Karin.'

Karin slapped the envelope down onto the table.

'So, what are you going to do then, if you're not prepared to do that?'

'Ignore it,' Karin replied. 'It's Louie, she's just playing games.'

Karin's phone vibrated on the table. It juddered, and seemed as startled as they were. When a message flashed up, Karin flipped it over, but it was there long enough for Mel to see it contained the words

Meet me at the edge.

She wished she could have seen the whole thing.

'Was that her?' asked Mel.

'I've got to get to work,' said Karin. She stood up, snatching her phone off the table.

'Can't believe you gave her your number as well! Hey, wait,' said Mel, catching her by the arm. 'Look, I'm sorry. I know you didn't mean to. It just shits me up, that's all.' Karin nodded, apologetically. ''Course I'll come with you on Thursday. But you do realize, you should be asking the police for help, not me.'

Karin marched off into the hallway.

'You're playing with fire,' Mel shouted. 'Do you realize that?' She heard the front door close before she had even finished her sentence.

Too late. The fire's already started, thought Mel.

16

Karin

The traffic was doing its usual crawl through Headingley. A cricket match down at the stadium was making it even busier than normal, and Louie's face was everywhere in the crowds. Aware that Louie now had everything she needed: phone number, *her* address *and* Aaron's, was feeding Karin's paranoia.

As she waited for the beep of the pedestrian crossing at the end of the Arndale, her heart was pumping so fast she thought it might actually explode out of her chest. Holding onto the box of cakes she had just bought from Greggs, she was trying to focus on work, not on Louie. They were almost over the finishing line now, but she needed everyone to pull together on this final push for next Saturday's launch.

She hoped Will understood that. Surely he did. This meant everything to him. His behaviour this morning had perturbed her, not to mention the disturbing things Mel had said about him afterwards. She would speak to Will as soon as she got to work, get his version of the story.

Will would never lie to her.

An angry driver tooted his horn when she stepped out before the lights had changed. She almost dropped the box of cakes. Her mind was full of too many other things.

I KNOW EVERYTHING KARIN

'Watch where you're bloody going,' the passenger in the car shouted.

Her hand shot up in a V-sign, the fury inside her coursing to her fingertips. It was the reaction of someone living rough. Or a school kid kicking back against the system. That's why the counsellor had suggested tossing the imaginary pebbles into the sea. 'Or try holding onto your wrist with your thumb and forefinger, Karin. Deep breaths. It all helps.'

Coping strategies. For when she really couldn't any more.

But she had been coping. That was the thing. Karin had worked hard to get her life to where it was now. Aaron was the man she wanted to marry; she had a job which actually meant something; some money behind her too, even if it was a hand-out from her mother. She finally had something which resembled a proper future. Karin could safely say that she was happy, and it was a happiness she felt she could trust.

But then the weekend happened.

And Louie, all over again.

It was a haze to her now, coming back in fragments. Excerpts of one mistake after another playing out in her head. The biggest of all was Louie. Why give her that shred of hope, then crush it immediately after? And why did Aaron have to wave the engagement ring in front of her like that? Not the way to treat someone who had saved you from drowning. Louie didn't deserve that. But it was *not* a mistake saying yes to Aaron. Her mistake was in not telling him about Louie. Before the weekend.

There may have been a momentary spark in the toilets again, a runaway desire for that raw passion which had once fused their teenage souls together, but Karin had let go of Louie a long time ago. The shock of seeing her had made her behave irrationally. It could have come out of pity, Karin supposed, or a sense of guilt. Really, she had no idea what happened, other than she bitterly regretted it now. Of course, Mel was right to advise her not to go anywhere near that exhibition on Thursday, but how could Karin stop that either? Tell her fiancé that she had had sex with her former girlfriend in the toilets just before he proposed?

Whatever she did now, Karin was on the back foot.

As if Louie had been reading her thoughts for the past forty minutes, the phone flagged up another message:

LOVE YOU TO SEE MY PAINTINGS.
MEANS SO MUCH.
YOU MUST COME.
LOU xx

With that, Karin was in Morecambe again. In their tiny bedsit, cold and damp in winter, a tropical hothouse in summer. Poorly lit, the shower no more than a trickle, and a room full of rickety furniture that smelt of old people. None of that mattered because it was their home. Their love nest. Sometimes she would laugh so much with Louie it would hurt, and all Karin wanted to do was drink up every last drop of her, in case Louie's love for her ran out.

But things had got out of control and she knew Louie would never let her go. Fearing the consequences if she didn't get out.

Mel had fixed things. As soon as she heard Karin had a 'stalking ex' on her case – as Mel referred to her – the next time Louie called she grabbed the phone. Karin begged her: 'Oh please, Mel, don't be cruel. She thinks I'm in the States.'

'I'll be your American girlfriend then,' said Mel. 'I'll tell her to stop calling you.'

It seemed to work for a while, but then Louie persisted again with texts:

How are you, please explain, when are you coming back?

In the end, Mel advised Karin to take the obvious action and change her number: *Why haven't you already done this anyway, Karin?*

It was a reasonable question. But changing her number was the last resort. It might get rid of Louie, but it would also sever the link to her mother. Karin longed for a call to say that Birgitta was sorry too and that she could go home. She wanted her mother to take some responsibility for what had occurred. In reality Karin knew this was never going to happen, but it had been mildly reassuring that at least a sequence of numbers still held the two of them together. Now there wasn't even that. So when Louie was finally eliminated from her life, Birgitta went too. It left Karin feeling both liberated and bereft, not sure which was greater for which person. Not that it mattered. They were both gone and that was what mattered.

It sent a shockwave through her now to consider the damage that Louie could inflict upon her current happiness.

I KNOW EVERYTHING KARIN.

Louie did know everything.

And, worryingly, so did Will.

Karin had met Will down by the River Aire under a bridge. She hadn't long stepped off the train from Morecambe and had no idea where to go in this vast city of Leeds. Apart from her few remaining possessions, everything else had gone, robbed on the train while she slept. So she gravitated down onto the towpath, because that was where homeless people went.

The last half hour of daylight was shared with cyclists and the occasional dog walker, which made Karin feel reasonably safe and she even received a few coins from a couple of them. But when it grew darker and colder, the shadows turned into angry, threatening faces as they got closer, and the wind was raw and uncharitable, biting into her skin. Karin was glad of her parka with the enormous hood. Not only did it keep her warm it also covered her face, hiding her vulnerability as a young woman.

She had spotted a cluster of hunched-over shapes gathered round a small flame flickering up ahead under a bridge. When she got closer she realized it was a cigarette lighter and five men passing a soggy cigarette and a bottle between them. They seemed out of it, listless, and didn't pay too much attention as she walked past. After, she heard a wolf whistle and some remark she didn't quite catch. Quickening her step, she decided on the next bridge instead.

It stank just as much as the other one, piss and excrement mixed with cheap booze and cigarettes. But she found a place under the curve of the roof, where, with any luck she might be able to sleep undisturbed. Then she noticed an unoccupied pop-up tent taking a battering in the wind. Shivering and desperate, Karin thought it was worth the risk and crawled inside. She must have fallen asleep straight away, but woke to the sound of two men arguing outside.

It soon became obvious that the dispute was about her, as it began to escalate into a drunken brawl. And yet, listening harder, she was sure it was only the one voice she was actually hearing. So maybe he was having an argument with himself?

'She's in my fucking tent, she can pay me in fucking kind.' Then it went quiet, followed by the same voice again: 'I don't know what you're fucking saying to me you fucking retard but just back off or you'll end up in that river and never get out again. Read. My. Lips.' A dog started barking, and then another, growling and snarling. 'Ah pipe down yer cunts,' came the same voice once more. 'You can fuck off the lot of you.'

The tent began to shake violently. Karin crawled out, holding her hood down over her face. She tried to make herself taller, stronger. Tightening her throat, she hoped her voice would sound deep enough. 'Sorry, mate.'

The man laughed, holding onto his stomach. He was solid-looking and mean. Through his bursts of coughing and snorting he finally managed to say: 'The bitch thinks she's a wee boy now.' More laughter. But then he stopped, stepped into her face and wrenched down the hood of her parka. 'I've already had a look at your tits and pussy, love, so you can—'

He was knocked off his feet. Lying flat on the ground, hit from behind.

The dogs, she could just make out their shadows, started barking again. This time their barks sounded different, like they were pleased.

'Shush now. It's all over.' That was an old man's voice, and Karin saw a large hand patting the dogs' heads. 'He'll look after you. Stick with him and you'll be fine.' She realized that the last comment was for her when the old man gave her a friendly nod. He settled the dogs and then lay down beside them. Karin had mistaken him for a heap of old rags before.

She felt a tap on the arm, jumped sideways and raised her fists.

The man was youngish, but hard to tell how old because of his long beard. He was using sign language and gesturing at her. It all made sense then, why she had only heard one voice in the conversation earlier. There was a girl at her boarding school who had been partially deaf. She had taught Karin a few signs, but Karin couldn't remember any when she really needed them. At one time she had known the whole alphabet.

'I really don't understand,' she had to confess, giving him an exaggerated shrug, throwing her arms out wide. 'But, thank you.'

The sign for that one suddenly came back to her. Hand flat, fingertips on the chin, hand moves away from you to show gratitude.

'And erm. My name's Karin.' She just about managed to spell out her name too. But struggled to decipher his, guessing wildly at the letters he was forming.

The old man piped up from his slumber again, and shouted, 'His fucking name's Will,' then went back to sleep.

'Hello, Will,' she said, laughing. 'Can you lip-read?'

Will nodded, and they shook hands. He led her away from the bridge to another area, through a secret canopy in the undergrowth to a place protected by tall trees and sheltered by the wall of a long, flat building. 'Welcome to my bedroom,' he said, or something similar. From his rucksack he produced a sleeping bag, and for himself a blanket. Karin tried to insist that it should be the other way around, but he was having none of it. They sat and chatted for a while and when she asked what he had said to her tormentor he made some rather dramatic signing. Something along the lines of: 'If you touch her I will rip your head off and feed it to those dogs.'

They stuck together after that.

Will taught her to sign and she became reasonably fluent again, but resorted to notebook and pen if necessary. In many ways Will's story was worse than her own: abandoned as a boy for being deaf and stupid, followed by a succession of children's homes and foster carers, locked into a system which ultimately failed him and left him to fend for himself. A loner and an outsider, not a single qualification to his name, Will was the kindest, most sensitive, intelligent person she had ever met. Always carried a book around with him, Russian history and literature being his thing. A notepad and pen too.

They would swap stories over a bottle of cider, or anything else they could get their hands on to numb the pain of their existence; the rest of the time, trying to keep warm, find a bed for the night or get a hot meal.

Karin promised to repay Will one day for all the times when, if it hadn't been for him, she would have been raped, drugged and possibly even murdered in those desperate months being kicked around the streets of Leeds. It was as though Will could smell danger, and even if they were separated for a time he always seemed to turn up whenever she was in trouble. This hideaway of his, Will's bedroom, became their regular meeting place down by the river.

Will was a special person and a friend for life.

So in the same way that Mel had shown kindness to her, putting a roof over her head, giving her the chance to make a go of her life, now Karin wanted to do the same for Will.

The world was not all bad.

17

Karin

Getting the *Room for a Night* and *Love an Empty* schemes properly off the ground had been a tough battle. It made Karin think she did have some of her mother's drive and tenacity after all.

The charity's aim was to help homeless people get back into society, giving them skills for life. The *Love an Empty* scheme fit this vision perfectly. Doing up unoccupied homes, they had a guaranteed roof over their heads at the end of it. Will was to be one of the first to move in next week to the Ashby Road project. Karin had the *Yorkshire Post* and local TV networks lined up to fanfare its completion. Of course, she dreamed of national coverage so that her mother might see her being interviewed on BBC *Breakfast* and *News at Ten*, or on the front page of *The Times* and the *Guardian*, maybe hear her on Radio Four. Erase all those years of being an embarrassment and disappointment to her. Sometimes she just wished they could start again.

No matter. This was a big achievement all the same.

The area around Ashby Road had once been popular with students but now many of the houses were left empty and neglected as the student population had gravitated towards the city centre into flats with en suites, gyms and on-site shops. For the past few weeks, Karin had been busy with garden maintenance, enjoying the run of long summer days.

Number sixty-eight was Will's house, along with seven other residents. In a couple of days the scaffolding would be gone from these houses and they would look lived-in and loved again. Karin spotted a yellow hat visible between the metal bars on the first level, but not much activity going on. As she walked up the path, the site manager was coming towards her wiping the sweat off his face with his forearm. He greeted her with the news that two people had called in sick and he warned her they were in danger of not meeting their deadline. There was no sign of Will yet either, but Karin felt sure he would show up at some point.

Will had needed a lot of convincing at first that this wasn't a trick or another half-hearted promise. He had had too many of those in his life. Karin assured him that this opportunity would never be taken away from him, as long as he worked hard. It was a chance to get qualifications, maybe go to university, with a well-paid job at the end of it. Like Karin, he finally had the option of a proper future. Will had been so keen throughout the project, helping out at every stage; the one person she could rely on to do whatever she asked.

'I'll get some agency help in,' Karin said.

The site manager shook his head, saying it would be expensive and there were no special rates for charities. But Karin had funds now, which she could use on the quiet in circumstances such as this. Maybe she could pretend to be an anonymous donor, the secret millionaire boss. It gave her a warm feeling to be able to put some of this money she had received from her mother to a worthy cause.

A string of messages and missed calls greeted her when she extracted her phone from her pocket to make the necessary arrangements. All were from Louie. Ignoring those, Karin gave Mel a quick ring instead.

'Mel, has Will come back to the house? He's not shown up for work yet.'

Mel said he hadn't, but offered to check his room just in case.

He wasn't in there either. As she was working from home today, Mel promised to let her know if he appeared.

When a message came pinging through, minutes later, Karin hoped it might be Mel to say that she had seen him.

But it was Louie:

SO PLEASED YOU CAN MAKE MY EXHIBITION.
YOUR OLD MAN JUST CONFIRMED!
SEE YOU THURSDAY.
LOU XX

Karin deleted it. There were far more pressing things to worry about right now.

There was very little she could do about Will for the time being. His refusal to have a mobile phone, despite offering to buy him one, meant that no one could reach him. And with their big launch only around the corner, Karin couldn't afford to go chasing across Leeds to find him. She just had to hope that he would emerge at some point, which, knowing Will, he more than likely would.

He didn't.

By six o'clock Karin had had enough. Her back ached from a day of pulling up weeds and chopping down overgrown shrubs. She packed up her things and promised to return tomorrow morning. Walking home via Woodhouse Ridge, a woodland shortcut that was once an Edwardian park, she wondered what she should do if Will wasn't back at the house. She had asked a few people working on the project if they had seen him, made a few calls, but no one had. At what point was a homeless man – and technically he still was until next week – a missing person?

Despite feeling like she was being watched, her mind was still distracted. She didn't notice the cyclist shooting past, bouncing her into the wall. The brightly-coloured graffiti sprayed along the old stonework was also a reminder that the beat and throb of the city was never far away. For all the beauty of the Ridge, it paid to stay alert at any time of day and to avoid the area at night. Karin continued on her way, quickening her pace due to a growing unease. Once or twice, a movement in the dense shrubbery caused her to turn, the sound of branches snapping, but as soon as silence was restored she was back in the tangle of her thoughts once more.

A tap on the shoulder soon pulled her out of them again.

She yelped, turning round quickly.

'Will! Thank goodness, where have you been?' She signed the words, as well as saying them, resisting the urge to throw her arms around him. There were boundaries not to be crossed these days. Even though Will was a good friend, he was part of her professional life now and for both their sakes it was better not to show any favouritism or affection, at least not in public. The Ridge was quiet, but there were always people about, hidden by trees in the maze of upper and lower paths.

'Are you okay?' she asked.

Clearly he wasn't. He seemed agitated, more than she had ever known him to be.

Will signed something back to her. It came across as angry. 'I'm leaving,' he said.

'What?' She thought she hadn't understood properly. Karin still wasn't completely fluent in sign language but she could usually get the gist. 'Did you really say *leaving*?' She noticed his rucksack and the sleeping bag attached to it, dangling by its cord.

'I wanted to say goodbye first, and to thank you for all you've done for me, Karin. You are a good person.'

'But why? Your home is here, it's almost finished. You can move in next week.'

'Give my room to someone else.'

'Will, I'm really struggling with this. You've worked tirelessly these past weeks. How can you throw all that away?' Karin let out a despairing sigh. Will was one of the reasons she hadn't given up on this project when things weren't going to plan. He was always there, offering words of encouragement, making other members of the team work as hard as he was prepared to do. Do it for Karin, he would say. And then she would have to remind him that it was for himself. They were doing it for themselves, all of them. Helping each other.

Will started to sign again. 'It's time to move on. You're getting married.'

'Yes, but I'm not going anywhere. I'll still be in Leeds and working for the charity. Come on, Will. We're a good team, you and me.'

There was no denying it would be a challenge for someone like Will to live in a communal environment, but they had been over this many times. Karin knew this wasn't the issue now.

'It's Mel, isn't it?'

He gave her one of his looks, reaching into her thoughts, rifling through them. She was used to it, others found it unnerving. Will thrust his hands into the pockets of his overcoat; too warm for this weather really. Karin had bought it for him second-hand as a gift when she first started working properly for the charity. She noticed, though, that his pockets were weighed down for a life on the move. Will extracted a book, clearly looking for something else. Karin noticed a bottle and pulled it out.

'You're drinking again?'

Will snatched it from her, but in his frustration he put it back into his other pocket, clanking it against another bottle.

Karin removed them both, holding one in each hand. 'Why, Will?'

Finally he found what he was looking for and held up a set of keys. Karin recognized them as the ones to their house in Headingley. They jingled together in a happy dance, as a dog might wag its tail to cheer up a sad owner. She returned the bottles of cheap whisky to his pockets and accepted the keys with painful reluctance, staring down at them in her palm. She nudged her thumb over the rainbow keyring that she had attached, so they wouldn't get mixed up with her own set or with Mel's. Karin could feel tears burning her eyes, doing her best to hold them back.

Will flicked his elbow in the air, hooking the strap of his rucksack over the other shoulder. 'Goodbye, Karin,' he said, and took off towards town, taking the lower path.

'Will.'

She caught up, running in front of him so she could sign. He didn't make any effort to stop and Karin had to put her hands up to prevent him from going any further. He slammed into her hands deliberately. There was so much anger behind his eyes.

'Mel told me what happened about the jewellery. I knew you weren't stealing it, Will. I mean, you wouldn't do that, would you?'

He looked down, kicking at the dried-out soil on the path.

'If you have to ask me that,' he signed, 'then I really don't belong here.'

'No. No, wait. I explained to Mel it was probably just some mix-up and— what's that?'

Will was unfolding a piece of paper. It looked vaguely familiar.

'NO HOME FOR YOU HERE. LOSER.'

'Oh God. She's got to you too then,' said Karin, inspecting it more closely.

Will didn't give her time to explain. He snatched the note back and set off, forcing Karin to run in front of him once more to slow him down. 'Wait,' she shouted, putting her hand up again to make him stop. 'It's Louie who sent that note. She sent one to me this morning.' Will looked confused, then Karin remembered he wasn't up to speed. 'Sorry. I didn't tell you everything about the weekend and – and maybe I should have. But Aaron took us to The Midland hotel – he thought it would be a special birthday treat – and I bumped into Lou again.'

As she was saying the words she felt Will picking up on her embarrassment. He always knew when she was hiding something, which made it even worse. 'I think she might be in Leeds,' she continued. 'She has an art exhibition here on Thursday. I know exactly what she's up to, Will. She wants to isolate me, get rid of the people I'm close to, stop me having friends.'

The way Will was looking at her, Karin knew she wouldn't be able to prevent him from leaving. And maybe he had been her protector for long enough. After all, he was free to live his life the way he wanted, and if he didn't require any more of her help, then that was his choice.

Karin extracted a wad of money from her dungarees. It was intended for one of the contractors at Ashby Road, but she could easily get some more. She pushed the roll of notes towards Will.

'Two hundred pounds. Take it. We couldn't have got to this stage without all your hard work. At least accept this.'

Will rolled an elastic band down his wrist and put it round the bundle of notes, stuffing it into his jeans pocket.

'And you deserve way more than that,' she added, 'but it's all the cash I have on me.'

Will threw his arms out to the side and took a step back, signing something else. 'It's enough, Karin,' he said. 'You need to watch your back.'

He was on the verge of leaving again but when he saw Karin's fingers fumbling to remove the rainbow keyring, he waited for her to take it off.

'For luck,' she said. 'And friendship.'

'Thank you.'

Will pushed it through the hole in the bundle of notes she had just given him, then returned it to his pocket, doing a half-circle around Karin, staring in that way of his as if to say this really was it.

He didn't look back.

She wanted to cry as Will became smaller, obscured by the green wilderness of Woodhouse Ridge until the bend in the path took him out of sight completely. It was too final. Karin couldn't bear to be parted from him. In a world where their only choices were either to survive or give in, the two of them had stuck together in the hope that something better would come along. She always assured Will that things would improve if she could make it to her twenty-second birthday. In the end they didn't have to wait that long because Mel had come to her rescue long before that.

They had both been thrown a lifeline. So why was he prepared to throw it back again? After all they had been through. Sitting on pavements side by side, they knew the rhythm of each other's heartbeat, the length of the other's breath while one slept and the other kept guard.

And yet.

She had to let him go.

Retracing her steps back up onto the path which led home, Karin left a tearful voicemail for Aaron. And then turned back again, racing down the path to Will.

She was completely out of breath by the time she caught up with him.

'I'm so sorry, Will. I just wanted to ask you—' Karin signed as best she could, realizing he might struggle to lip-read with her panting so heavily. 'It's really – well, I'd be grateful if you didn't go to the police about the note. I mean, I know it's unlikely and everything. But – well, you know why.'

The intensity of his stare made her shrivel all the way to the ground. Will deserved better than this.

'They won't listen to a homeless person anyway,' he replied.

'Oh. But. Do you mind if I have it? I mean it's only to compare it with the one I got this morning. It's not because I don't trust you or anything.' Her voice faded into a trail of shame.

Will certainly deserved better than this.

He handed the note over and she bit hard into her lip, avoiding his gaze. The gentle sway of the trees, the thin clouds tearing themselves apart in the sky, and even the faint buzz of traffic on Meanwood Road, all were saying that her secrets were safe with Will, so why had she had doubted him twice in the space of ten minutes? First the jewellery and now this.

'Don't worry,' he said. 'I know everything, Karin.'

'What?'

Her insides turned cold at that phrase.

Will was already walking away.

18

Mel

'What did you *actually* say to Will?'

Karin was straight onto her the moment she walked through the door. Mel had only just walked through it herself, dumped her things in the hallway and sat down. Aaron had phoned her on the way home, having picked up a tearful voicemail from Karin and wanting to check his facts before speaking to her. He had adopted his landlord tone, and Mel was rather put out by that, asking questions like: *Did she know that Will was intending to leave? Had Will said anything to her about going? Why hadn't she reported it to Aaron that she was having problems with him?* So she really didn't need it from Karin as well. Mel had done her best to accommodate Will and he just hadn't helped himself in the end. He could have played by the rules.

'I haven't said anything to Will,' she said, replying to Karin's question. 'Where do you think he's gone?'

'He's out there on the streets I guess. I gave him money, so maybe he'll find a hostel. But I just hope he comes back.' Karin dumped a set of keys down on the unit, presumably Will's, although there was no keyring attached. 'So tell me what happened then.'

'Hey all I did was have a discreet word with him, after I caught him doing whatever it was he claimed he was doing with your jewellery,' Mel replied, rolling her eyes. 'Exactly like I told you.'

Mel hesitated and let out a sigh. 'Okay, you'd better sit down,' she added, pulling a chair out for Karin.

'Why?'

'Because I didn't want to say this.' She waited for Karin to take a seat, but she clearly wasn't going to. 'Some of my things have gone missing too over these past weeks.'

'Well like what?'

'Money, if I've left any lying around. A really expensive pen. My mum's bracelet, which I'm so upset about. Too many things for it to be a coincidence, Karin.'

'So why didn't you say something to me?'

Karin looped her bag over the chair, flopping down into it after she had done a full circuit of the room.

'Because I knew how important it was that Will had a roof over his head until his place was ready. Important to you, important to him. I didn't want to cause any trouble. To be honest though, it's a bit rich of you and Aaron to start accusing me, when you two were never around. You did abandon me with him.'

'I'm not accusing you of anything. I'm worried about Will.'

The pipes howled and juddered, because Mel had got up to fill the kettle and turned the cold tap on too far. She had to wait for it to stop before she spoke again. 'Look I didn't tell him to go, if that's what you're *asking* me.' She used the kettle to make her point, swinging it round to plug it into the wall. 'There could be a whole host of reasons why a guy like Will has to move on.'

Karin pressed her nails into her head, scratching it like there was some unwanted thing inside. Mel had seen her do this before, but not for a long time. She stopped and looked up at Mel.

'Will got a note too,' Karin said.

'No. From Louie? So what did it say?'

Karin was struggling to get her words out, on the verge of tears. 'It's so hurtful,' she said, taking the note from her bag. 'It says, "no home for you here. Loser".'

'Wait a minute,' said Mel, banging two mugs down onto the unit. 'How the hell does Louie know about Will?'

'Because she's already in Leeds setting up for her exhibition. Been texting and calling me, and I think she must be spying on me. It's really creepy what she's doing, Mel.'

Mel placed a steaming mug of tea in front of Karin and sat beside her, gently rubbing her back. 'She's sick in the head, that one. What do you think we do now?'

Karin seemed to regain her strength. She sat up tall and said, 'I'll speak to her on Thursday at the exhibition.'

'What? You're still going, even after this?'

'I've tried telling Aaron that Louie can be a bit weird and that I really don't want to go, but he says it's business and he's quite capable of going on his own. Obviously, I can't let that happen. He thinks he can sell Louie's work to the corporate market, but it's all so mixed up because I really want her to do well and it could be the making of her. It might even get her off my back in the process.' Karin used her pleading face and Mel could predict what was coming. 'You'll be there, won't you, Mel? Please, I could really do with your support.'

When Mel didn't give an answer straight away, Karin grew agitated, then desperate. 'You've always been there for me and you know I'm so grateful for that. I've booked us a table at Swank. Just me and you, because I want to say thank you, and Aaron is fine with—'

'Of course I'll be there! Don't worry. I'll be there.'

Karin collapsed into her.

Mel was used to her being an emotional pressure cooker, in the early days, but it all seemed to be starting up again. She asked if Karin wanted to talk some more, but she said she didn't. Mel still sat with her, forcing her to finish her tea. Then when she had, Mel studied the note and folded it up. 'I'll put this safe in the drawer with the other one, shall I? I really don't think we should throw them away. It's evidence.'

Karin looked fearful. 'I'm not going to the police, Mel. I can't.'

'Do you want to tell me why not?'

She shook her head.

19

Louie

Louie stood back to examine how the exhibition was taking shape. It wasn't quite what she had in mind. Her artwork was mounted onto thirteen felt-backed panels, which made it look more like a museum display than an art exhibition, and much smaller than she expected. She had requested some extra panels; the arcade in the Victoria Quarter was plenty big enough. She really needed Karin to see the full effect. Without Karin, there would be no exhibition. And this was her moment to come back to Louie.

The management team at The Midland were being very accommodating, allowing her the time off that she had requested. As a rule, they were supportive to employees in endeavours of this nature, so Louie had always assumed there wouldn't be a problem asking for unpaid leave. The exhibition sponsors were paying modest expenses for her to stay in Leeds during the set up and preview night, and the rest she was covering herself. Even if it was only a room above a pub in a seedy part of town, at least it was the same town as Karin, which, in itself, meant as much as the exhibition.

Louie took the scarf from her pocket and ran it under her nose. It went everywhere with her, since retrieving it from the beach that day. She had seen roughly where it had landed after it broke free from Karin's neck, and she had gone out in search of it. It was a different perfume to the one Louie was used to her wearing, more expensive probably as Karin could now afford to splash out on such luxuries. The scarf would be waiting for Karin in Morecambe when she came home; she could have it back then.

Louie was rather surprised by the interest that old bastard was showing in her work. Despite being flattered, she was also sceptical. With his percentages and sales-projection jargon, he may as well have been speaking a foreign language, but she understood the gist of it to be that her commercial work had potential in hotels, offices, bars, and that he could place it for her. She did wonder if he was playing some sort of cat-and-mouse game but, when he spoke of drawing up a contract, she said she would give it some serious thought and agreed to discuss it further with him at the preview night. If it had been anyone else making this offer she would have jumped at it immediately.

For the moment, though, her focus was on getting these paintings displayed correctly. She couldn't wait to see Karin's face tomorrow night when she set eyes on them.

She would do whatever it took to get Karin back in her life again.

20

Mel

Mel was secretly furious with Aaron for cutting it so fine. She knew, from his point of view, this was neither reasonable nor rational, but having promised to come and sort out the dishwasher before the end of the week he had finally showed up today, only four hours before the exhibition. Confiding in her about his marriage proposal was all well and good, however a follow-up conversation to that might have been polite. The one phone call she did receive from him was the scolding about Will, which she could really have done without, particularly when Aaron's biggest concern now ought to be Louie. Of course he still didn't know this, nor could she tell him.

He arrived in a steaming temper. Not only was he still showing resentment for her not informing him of Will's snooping and thieving habits, he also let slip that some property deal had fallen through.

He crouched down to look in the dishwasher.

'You're not really dressed for that you know,' said Mel, teasing him. 'Hand over your jacket. Come on.'

Aaron stopped what he was doing, looked up and smiled at Mel who was standing with her arm out. He removed his suit jacket, which she hooked neatly over the chair for him.

'Sorry. I know it's not your fault about Will,' he said. 'It upsets Karin, you know how it is.'

'Yes, I do know how it is,' she replied. Mel admired these qualities in Aaron: his willingness to apologize, his loyalty to Karin. 'Congratulations on your recent engagement, by the way,' she added.

'Oh thanks. Even though you don't approve?'

'I never said that, Aaron. I just don't want either of you to get hurt. You know how much I love that girl, so if your intentions are less than honourable, you'll have *me* on your case.'

Aaron laughed. 'Noted,' he said, diving back into the dishwasher.

'Good. Right, well I'm going upstairs to get changed. If you want to strip down to your underwear, I'll be gone approximately thirty minutes. I'll hum loudly when I'm on my way back.'

He laughed again. She liked to hear him laugh, and to know they were on good terms again. Mel left him in the kitchen, going upstairs to get ready.

When she reappeared, Aaron was shouldering his jacket and looking at his watch. He did a double-take when he saw her.

'Wow. You must be going somewhere "swanky" tonight.'

She was wearing a black cocktail dress, above the knee, and heels. Nothing too over-the-top but she supposed he had never seen her dressed up like this before. Plus she had been to the hairdresser that afternoon, so her black bob was looking neat and slick.

'I take it you can spare your fiancée for a few hours,' Mel said. 'She did run it by you?'

'She did, and I'm sure I can.'

He was already on his way out, walking hurriedly into the hall checking his watch as he went. Mel knew this was her moment if she was going to say something.

'I'll see you at the art thing though,' she shouted. Aaron gave her a backwards wave, almost at the front door. 'It's her friend's exhibition, isn't it? Louie somebody or other. Think she knew her in Morecambe.'

109

Aaron paused, the door half open. 'Actually *not* a friend as it turns out. But she's a bloody good artist.'

'Ah. So you do know? I'm glad she's told you. And you're obviously okay with that?'

Aaron was looking puzzled now, letting go of the door handle. 'She's told me this Louie can be a bit weird sometimes. Artistic temperament and all that.'

'Well yes, that's what I meant. And erm, well Karin mentioned you really like her work, and she's finding that a bit awkward I guess. Doesn't want it to look like she wants to suddenly be friends. I suppose.'

Aaron stepped outside. His parting words were: 'Karin knows she doesn't have to be involved. I've told her that. See you later.'

Mel decided to take a quick blast of air in Hyde Park to clear her head, once Aaron had gone. She was finding the role of go-between quite a strain. She slipped off her heels and slid into a pair of trainers, draping a long cardigan over her shoulders to protect her dress.

There were students everywhere, having barbecues and getting drunk, teenagers going back and forth on the skate park, litter overflowing from all of the bins.

After half an hour she headed home again, calling by the florists at the bottom of the road to pick up some sunflowers for Karin. She needed cheering up, with all that was going on.

Closing the front door, Mel thought she could hear someone upstairs and assumed it would be Aaron, perhaps forgotten something. But she hadn't noticed his car outside, which then made her anxious. It was unlikely to be Will, as he no longer had a key, and she had arranged to meet Karin later at the exhibition. Unless Karin had changed her mind, but that also seemed unlikely.

It only left one other person.

Could it be Louie?

Mel removed her trainers, putting them down silently in the hallway along with the flowers. She hitched up her dress so she could creep upstairs, her heart pumping. Should she be armed with a heavy implement of some kind? But it was too late for that now. Her phone would have to do as her safeguard.

The noise was coming from her bedroom.

Nudging the door a fraction, Mel peered through the crack and saw that it was Karin.

'Have you lost something, Karin?'

She was leaning over Mel's desk, shuffling papers around.

Karin froze. Her body turned slowly, although her head was a few seconds behind because she didn't want to look Mel in the eye. 'Oh erm. I thought you'd gone into the office today and were meeting me straight from work.'

'I ended up working from home because Aaron phoned to say he could come and have a look at the dishwasher again. I thought if I could show him the problem it might actually get fixed this time. What are you after?'

'I-I was trying to find the notes and couldn't remember which drawer you said you'd put them in. Thought I might take them tonight, just in case. I'm sorry, I should've asked you just to bring them, but my head is so frantic I can't think.'

'Sure,' said Mel. She opened the drawer of her dressing-table and took out the notes.

'Thanks.' Karin was digging her nails into her head.

'Come on, sit down.' Mel guided her over to the bed and sat beside her, pushing her hair back and stroking her cheek. Karin looked so lost. 'I *am* here for you,' she said. 'You know that, don't you? You can't deal with this alone.' Karin dipped her head into Mel's shoulder as she continued to stroke her face. 'Louie sure knows how to push your buttons, I'll say that for her.'

'It's not just Lou,' Karin muttered. 'It's something Will said too.'

Mel knew it was often better to leave her rather than try and tease it out of her. Karin did continue, after a brief period of reflection, staring at the notes in her hand. 'He told me to watch my back. But then said something else, which I can't stop thinking about.'

'Well, like what?'

She seemed to have gone into a trance, as if trying to work something out in her head. 'Will said: "I know everything, Karin".' She held up the note with those exact words, amateurishly stuck onto it, and then looked at Mel. 'I'm sure it was a coincidence. But isn't that weird?'

'Wow,' said Mel, whistling her dismay, having to get her own head around this. 'So you think Will *is* sending these notes? Not Louie?'

'No. I don't know.'

'Karin, why won't you just go to the police? Let them find out who it is. Who are you protecting? Is it Louie?'

Karin shook her head. 'She did save my life.'

'Huh. And she's trying to ruin it now. Look, even if it's not her sending those notes, she's clearly getting to you again.'

Karin was on her feet now. 'She is *not* going to do this to me. I'm going to speak to her tonight and put a stop to this.' Holding the notes up defiantly as she spoke, she must have noticed the time on Mel's clock because she quickly added: 'Oh God, I need to get going, don't I?' She blew air out of her cheeks, as if to give her courage. 'And you look great by the way, Mel. That dress really suits you.'

'Thanks. Look, why don't you just get Aaron to meet us there?'

'Because I don't want to let him out of my sight this evening.' She was heading for the door, but stopped in her tracks. 'What's up? Why are you looking at me like that?' There was dread in her voice.

'I wasn't sure when to tell you this,' said Mel.

112

'What?'

'I got one too.'

'One what?' Karin's frown deepened. 'Oh God, you didn't, did you? Shit.' She sank down onto the bed again, holding onto her wrist; that thing she did when she was stressed. Deep breaths, eyes closed.

Mel held the note out ready for when she opened her eyes. It was the same as the other two: cut-out letters from newspapers, crudely stuck on.

Karin unfolded it slowly. She put her hand to her mouth when she read it: '"You know she hates you."'

'I'm so sorry, Mel,' she said, after a while. 'You know that's not true.'

'Don't be silly, why are *you* sorry? It's not your fault.' She pulled Karin towards her again.

'I know what she's doing, she's trying to isolate me. Wants to get rid of everyone so I'm totally alone and then thinks I'll go back to her.' Karin must have seen that Mel was looking alarmed at that. 'Oh, I don't mean get rid in that sense. She's not dangerous or anything.'

'Well I hope you're right about that,' said Mel, half-laughing, but only just. 'She was pretty scary the last time, I seem to remember. One crazy bitch all right, and looks like she wants to shit you up as much as possible. Or Will does.'

Karin shook her head. 'No. It's definitely Louie.'

'Does Aaron know about these vile notes we've been getting? Has he had one?'

Karin was holding onto her wrist so tightly now her fingers had gone white, cutting the circulation off in her other hand.

'He hasn't mentioned it and I'm sure he would. Please don't say anything to him, Mel. My god, you don't think she's going to send him one too, do you? But she wouldn't though. He's helping sell her artwork, it'd be a stupid thing to do.'

'Depends what's more important,' said Mel. 'You. Or the artwork. Look, Karin, you've got to tell me what's really going on here. I'm getting nervous now.'

Karin was hastily on her feet again, heading out of the room. 'I don't know what's going on. If I did I'd tell you.'

21

Karin

Aaron's apartment was in the centre of Leeds overlooking the river. Modern and spacious, usually Karin found it relaxing here, but she was running late and under pressure. Not only that: in both her homes, Headingley *and* here, she felt as though her privacy was being compromised, constantly being watched.

Karin could hear the TV on in the lounge, reinforcing the fact that Aaron was waiting for her to get ready. The sensible thing would have been to meet him at the exhibition, as Mel had suggested, but she still didn't want to risk leaving Louie alone with him.

Although Aaron was without prejudice per se, his own outlook on these things was very traditional. Even if he could accept that Karin's previous relationship was with a woman, he could never forgive her for what she did with Louie at The Midland. Of course, she would say it was a one-off, a big mistake, all those excuses people give in these situations. Which it genuinely was; she still regretted it as deeply as she had the moment it happened. But hers was an indiscretion driven by fear and surprise; she certainly hadn't set out to hurt the man she loved. How would *she* feel, though, if Aaron suddenly announced that he had recently slept with his ex-wife? Would she be able to forgive and trust him again?

As they walked towards the exhibition, she reached for his hand. It felt cold. She tightened her grip and he gave her a half-smile, but it seemed rather forced. Karin felt that something had broken between them. Something invisible.

The Victoria Quarter was even more beautiful at night. When the decadence of the shops had been packed away, doors locked, lights extinguished, it was time for the arcades themselves to shine, allowing the mosaics, marble, and the stained-glass roof to really come alive. A security guard approached as they entered through the glass doors. He was about to check them off the guest list but, on recognizing Aaron, guided them through to a private partitioned-off area.

The exhibition was already buzzing with Leeds' trendy set out in force, as well as a cluster of art students, easy to spot by their hairstyles and piercings. The after-work gate crashers were also there, lured in by the prospect of free wine, and maybe the odd canapé besides no doubt. Louie came over to greet them. She was her usual relaxed self. Karin recognized those jeans she was wearing, loose-fitting, faded and torn in places by genuine wear and tear and not by any fashion dictate, and she recognized the white shirt too, the ends of which were tied in a knot showing off her toned stomach and pierced belly button. It was Karin's shirt. She used to wear it for work at The Midland.

She still looked good, despite losing weight. Perhaps Karin was the reason for the weight loss but she didn't want to dwell on that thought. Louie made a point of kissing Karin on both cheeks and shook Aaron's hand. Karin was worried how this might look to Aaron: a waitress whom she first of all claimed to barely know, who then became *a bit weird*, now giving her an intimate welcome at her art show. Aaron had been asking questions on their walk down here, and Karin merely implied they just didn't hit it off, fearing if she said any more it would only make him suspicious.

The partitions made the arcade seem small, even though it was vast, and Karin felt hemmed in. She managed to convey a weak smile to Louie. Polite. But clear enough to suggest that she really didn't want to be here.

'Come and get a glass of wine,' said Louie.

Karin didn't respond. Sensing Aaron shifting away from her, she found herself rooted to the spot by what had unexpectedly caught her eye. The artwork on display had suddenly become far more important than allowing Aaron to go off with Louie unsupervised. People were floating around her, chattering and smiling. She stood alone. Feeling like someone had pulled the plug on her lungs and emptied all the air out of them.

The panels began to spin as her eyes swooped from one painting to the next. Familiar places. Sounds and smells rushing back to her in huge nostalgic waves that she couldn't hold back, drowning in them all over again. She recognized herself in a couple of the images, recalling the poses Louie had asked of her, even what they had talked and laughed about as she feverishly worked away on them.

She tried to resist their pull, but there was one in particular which drew her in.

Ophelia.

It was Karin posing as Ophelia, drifting on flat mirrored water at Morecambe Bay. Her hair trailed like silk behind her head, wild flowers trapped in the ripples fanning from her dress. The bay never looked like that but she recognized the pebbles piled up by the waters edge. Each one had a tiny letter on it, an *L* or a *K*, which probably only Karin would be able to spot. She stepped in closer. The canvas smelt of oils but also, faintly, of the sea. It wasn't quite finished by the time Karin had left. She was seeing the final version now. The dress was new; only her head and the outline of her body were there before. The hair though. Something about the hair which made it seem real. Karin reached out to touch it, and flinched, trying to hide her reaction from the people standing behind her. On closer inspection she saw that a few of the strands were in fact real.

Long, red and wavy.

'There you are,' said a voice, a hand curving round her shoulder. 'You okay? You look like you're not. What's wrong?'

It was Mel.

'Oh God, Mel.'

'What's up?'

'These paintings.'

'Pretty good actually,' she replied. 'Bit abstract and weird, but that just about sums her up. She's prettier than I thought she would be. Have you spoken to her yet?'

'Shit,' said Karin. 'I've lost Aaron. Have you seen him?'

'Not for a while.'

'I'll be right back. Sorry, Mel.'

'Do you want me to come?'

Karin heard Mel call out to her, but didn't respond. Why had she let Aaron out of her sights? That was the sole purpose of her being here this evening and she had let him wander off with Louie as soon as they arrived. She should never have allowed them to come here in the first place. It was a terrible mistake.

22

Mel

Mel spotted Aaron talking to Louie over at the drinks table. She thought it strange there was no Karin to chaperone, so had moved swiftly in and stolen Aaron away to enquire where she was. He told her they had come together, but that Karin must be looking round the exhibition on her own somewhere.

It was even busier now than when Mel had arrived. She didn't really do this as a rule, art wasn't her thing, so she hadn't known what to expect and was surprised by the number of people.

'Have you been round yet?' she asked Aaron.

'Not yet. I've seen some of her work online though. This stuff looks much less commercial, but I reckon she can make a good living out of her talents if steered in the right direction.' Aaron waved his arm over the paintings. 'I don't mean with this kind of thing, although it looks interesting,' he added.

'Yes,' replied Mel, feeling an obligation to agree with him. They found themselves having to raise their voices as the general noise level increased. Mel took a sip of wine, Aaron doing the same, and they made a start at the first panel. 'I do find them quite odd though. I had a quick look as soon as I got here. Some of them give me the creeps.'

'You never know, these might be worth something one day,' Aaron said, amused by her response.

As they shuffled down the display it was like a kind of dance they were doing, moving in to read the title, standing back to get a better angle. Mel felt she had to say something. Aaron needed to know what he was dealing with, or at least be able to work it out for himself. That the artist behind these paintings was a potential threat and not to be trusted.

'Have you noticed anything?' she asked.

'What's that?'

'Some of these have a striking resemblance to Karin. Don't you think? See this one. *Woman Standing on Pier*. Look at the hair for instance. And this one too. That could almost be Karin.'

Aaron seemed to be giving her theory some consideration, going from one painting then back to another he had already seen. 'Can't see it myself,' he replied. 'And certainly not in these.' He laughed because the next set of panels featured a female mannequin, dressed or undressed, positioned in various real-life settings. Standing in a queue at the hotdog van. Sitting in a deckchair on the beach. The last one in the series was titled *Woman Standing on Pier II*. It was identical to the first painting with that name apart from the woman in the other was real.

Aaron was examining each of them closely.

'So what do you reckon to these mannequin ones?' asked Mel, hoping to recover his attention.

He straightened up, took a sip of wine and pulled her to one side. 'Playful?' he said. And then whispered: 'Actually I'm not too keen on these, but don't tell the artist I said that.' He may have been about to say something else but stepped out of the way for a couple trying to push their way through, and then moved off down the other panels.

Mel left him to it.

On her way over to the drinks table she had that feeling she often had, ever since childhood in fact, of playing a part in other people's lives yet not really featuring in her own. She looked around at the throng gathered here tonight, trying to work out who were the couples among them, imagining what their lives

120

were like. Mel hoped she hadn't left it too late for herself, and just had to trust her time would come.

'Red or white, madam?'

'Oh, erm. Red please,' she answered, realizing this probably wasn't the first time she had been asked the question. But she was convinced that she had just seen Karin disappearing with Louie behind one of the panels, into an area which said:

'NOT OPEN TO VIEWING PUBLIC.'

23

Louie

Karin had been hovering nearby for some time, making it obvious that she wanted to speak. She was chewing her nails, a habit she used to berate herself for, and when Louie gave her a knowing smile she immediately stopped doing it.

She looked incredible tonight. Bottle green dress against red hair, black lace-up boots. Striking. Sassy. Sexy. Louie could hardly contain herself. She mouthed the words 'two minutes', holding up her fingers to reinforce the message. At the same time, Louie was trying to extricate herself from the man who had been monopolizing her for the past fifteen minutes, but without being rude as he was expressing a keen interest in making a purchase.

So Karin had finally come to her senses. Seeing these paintings had done the trick. Brought it all back to her how much they meant to each other. What incredible times they spent together. Here to tell Louie that she was ditching the old bastard, so they could pick up from where they left off. Or make a completely fresh start.

Anything Karin wanted.

Louie's training from The Midland kept her on the right side of politeness. 'Tell you what,' she said to the man, managing to interrupt him at a convenient place, 'why don't you have a good look around and then come and find me again? Maybe we can agree on a price later.'

When Karin saw him move off, she immediately hurried over, pushing Louie behind one of the screens.

'Whooh! Can't keep your hands off me, can you?' said Louie. 'Shagging at my own exhibition, that's very rock 'n' roll.'

'What the hell are you playing at?' said Karin.

She was in a beautiful temper, her cheeks as red as her hair.

'Oh I'm certainly not playing. But we can do if you like, it's private enough.'

'This is too much, Lou. These paintings.'

'Relax,' she replied, moving closer. 'No one knows it's you, so don't be so paranoid.' Standing taller than Karin, she couldn't resist lowering a whisper into her ear: 'Even your fiancé doesn't recognize you naked.'

Karin was about to slap her, pulling up at the last minute.

'Be my guest,' said Louie, opening her arms out as an invitation. 'Any time.'

'I know what you're doing.'

'Good. As long as it's working.'

Karin pushed her lips forwards and sighed. It made her mouth fuller. Kissable. Despite Louie not liking the words coming out of it.

'I don't want to be with you, Louie.'

'Yes, you do. You love *me*.'

'I don't, not any more.'

Louie knew she didn't mean that, although it still hurt to hear her say it. And then Karin proved she was in denial because she placed her hand on Louie's cheek. Tender. Her tone soft this time when she spoke.

'I want you to be a success. You have a very special talent. Aaron clearly wants to help you and you should definitely take that chance. But you have to forget *me*.'

'How can I, when I know you feel the same?'

Karin removed her hand. 'No. You need to find a new obsession. I'm with Aaron now, you have to let me go. I know I hurt you but please don't ruin my life.'

It was captivating to see her eyes swirl with tears like that, like cream going into coffee. Louie wanted to paint them right now. At the same time, it made her angry because Karin just wasn't seeing what was happening.

'Like you're ruining *my* life you mean?'

'Stop!' Karin shouted, raising her arms, elbows at right angles over her ears as if shutting herself in a box. Louie knew to leave her alone until it passed. When it did, Karin looked up again, slowly. 'I can't have you messing with my head, Louie.'

'Hey if I wanted to ruin things I'd just tell granddad out there what a good time we had in the toilets at The Midland, before you agreed to marry him. I trust you haven't told him that one yet, because he's being awful nice to me. Don't get me wrong, I appreciate his help, but I'd much rather have you.'

Karin tried to leave, but Louie was quicker and blocked her way. She put her hand out, forcing Karin to walk into it, her chest pressing against Louie's palm. It was a moment. A feeling of warmth and softness between them. Until her hand was swiped away again.

One of the stewards stuck his head round the screen. 'Erm, are you going to be long? People are wanting to speak to the artist.'

'I'll be right with you,' said Louie.

The steward nodded and disappeared.

Louie moved in close again but without touching.

Karin stood firm.

'Come back to me, Karin. Just don't take too long about it. If you marry him, you'll be sorry.'

124

24

Karin

Karin found herself alone again. She took a moment before going back out, heading straight for the toilets to try and recover. Her head was screaming, and she desperately wanted to escape from here now. Go home. Back to Aaron's place preferably. She was in no mood to go to a restaurant with Mel, although she could hardly bail out of that one at such short notice, having built it up to be the big *Thank You* meal. It was the least she could do, and especially as Mel had been on the receiving end of one of those appalling notes. Will was gone. She didn't want to lose Mel too.

Where was Will now? she wondered. Wandering round Leeds looking for a place to put his sleeping bag? Had he gone back to 'his bedroom' down by the river? Karin hoped that after a couple of nights in the open, he would change his mind. In spite of not seeing him as often as she once did, she still felt her life was somehow incomplete without him. It continued to baffle her as to why he would walk away from the opportunity of a proper home and the chance of a better future.

'Darling,' said Aaron, handing her a glass of wine when she re-emerged. 'I couldn't find you anywhere. And your friend, or whatever you want to call her, wants us to choose a painting. As a wedding present!'

'What?' The word got stuck in her throat.

'She's offering us one of two, but I said I'd leave it for you to decide. Let me show you.' He took her by the arm. 'I was saying to Mel earlier, I really think these could be worth something one day. We shouldn't look a gift horse, as they say.'

Karin had a fainting taste in her mouth. Metal. Like eating tinfoil. And a blurry sensation in her limbs was making it impossible to put one foot in front of the other. Somehow she made it over to *Ophelia*. She must have, because she was standing in front of it now.

'What do you think?' asked Aaron, raising his arm as if he already owned it.

'Yeah, it's—'

'Oh. You don't like it.' Aaron sounded defensive. Or disappointed, she couldn't tell which.

'Well yes, it's just—' Karin swallowed. She was on the verge of giving him some sort of explanation when she saw him waving his hand at Louie to come over.

'Right,' said Louie, rubbing her hands, 'so which is it to be?'

'You don't have to do this,' said Karin.

'No, I insist,' said Louie. '*If* you're getting married.'

Karin was desperate to locate Mel, frantically searching for her in the crowd. She badly needed Mel's strength and support right now, but couldn't spot her anywhere.

'Is there a problem, Karin?' Aaron made it sound more like an accusation than a question.

'Erm. Not really. It's just the woman in this picture is – well, she's dead.'

'Of course she is, it's Ophelia,' he said.

Karin could feel Louie's eyes burning into her cheek. Then Aaron pulled her to one side.

'Being a bit ungracious, aren't you?' He spoke in a low whisper. 'Is there something you're not telling me? I just wish you'd open up to me, I'm not a mind reader.'

'I told you, Aaron, I nearly drowned once.' She was also whispering, trying not to sound angry.

'Yes, I'm aware of that. But it's Ophelia in the painting, not you.'

Karin felt faint again. Had Louie said something? She really couldn't tell by Aaron's tone.

'It still makes me think of my bad experience,' she said, reminding herself of the fact there was no real resemblance. Not unless you knew. It wasn't her face or anything. Not in any of the paintings. You really did have to know in order to make that connection. She was just being paranoid.

'Any thoughts?' said Louie, interrupting. 'Maybe you'd prefer the other one if you're not so keen on *Ophelia*.' She linked arms with the pair of them and continued talking. 'And if you don't like that one, then you just choose whichever you like.'

The next painting was titled *Meet Me at the Edge*. Karin remembered Louie starting it just before she left Morecambe. An enormous canvas, spread thickly with creamy blues and whites and two vague outlines in the distance, standing side by side like ghosts. It was a romantic painting in its innocence.

Louie's eyes were on her once more from behind, burning into her back. At least this painting didn't feature any of her body parts, as far as she could tell. No hair. No blood, no fingernails; she wouldn't put it past Louie to stop at just hair. And the figures were pretty abstract, despite Karin knowing exactly who they were.

'Yeah, I guess this one,' she said, feebly.

'You still don't sound keen,' said Aaron.

'No, I am. It's a beautiful painting. I always loved it.'

'Great, well let me put the red dot on it then,' said Louie, stepping forwards to do just that. It seemed like she was making an attempt to rescue Karin by moving in quickly. Perhaps to deflect from her use of the word *always*?

Did *always* say too much about the two of them? Karin didn't know any more. She was drowning in lies, pulling her under.

'Gone to a very good home,' said Louie.

It helped Karin recover, whatever Louie intended by it.

'Thank you,' she said, smiling thinly at Louie. This was all part of her carefully choreographed game of course, Karin realized. She wouldn't want to jeopardize things with Aaron, acting in a way to protect her own interests.

As well as doing her best to unnerve Karin.

She felt Aaron's hand brushing her hair to one side, and assumed he was going to kiss her. Instead he whispered: 'We need to talk, Karin.'

It made the blood empty out of her again as the Victoria Arcade rotated in a kaleidoscope of marble and coloured glass. Karin had to excuse herself, abandoning Aaron with Louie for the second time this evening. But she knew, if she were to faint now, it would be an even worse disaster.

She had in her sights a marble pillar to lean against. It was a long way off. Trying to keep her breathing under control, fingers tight around her wrist, she stumbled, reaching into thin air to stop herself from falling. An arm linked through hers. A sturdy shoulder bolstered her upright and she heard a voice say: 'You okay, Karin?'

'Mel. Thank God. Let's get out of here.'

As Mel steered them towards the glass doors at the bottom end of the arcade, it occurred to her that she hadn't told Aaron she was leaving but couldn't face going back. She would text him. It was a risk leaving him here alone with Louie, although the damage had already been done.

25

Mel

'Well I didn't *tell* him, obviously,' said Mel. 'I made an innocent suggestion that it looked a bit like you in one of the paintings, that was all. I guess I just panicked, I'm sorry. Look, you asked me to help out, Karin, but I've no idea what I'm supposed to do. I'm doing my best here.'

'Yeah, I know,' she replied, staring out of the window.

'*Do* you though? There's a nutcase out there on the loose. *Again*. Sending shitty notes to people, and God knows what she'll do next. Yet you refuse to go to the police. Personally, that makes me a little bit uncomfortable.'

'It's fine,' said Karin, looking apologetic this time. 'You did fine. I'm glad you were there, Mel. It would have been a million times worse without you. Let's try and enjoy ourselves now. Cheers.'

The restaurant lived up to its name. Understated and minimalist, but with a swank that gave it a touch of the New York loft. A rippling of jazz notes from a live pianist twinkled in the background. Their table was overlooking the river. They had placed their order and got settled with a bottle of wine, enjoying the lights reflected in colourful zigzags on the water from neighbouring bars and buildings.

'The good thing to come out of this,' said Mel, 'is that Aaron must have sussed that you don't want to be around her.' She waited for a reaction but there wasn't one. 'Oh come on, Karin. So you have one of her paintings, it's no big deal. Aaron says they'll be worth something one day.'

The ridiculously expensive bottle of wine that Karin had selected was being wasted on her bad mood. Mel watched her send a large mouthful of it down her throat as she stared out at the river.

'He seemed to be pushing me tonight though,' she said, still pensive. 'I could feel it.'

'Do you really think so?'

'Yeah, he was just different with me.'

'Maybe Louie said something to him then. The thing is, she might, Karin. So maybe it's time to come clean?'

'If I tell Aaron now, I'll lose him,' she snapped. 'And then I've lost everything, haven't I?'

Their food came and went. Mel cleared her plate, commenting on how delicious it was, several times, but Karin hardly touched hers. They barely spoke at all during the meal. Karin drifted off into the muted piano sounds that weaved in and out of other people's conversations, while Mel studied her, trying to read what was going on inside her head.

After their plates were cleared away, Mel attempted to pull her back into the moment. 'I know you still think some of this is my fault but if you don't tell me what Louie has on you, how do I know *what* to say? It's not fair to put me in this position. You asked me to go along to that exhibition when I didn't even want to.'

Karin was still distant. After a while she reached for Mel's hand and Mel accepted. 'Listen Karin, the police can put a restraining order on Louie,' she said, stroking her hand. 'Did you tackle her about those notes?'

Karin shook her head. 'No point. She knows exactly what they're doing to us.'

'And what *she* is doing is against the law, stalking and harassing you like this.' Karin's head dropped, but Mel wasn't going to stop there. 'And what about all the other stuff you carry around with you? It's no wonder you're a wreck, Karin. Your dad dying, the way things are with your mum, your stepdad committing suicide. Are you sleeping okay? You don't look like you are. Maybe you should go and see someone.'

Karin rolled her eyes, twirling the wine she had left round her glass before finishing it.

'I mean like a counsellor or something.'

She let out a mock laugh in reply, holding her glass out for a refill. 'Been there, tried that. Thanks for your concern, Mel. I appreciate it, I really do.' Karin gulped the refill down then faded back into her thoughts again. After a while, she began looking round for the waiter.

'Okay,' said Mel, seeing Karin gesturing for the bill. 'Well you just tell me what to do about Louie and I'll do my best. As long as you don't ask me to kill her, that is.'

Karin's face dropped.

'Hey that was a joke. All I'm saying is, I'm here for you. Okay?'

'Thanks. Sorry for being such terrible company tonight.'

'No, you're not. You're doing okay, Karin. It'll be okay.'

Mel knew it wouldn't be. *It'll end in tears*, her mother used to say, but that wasn't what Karin needed to hear right now. She had floated off again, staring at the river.

Eventually Karin pointed to something. 'That was Will's spot down there,' she said, sinking deeper into the memory. 'Just a bit further along by the bridge. He called it his bedroom.' She paused to drink up the last drops from her glass, still looking out of the window when the waiter brought their bill, which she settled without even checking it was right. Mel thanked her, and when Karin left a £20 tip on the table she cringed at how much this meal must have cost.

They stood up at the same time, gathering their belongings.

A chilly wind greeted them when they stepped out into the night. As they pulled their thin layers over their chests, a young man came shuffling towards them with a mangy-looking dog on the end of some string. He asked for money, Mel shaking her head at that request. Predictably, Karin stopped to talk to him and Mel saw her putting some coins into his hand.

'He's seen Will down on the river,' she said, trotting back to Mel.

'Well just you promise me that you're *not* going to do anything stupid. It's dark and dangerous as hell down there.'

'That used to be my life too, remember,' said Karin. There was strength in her voice when she said that, but it faded quickly. 'Seems a lifetime ago now.'

'Fortunately those days are over.' Mel gave her arm a reassuring squeeze and Karin patted her hand in appreciation. 'Thanks for tonight,' Mel added. 'But you don't have to treat me any more. I mean you've done it now, and it was lovely, but I'd rather you just look after yourself. Okay?'

Mel rubbed her own shoulders, feeling the goose bumps ripple down her arms as the night air started to bite. 'Right then, it's bloody cold standing here. I take it you're staying with Aaron tonight, not coming back to Headingley?'

Karin gave her a guilty shake of her head, quickly offering to pay for Mel's taxi and trying to flag one down as it passed, but the light was off. Mel said she would walk on a bit further in any case, to the taxi rank, as she needed to pick up a few things from Tesco Express before it closed.

'Karin, no!' she shouted when Karin began extracting a £20 note from her purse, trying to push it into Mel's hand. 'I have my own taxi fare, thank you. Put it away. You don't need to buy my friendship, Karin. Or anyone else's.' Mel was about to add that she really shouldn't be flaunting her money about like that because it made her look vulnerable. But it would sound like another lecture and she concluded that Karin had more than enough to deal with for now.

They parted company with a meaningful embrace, brief enough to keep their emotions at bay. Until Karin flung herself at Mel again. 'Sorry,' she said with a sniff, wiping the tears off her face.

'Don't set *me* off,' said Mel, but she was crying too now. 'You can get through this, Karin. You're a fighter. Just tell me how I can help and I will. Don't worry about Aaron, I'm sure he'll be fine. You'll work it out. Now go get some sleep.'

Karin nodded. She looked so alone.

As Mel walked away she blew her a kiss, which Karin mirrored back to her. They went in opposite directions. Mel checked several times to see that Karin was going where she was meant to be heading and hadn't changed her mind.

26

Karin

Karin knew that Mel would be watching. She looked back once to wave, then hurried along to the end of the road, where she turned the corner and waited another ten minutes before returning to the bridge.

Leaning against the railings, the chill from the metal bars passed through her chest into her veins, sending a shiver round her whole body. What a dark, lonely place it was down there. Back then it didn't used to bother her, because that was how it was, and Karin soon learned to creep about like a dirty shadow. During the daytime most people would hold their breath and walk by.

Homeless. Invisible.

Those words went together like night and day.

The truth was she was too scared to venture down there now, even if she wanted to try and find Will. Grown soft on central heating, lights that come on at the flick of a switch, and doors which locked and bolted, keeping her safe. A solid roof over her head to block out the snow blizzards and gale-force winds.

Modern comforts turned people into cowards.

Karin considered the number of times Will had come to her rescue. He had always been there for her, by her side. Spending their days and nights together as street companions. Friends for life. Then a sudden thought pricked the back of her neck. So could it be that Will was somehow jealous? Of Mel perhaps. Aaron. Even Louie. She thought of those hateful notes and Will's parting words to her on the Ridge a couple of days ago.

I know everything, Karin.

She didn't hang about for much longer. In the end, resorted to ordering an Uber because she was too cold and afraid to walk back on her own.

It was after midnight by the time she got in. Turning the key silently, she crept in like a cat as Aaron was probably in bed by now. Slipping her boots off at the door, tiptoeing across the floor-boards, she noticed the light was still on in the kitchen, dimmed.

When she nudged open the door, it was the first thing she saw.

The painting. Lying across the breakfast bar.

There was a delay of a few seconds before she realized Aaron was standing on the other side of it, glass of brandy in his hand.

'My god, Aaron!' she said, her heart pounding. 'Why didn't you say something?'

Shaking the ice cubes around his glass, he took a sip, keeping his eyes on Karin. The painting was like a giant tree fallen between them.

'How did you get it back here?' she asked. 'It's massive.' She moved towards him, stopping at the chair to put her bag down and then deciding that was close enough.

'People can be easily bought,' he said, taking another sip of brandy. Something in that comment made her heart thump against her chest, until he added: 'I bunged a couple of security guys a tenner. They carried it back for me.'

Aaron knew a lot of people around Leeds, so could always get favours. Something Karin was grateful for because he had managed to secure plenty of them to assist with the housing project.

'We don't have to keep the painting here, if you don't want,' he added. 'I can put it in the office. She'll never know.'

'Oh. No, it's fine. I was just a bit shocked when she said it was a wedding present. That's what threw me.'

Aaron flung his arms out in exaggerated surprise. 'Really? So what's that on your finger then? I could've sworn it was a ring.' He raised his eyebrows, bringing the glass to his lips again, placing it down on the unit when it was empty; the hollow clanking sound causing her to shudder. Karin told herself that they were both drunk, probably. And tired. Her insomnia was unbearable just now, too many thoughts racing through her mind that never seemed to stop.

'Oh come on, Aaron. You know I love Louie's work, but you must have seen it's a bit strained between us.'

'Why?' He began to pace around. 'Why? You're always so secretive, Karin. I almost feel like I don't know you. We're supposed to be getting married, but sometimes I wonder who it is I'm marrying.'

The pain came as it always did, catching her off guard. The sharpened icicle between the eyes. She staggered backwards, aware of Aaron helping her onto a stool and asking if she was okay. She tried to tell him that she just had to let it work its way through her body.

Legs swinging side to side. A human pendulum. The smell of his sweat in her log cabin. Her mother's screams. She sees the steps kicked away in slow motion, clattering against the wall. Birgitta says it's all Karin's fault for making false accusations. A creaking sound as the rope cuts into the beam.

She hears Aaron asking for the second, third time: 'What is it, Karin? Should I call a doctor?' and she knows where she is now, but his words swirl around the kitchen sounding blurry.

Karin remembered asking if they could go to bed, promising she would be fine in the morning.

Her insomnia was made worse by the amount of alcohol she had consumed, and each time she managed to snatch a few seconds

136

sleep she was soon chasing after it again. Whenever she tried curling herself round Aaron, his body edged further away from hers. Then at one point her phone came to life, lighting up the whole room, so she fired it across the floor knowing it would be Louie. But that just made things worse, not knowing for sure.

Peeling the duvet back she went over to check.

BETTER SEE IF THE OLD MAN'S STILL BREATHING

It was irrational, but she still rushed back to Aaron to do just that. He was lying across the bed with his legs in a mid-run position, one arm above his head, and Karin smiled when she detected a light snore. It was a huge bed, so it didn't matter if he spread out, but she felt a sudden need to wake him and tell him that she loved him. Knowing where that would lead, she decided to leave it. Immediately after sex he would begin questioning her again and maybe she would feel inclined to say too much. At least by morning she would know what *not* to say.

I knew Louie from my past. We flat-shared for a couple of years and she helped me get through a really difficult patch. We must have had a fall out I suppose, I can't remember now. But I left Morecambe anyway, not long after, and we just lost touch.

That was all she needed to say.

In the morning.

Daylight flooded in through the blinds in thin slices of light and shade slatted across the bed. Aaron's questions began immediately, and the words Karin had rehearsed during her sleepless hours were now lodged in her throat. The danger of leaking something out that would jeopardize their relationship even further, paralyzed her. Whatever she said would lead to more questions, followed by another episode like last night. Until now she had succeeded in keeping her attacks from Aaron. He knew she got headaches, but not like that.

Aaron ate his breakfast, still waiting for her to begin, looking repeatedly and impatiently at his watch. In the end he thrust his arms into the sleeves of his jacket and said he needed to get to work, taking one last slurp of coffee.

'No. Wait. I'm sorry, let me explain, Aaron. Please,' she said, scurrying after him down the hallway.

He made her go back into the kitchen, taking a seat next to her at the breakfast bar. Louie's painting hadn't moved, still nestling on its bed of bubble wrap, the two figures facing away from them going towards the sea.

'Right. I'm listening,' said Aaron, folding his arms.

'Okay. Well,' she began, gathering her thoughts. 'The reason this and the other painting disturb me so much is because it was Louie who saved me from drowning on the beach at Morecambe. It wasn't just some bloke. Louie happened to be out that night walking around in the fog. She's an artist, she does stuff like that. She saved my life, Aaron, but I didn't want to tell you.'

'Why not? I'd have given the girl a medal, if I'd known.'

'Because.' Karin sucked air through her teeth, afraid of letting the words out. 'Because I *wanted* to drown. I was trying to end it that night. I was so screwed up after my dad dying, and my stepdad committing suicide. Then when my mother threw me out I just thought there was no point to life. Not to my life.'

'Oh Karin. Why didn't you tell me?' He pulled her into his chest, holding her tight and stroking her hair. She wanted the discussion to end there, in his arms, but she knew she had to go on.

'I thought that me living rough was bad enough for you to come to terms with, without hearing that I was suicidal as well. I suppose I was afraid you'd think me a complete basket case and ditch me. I'm totally fine now. Mel helped me get my life back together, when I came to Leeds, and you have too, obviously. But I should have told you about Louie, I'm sorry I didn't.'

Aaron was looking so lovingly at her, she was wondering if he might actually be able to cope with more than this.

Tell him the rest.

'Don't worry,' he said. 'I'll definitely hang that painting somewhere else.'

'No, let's keep it. Now that I've told you it's fine.'

Lose this moment and the opportunity may never come again. *Do it, Karin. Tell him.*

'Aaron.' He was studying the painting, leaning over to examine it more closely. Karin waited until she had his full attention. 'There's a bit more to it than that. Have you er – have you got time?'

'Of course. What is it?'

'I used to live with Louie when I was working in Morecambe. We were just kids, it wasn't serious or anything.'

'Okay. So let's rewind that. What do you mean by "it wasn't serious or anything"?'

'I needed someone, and she was there.' Karin felt a tear rolling down her cheek, betraying her. Aaron wiped it away. She realized this could be the end, but there was no going back at this point.

'What, like a friend? You mean like Mel is?'

'Not exactly. I needed someone to love me and there was nobody else. I'm so sorry for not telling you.' The tears were falling like rain now down her face. 'I was trying to find myself, I was totally lost. But I had no idea where to start looking.'

He took a moment to process what she had said, then slid off the stool to walk around. He combed his fingers through his hair, making thick grooves in it. 'So-so did you love her? Is that what you're telling me?'

'Yes, but more like a friend really. Even though it was—'

'Physical?'

'Well, yes.'

'And now?'

'No! Absolutely not. I left Morecambe when Louie became all needy and possessive. The whole thing wasn't really me. I'm not – I'm not gay, Aaron. I was just … grateful.' By now she was

139

sobbing and her words were coming out choked. 'She saved my life. Nobody had ever loved me that much. I didn't know what it was I was getting into.'

Aaron did two circuits of the kitchen.

'Aaron, please, it was nothing. We were young and I think Louie thought it was much more serious than it really was. She thought I'd gone to the States, that's what I told her when I came to Leeds. I had to escape, and I didn't have any money. I got robbed on the train on the way over, as you know. But in a way it was safer to be on the streets.'

'Safer? Are you saying she's dangerous?'

'No. No, not that. I don't think so. But Mel saved me from her.'

Aaron looked startled by the contradiction.

'Well when I say *saved*, I only mean that Mel pretended to be my American girlfriend. You see, Louie is – Louie is just Louie and I didn't end things well with her. Basically I ran away. As I say, we were young and immature. I was probably naive too.'

'Mel knew all of this? The whole world knows this stuff but me?'

Karin was only too aware what that felt like to be the last to know something. Being kept in the dark for four days before she found out her dad was dead was the cruellest thing, and her mother getting remarried without even bothering to tell her just a few weeks after he died hurt almost as much.

Aaron's eyes flickered with disappointment, and for a moment Karin feared he could see all the other awful things she had done besides: sleeping with strangers, drinking herself to oblivion, her only ambition in life being to end it. Not to mention what happened with her so-called stepdad.

'If you still have feelings for this girl then you need to tell me now, Karin. And I mean *right* now. Because if I find out there's anything more … I need your honesty.'

'No! I don't, it's really not like that.' Her voice tailed off, the memory of what she did with Louie in the toilets gnawing away at her.

'My wife fed me a pack of lies and I am not going to allow you to do the same.'

'I'm not going to run off with her. If that's what you're thinking, Aaron.'

'I didn't think my wife was going to do that either.' He rubbed his face, bringing his palms down on the painting, the sound of his fingers cracking and the bubble wrap bursting underneath them. 'She's been playing me like a fool then. All that business with the painting last night, and still allowing me to help her with contacts and commissions. What a cheek.'

'Please still help her, Aaron. She deserves a break. She's so talented.'

'*And* at The Midland.'

'At The Midland? What do you mean "at The Midland"?'

So he had it all worked out then. He knew. Aaron was not a fool.

'That fake celebration with the champagne, and being so attentive to our every need, when really she must have wanted to stick a knife into my back.'

Aaron swiped his keys from the unit, Karin following him again into the hallway.

'Wait, Aaron. Let's do something special tonight, shall we?' She touched his arm as he was unlocking the door, immediately feeling his resistance.

Next Saturday's launch for Ashby Road was getting scarily close and she had intended to work late tonight, but this was more important. She could still make up the time over the weekend.

'I could cook us a meal, get a nice bottle of wine in.'

'I can't,' he said, retrieving his arm, snatching it out of her grasp.

'But why?'

141

Karin felt like she was about to break. It was all over between them.

'That property deal fell through and they're biting at my heels. Buying my ex-wife out has proved rather expensive. I must be insane even considering getting married again.'

'Aaron. Please, wait.'

'I have a meeting tonight, Karin. That's why I can't make it.'

He opened the door and was about to step out into the corridor when he realized Karin was on the verge of saying something else. He hung on, even though she was still prevaricating.

'How much is it you need?' she asked finally.

'Puh. More than you've got, that's for sure.' He went out this time, heading for the lift.

'Try me, Aaron,' she called.

Thinking about it, he then came back. 'Well, if you've got a spare two hundred grand kicking about, that should pretty much cover it.'

Aaron closed the door so that Karin couldn't detain him any longer.

It made her feel empty. She was back at the gates of her boarding school saying goodbye to her dad, eight years old; her mother didn't even bother to go with them. The gates clanked shut and she was led away. Everyone she cared about seemed to desert her in the end. Even Will. Perhaps Mel would one day, if Louie got her way. Last night Mel had seemed quite despairing of her.

And now Aaron.

Karin returned to the kitchen, looking for something to lash out at. She kicked the unit with a stifled yell of frustration. Louie's stupid painting was still lying across it. She grabbed one of the knives from the magnetic strip on the wall, about to bring it down onto the canvas, stopping herself just in time. What would that achieve exactly? Instead she managed to manoeuvre the painting to the floor, struggling under its weight, and leant it against the unit so she wouldn't have to look at it any more.

Her breathing still heavy and angry, she stood away from the painting, staring at the back of it and noticed something in one corner. As well as the paint spatters, there was a tiny image of one of The Midland seahorses. Louie had got into the habit of drawing them on any notes she left out for Karin, or on cards that she gave to her. The seahorse became their symbol. 'I only ever do them for you, Karin,' she would say.

Seconds later, her phone started to ring in the bedroom. She raced to get it, hoping it was Aaron.

'Aaron, hi.'

'Have you seen it yet?'

'Seen what? Louie, for God's sake. You need to stop all this now.'

'I know you've found it.'

How could she know that? Karin moved to the window, creeping along the wall to peer through the vertical slats of the blinds, not daring to disturb them. There was only the river below. Of course Louie didn't know she had found the seahorse; she was just trying to unnerve her.

Yet again.

'Meet me,' said Louie.

Karin drummed her head against the wall. 'No, Lou. Stop doing this.'

Louie. The pebble who always came back. Louie. The girl who saved her life. Louie. The girl who loved her too much.

'It's important, Karin. I'm trying to help you.'

'I'm not meeting you and that's the end of it. Leave me alone.'

For some reason, Karin still didn't cut the call.

'You owe me this at least,' said Louie. 'Listen to what I have to say. That's all I ask.'

'Okay. Okay,' said Karin, eventually. 'I'll meet you. But it's the very last time and then you disappear out of my life. I mean it, Louie.'

'I'll see you at the Doors Café at twelve. It's by the Corn Exchange. You probably know it.'

27

Louie

The café was already filling up with Leeds' workers on their Friday lunch hour, shoppers loaded with shiny Harvey Nichols bags and hessian sacks full of fruit and veg from the market. Everyone seemed to be rushing from A to B. Louie was used to the ebb and flow of Morecambe where the busyness came in waves, small ones, never like this.

No sign of Karin as yet, but she had got here early in order to secure a table by the window so that she would see Karin coming.

She spotted her flush of flaming red hair. It stood out, shining in the sunlight, beautiful as fire. Louie took a photo. Karin's pale skin, the silky warm feel of it, she was longing to touch it now. It actually had a light suntan to it, which she hadn't noticed in the more subdued lighting of the exhibition space last night, nor even in Morecambe a week ago. But it suited her. Perhaps she was more athletic-looking too these days.

'Right. So this is the very last time we do this,' said Karin, planting her bag down on the chair after she had fought her way over. 'What do you want to drink?'

'You mean you're not going to have sex with me in the toilet first?' Louie hoped to provoke a smile at least, but Karin just looked angry. 'They come round to take the order I think.'

Karin sat down, folding her arms and staring at Louie. In the old days they would sit or lie for hours like this, staring into one another's eyes. 'What's going on? What do you want, Louie?'

'Apart from you, you mean?'

'Just get to the point. I need to go to work.'

'Okay. Well I'm pretty sure your old man knows you're sitting on a fortune.'

Karin leaned across the table and Louie could catch her perfume in the sweet-smelling heat off her skin. Karin kept her voice to a discreet level. 'For one thing, it's not a fortune, it's a sum of money. And secondly, he doesn't even know I have it.'

Louie leaned in too, their faces almost touching, and Karin didn't pull away. She could detect that Karin was on her period; their bodies were always in tune, that's how she knew. The curve of her breasts was just visible down her top. Louie had to pull herself together before she could reply. 'If it's what you told me it would be, then nearly a million quid is a bit more than *a sum of money*. More like a shitload.'

'So this *is* about the money then.'

The waitress interrupted to take their order and they sprung apart. Louie ordered a sandwich and a beer. 'I'll just have a black coffee,' said Karin.

Louie waited for the waitress to go, leaning back in again when it was clear. 'For sure it's about the money. He's been asking questions about you.' She watched the panic spread over Karin's face.

'Like what? What have you told him?'

'Me? I keep it strictly business.'

Karin unfolded her arms, which, until now, had been tightly locked across her chest. She puffed out a sigh of relief but also seemed embarrassed, avoiding eye contact. 'I told him about us this morning,' she said. 'About us living together in Morecambe.'

'Yeah?'

Louie wondered whether to believe that, tapping her fingers on the table. 'And did you tell him how great we are together?

How great the sex is? How much you're still in love with me?'

'What do you think?'

'And what about all your other secrets? You told him any of that stuff?'

'If you're trying to intimidate me, it won't work, Lou.'

It wasn't how she wanted to do this. Sadly, it was looking like the only method to make Karin see sense.

The waitress smiled as she put down some cutlery and a napkin for Louie. Louie glanced up at her and smiled back, making sure the waitress had moved onto the next table before returning to Karin. 'I didn't get you here to upset you, okay? You can totally trust me, you know that.'

Karin let out a laugh, disbelieving and spiteful. 'I know you want to punish me, Louie, but it won't make any difference. I'm marrying Aaron.'

The waitress appeared again, bringing their order this time. Karin began to stir her coffee round in circles, waiting until the waitress had gone. She was back on the defensive. 'And you're wrong about him anyway. He owns half of Leeds, so why would he need my money?'

Karin licked her spoon, to emphasize her point rather than to be seductive, no doubt, but it was having an effect on Louie. As soon as she put it down, Louie made a grab for her hands. Karin tried to pull them back, but Louie's grip was too tight. 'We'll start afresh, Karin. We'll be perfectly happy again. Maybe this break has done us some good. We can be as boring and normal as you like, if that's what you prefer these days. I'd love that too. Get married, have kids, the whole deal.'

'I'm engaged.'

Louie loosened her grip and Karin didn't seem to know what to do with her hands then. They found their way to her cup, bringing it to her mouth, but she thumped it back down on the saucer without drinking anything. 'Have you been spying on me, Lou?'

'Has he ever asked you for money?'

'I'm not even answering that.'

Louie took a sip of beer, feeling a cold hit at the back of her mouth. She wiped her lips, her focus on Karin throughout. 'If you're stupid enough to marry him, he'll walk off with the lot. I'm just warning you. I'm trying to keep you safe.'

Karin asked for the bill. Louie hadn't even started her sandwich yet, but she didn't protest. She just wanted to dive across the table and kiss her, undress her, feel the softness of Karin's skin pressing firmly against hers again, run her tongue over her breasts and put her fingers inside her, her hand pushing just below the pubic bone. Hear Karin moan and call out her name.

As she was preparing to leave, Karin fished something out of her bag. It was a cheque for £900, which she slapped onto the table. 'What's this for?' asked Louie, taking a bite of her sandwich.

'It's for the painting. I'm afraid we can't accept your generous gift.'

Louie managed to swallow the lump of bread she had bitten off but she hadn't chewed it enough and it made her cough on its way down. She hit her chest as she spoke. 'I insist. Excuse me.'

'All I'm asking is for you to leave me alone so I can get on with my life, and you should do the same. This is your big chance, Lou. Don't mess up.'

Louie inspected the cheque and whistled at the amount. She tore it up, sprinkling it like confetti into Karin's face. '*I said*, it's a gift.'

Karin slapped down a £10 note for the bill, a couple of pound coins for the tip. 'You should chew your food more,' she said, 'or one day you might choke. Guess you'd like that, give yourself a thrill.'

'Karin, wait.' Louie grabbed her arm as she was about to go.

It revealed a seahorse tattoo on the inside of her wrist which Karin noticed but tried to pretend that she hadn't.

'Sit down, Karin, or I'll tell him.' Louie held onto her gaze as

Karin slowly lowered herself back into the chair. 'So which bit don't you want me to tell him the most? Us in the toilets, or the bit about you killing your stepdad?'

'Keep your voice down,' said Karin through clenched teeth.

'No one can hear us,' replied Louie, wanting to kiss her again. 'Look I know what you did. And your Swedish mamma knows too. I know everything, remember.'

Karin slapped the table with both hands. 'What did you say?'

'*I said*, I know everything, Karin.'

'Fuck you, Louie!' she said, scraping her chair back as she sprang up again.

Louie laughed. 'What, right now? Here, on the table?'

Karin passed in front of the window with a sideways scowl. It was meant to be a warning, but Louie just found it sexy. After a few seconds, she sprang up too. Pushing her arms through the sleeves of her jacket, sandwich in her teeth, she shot out of the door.

Keeping a safe distance, she followed Karin through town.

28

Karin

The number six bus to Headingley had slowed to its customary crawl up Otley Road. Overheated and overcrowded, Karin wished she had jumped into a taxi. All that money sitting in her account, she could afford to do that now. She was out of the habit and it felt decadent when there was no real need.

People on the bus were staring. Louie's words thrashed against her head. Hot tears rolled down her cheeks. Fingers were pointing.

Accusing.

Five years on, the memory is still as sharp. Her mother, running into the log cabin, yelling at her to get him down.

Go hang.

Of course, she had told him to do that. He wasn't her stepdad; he was an imposter with no right to be there in the first place, and certainly not when her dad had only just died. How could Birgitta not mention the fact that she had married a complete stranger? That's what he was to Karin, and waiting until the summer holidays to tell her daughter that she had *a new dad, Karin*, only highlighted her guilt as far as Karin was concerned.

Go hang.

It was an expression, a figure of speech. Of course, she wanted him out of the way. But that was all she meant by it.

A long queue of students was waiting to get on the bus outside the Parkinson Building. Karin watched them shuffling along, chatting about the lecture they had just been to and what pub crawl they were going on this evening in what fancy dress outfit; things she might have been a part of herself if her life had been different.

The door of the log cabin is slightly open. She can see that, and races down the garden towards it. Her instincts were right.

This is where he is.

Karin closed her eyes as the bus rumbled on and she was forced to relive the minutes before her mother got there:

The rope around his neck is hooked over the beam. His feet are resting on the steps, carefully positioned beneath them.

She hears Birgitta. Yelling at her to get him down.

But before her mother even gets there, he begins to tell Karin why. She hasn't asked him to explain, he just offers and she listens. The reason he gives is not what Karin is expecting.

Not at all.

In those final few moments of his life, her own changes forever as she runs towards him, shrieking: 'Just do it then, you coward. Do it! I hate you and I always fucking will.'

In a split second of fury, she kicks the steps from under him and his neck snaps. She hears it. His legs start to swing. Side to side. Like a human pendulum. He doesn't fight it. He totally wants it and fully deserves it. A few moments later, her mother is screaming. It isn't what she does. The sound is primal and raw and she yells at Karin to get him down.

It is too late.

It's always too late.

'What have you done, Karin? What have you *done*?'

Birgitta is there in those final moments. Hears the words Karin shrieks as she runs towards him. Sees her kick the steps away, his neck snap and his legs swing. But this is *all* she hears and sees. And Karin is never allowed to explain. Not that she would be believed.

'How could you *do* that, Karin? How could you do that?' her mother wails.

Karin put the key in the lock and felt her whole body collapse as the door opened. The bus journey had left her traumatized. Sweat was pouring from her brow and she was desperate to get inside.

The house felt cool. Tranquil, except for the usual creaks and groans of floorboards and pipes. She called out Mel's name just in case she was home, but no answer came back. For a moment Karin even considered shouting for Will, despite knowing he wouldn't be here. And if he was, he wouldn't have heard her. She raced upstairs to check his room all the same, and then went into her own, closing the door.

Karin snapped the curtains together, began unbuttoning her shirt in an attempt to cool down. Opening the drawer, she removed the box of letters and sank onto her bed, turning the numbers on the padlock until it released. It was time to get rid of these now. How could she move on if she didn't do that? Her mother didn't care about her and the past had no place in the present. Certainly not in her future.

The smell of her mother wafted up from the bundle and Karin couldn't resist putting it to her nose, until she felt brave enough to untie the knot one final time. She extracted the last letter she had ever received from Birgitta.

Karin

I want you out of my house, my life. That a child of mine would do such a thing. Why, Karin? Do you hate me so much?

This will never go any further, between the two of us only. However, if you come anywhere near me again, try to contact me, I shall go straight to the police.

For money you should liaise with Elliott, my accountant. He will contact you in due course and arrange for finances to

152

be paid into your account, once you finish your schooling that is, and go to university. Note, however, that I no longer have a desire to know what you are doing nor where you are. The money will be substantial, but there will be <u>no more</u> once it's gone, so use it wisely. I have paid your school fees until the end of sixth form. If you choose to leave before that, then NO MONEY will be released until your twenty-second birthday. That is your choice.

He could never replace your father, no one could, but it was a chance for me to have a life beyond him. Know that your father would be equally ashamed of you. You drove a man to take his life, accusing him of things he didn't do. Even worse than that – I saw what you did with my own eyes, and in that moment you killed my happiness too.

One day you will know that life is short and love is complicated. If you find a person who truly loves you and you feel the same about them, then hang onto them no matter what. No matter what other people might think or say. You will know who that person is when they enter your life.

This is the last letter you will ever receive from me, Karin. I no longer want to receive any more of yours either. Any you do send will be returned unopened.

It breaks my heart to say and do these things, but you have destroyed everything in my heart and left me with nothing.

You will have this on your conscience forever more, and I shall <u>never</u> be able to forgive you. You must find a way to live with that. I only ever wanted the best for you, to give you the best start in life. One day I hope you will see that, although I do not need to know if you do.

Goodbye.

Karin slid off the bed and lay on her stomach, weeping into the carpet. When she had nothing left inside her, she scrunched the letter into a tight ball and raised herself up again, tossing the letter onto the bed with the others. Stumbling into the bathroom she splashed cold water on her face and then went downstairs, not even sure what she was intending to do when she got there. She wasn't sure about anything any more. But then a noise from the kitchen suddenly stopped her in her tracks.

A banging sound.

'Mel, is that you?' she shouted. The dryness in her mouth made her swallow hard. She opened the kitchen door slowly. No reply came back.

Louie's name was on the tip of her tongue, but she couldn't bear to say it out loud. If it was Will, he wouldn't hear her. She hoped it would be Will, but something told her it wasn't.

Karin noticed the back door was open, which was strange when there was no one about. When she tried to close it again she was met with resistance, causing her to jump backwards as someone had been pushing against it on the other side.

'Oh my god, Aaron! What're you doing here? You scared the life out of me.'

'Sorry, I was passing. Had half an hour to spare. The neighbours have been complaining about the fence, and with Will gone it's not going to get done, is it? I need to put this place on the market.'

'Oh. So – but why didn't you answer me when I shouted earlier?'

'I didn't hear you. Been to fetch something from the car.' He waved a tape measure at her. Karin was trying to remember if Aaron's car was parked outside when she arrived home. Even if it had been she was probably too distracted to notice. 'Plus, I wanted to see you,' he continued. 'I called by Ashby Road, but you weren't there, so I figured you'd be here.' He took hold of her hands and kissed them. 'I'm sorry for this morning. I over-reacted about the painting. And about Louie. If you'd told me all of that stuff before, then I wouldn't have made you go to the exhibition. It all fits into place now.' He ran his fingers over hers. 'And I *would* like us to do something nice tonight.'

'Really? But, your meeting—'

'It's all fine. Selling this house will release plenty of capital. I should've done this anyway when I got divorced, but I didn't have the heart to turf Mel out.' He laughed. 'And I'd never have met *you* if I'd done that.'

Karin threw her arms around his neck. Why had she even doubted him? Of course he could accept that she once had a girlfriend. And why shouldn't he know that she had tried to kill herself? Aaron was loving and caring. Conventional maybe, but not unreasonable. She had misjudged him.

'Have you been crying?' he asked, brushing a wet strand of hair from her cheek.

'Oh. No, it was really hot on the bus, so I splashed some water onto my face.' Karin sniffed, giving herself away. 'Actually yes. A bit.'

'Not because of me, I hope.'

'I'm having a weird day. Started missing my mum on the bus coming home and I don't even know why.' Karin wasn't sure if she did miss her, not really, but at least it was some kind of an answer. Maybe she missed the idea of a mother, but not her actual one. It was all so mixed up. 'I just wanted her to love me, you know. It's what mothers are supposed to do, and all I ever wanted from her.'

Aaron released her again. 'Listen. I want to support you in every way I can. You know that, don't you? You *can* talk to me.'

Karin nodded.

Didn't he deserve to know a *bit* more at least? He had been honest and open with her about his divorce. After all, the two of them were going to be married at some point.

'My mother blamed me for his suicide,' she said.

Poor Aaron looked confused, trying to work out how Karin had come to make such a leap. 'You mean your stepdad's?'

'Well yes, but I was never going to call him that. Apparently he'd been on the scene for years, supposedly friendly with my dad too. Pretty strange, if you ask me. But then when he killed himself, my mother said it was all my fault. Accused me of trying to ruin her life, that I didn't want her to be happy. Things were said between us that can never be unsaid, and then she threw me out.'

'Does Louie know any of this?'

'Why?' Karin froze.

'Just something she said to me last night at the exhibition.'

'Like what? What did she say?'

'No, nothing specific. She seemed to be hinting at something, but I didn't take the bait. I was a little taken aback to be honest. Sorry, Karin. I should never have taken you to The Midland.'

'You weren't to know. And anyway, it's my fault for not telling you before. But it's all sorted now because I saw Louie today and she's going to back off. She gets it now, that we can't be together.'

Aaron seemed surprised by that. Was he even aware that's what Louie wanted?

Karin felt the blood rush to her cheeks, and tiny beads of sweat pricked through the skin above her lip. 'We met for lunch,' she continued, realizing that only made it worse. 'Oh but nothing happened. Don't worry.'

Karin! Just shut up.

She paused, giving him a moment to process her blunders, hoping he wouldn't read too much into them. 'But like I said, I do still want you to help her. Will you?'

He pulled away and turned his back.

'Aaron, what's wrong? Aaron?'

He spun round quickly again. 'Are you sure you're not using me as some kind of buffer against this – this former *girl*friend of yours?'

'No. No, 'course not. I wouldn't do that. I love *you*. I want us to be happy, have a life together.'

The way he was staring at her made Karin doubt that he actually wanted that as much as she did now. But then he raised his finger, saying: 'Just tell me if she bothers you again, Karin. I mean it. Just tell me.'

She nodded, desperate to change the subject. Make it about them and not about Louie.

'Listen Aaron. I've been doing some thinking and I might have come up with a solution. Well, it's just an idea really.'

He gave her a look to suggest he was listening, although he still seemed annoyed.

'As a matter of fact, I really do have money to put into a property – to follow on from our conversation this morning. It was released on my birthday – from my mother's accountant – and, well – why don't I buy one of the properties you need to sell? That way I have an investment, but you can release the capital to give to your ex-wife. If we stay together, the place is ours. I mean, that's just a precaution obviously.'

He was studying her like she might have lost her mind. 'How much do you have?'

'Enough.'

Aaron sat down, turning things over in his own mind. After a while he seemed to reach a conclusion and stood up. 'Okay. Why not? It's only office space you'd be buying. Or there's this place.' He looked about him to indicate he meant this house. 'Two fifty would probably cover it.'

Karin's phone started to ring, puncturing their excitement and causing Aaron to be suspicious again. He held out his hand to take possession of her phone. Karin felt she had no choice, extracting it from her pocket slowly, praying for it to stop ringing and that it wouldn't be Louie. If she looked at who was calling her that would make her seem guilty, so she resisted the temptation. It was still ringing when she handed it to Aaron.

Closing her eyes was about all she could do. And wait.

'Karin's phone,' she heard him say.

It was the site manager, Ron, wanting to know when he could expect her in at Ashby Road. He had a surprise for her apparently.

'Tell him I'm on my way,' she said, the excitement now restored to her mood. Aaron returned her phone and Karin kissed him, adding, 'It'll be Will, he's come back. I'd better go.'

29

Louie

She found it surprisingly easy to talk her way in here. But if the launch was next Saturday, then she could understand their desperation for volunteers. It looked like there was still plenty to do on the place. So Louie had only to say that she was a friend of Karin's and without a second's hesitation the site manager had her down for garden clearance, leading her to the pyramid of rubbish piled up in the front garden waiting to be thrown into the two giant skips out on the road. One of them was already rammed with dismembered sofas, broken chairs, endless beer cans and bottles, even old stereos, fridges, heaters, and before Louie set to work she had a good root around to see if she could find anything of interest. She couldn't.

She had asked the site manager if he would come and find her when Karin was on her way because she wanted it to be a surprise. He said it was the least he could do, as her help was much appreciated. In the meantime, Louie tossed things into the skip, keeping an eye out for Karin in case she arrived unannounced. Finally she heard that Karin was only five minutes away.

Positioning herself in one of the gardens backing onto those on Ashby Road, Louie had found the perfect view. Having already done a recce, she discovered that most of the houses on this side were also empty, so she was unlikely to be seen or challenged. Through the gap in the hedge, separating the two gardens, she could watch over Karin without her knowing that she was just a few metres away from her.

Louie spotted her walking down the path, fumbling with her gardening gloves. Karin had only just managed to slip them on when her phone started to ring and was now struggling to get to it. Louie smiled to herself, hearing her say *hello*, but when Karin stumbled and reached out to grab the dilapidated bird table she almost cried out for her to be careful.

'Are you okay?' Louie asked, refraining from running through the hedge to find out if she was injured.

'What do *you* think? Not until you leave me alone.' Karin's voice sounded angry, snarling out the words as she inspected her hand. She tucked it under her arm to dull the pain. 'What do you want now, Louie?'

'Have you decided yet?'

'On what?'

'Me or him.'

She had turned her back, so Louie could no longer see her face. Also the sway of some leafy branches meant she only had a partial view, although could still make out Karin's fiery red hair, tied back in a messy ponytail.

'I told you,' said Karin. 'Aaron knows everything now, so there's really nothing you can say or do to break us up.'

'Are you sure about that?'

Karin spun round, almost facing her, and Louie ducked down just in case. Had something made her aware of her presence? But as she didn't investigate further, Louie carried on talking. 'So what about The Midland? He knows about us in the toilets, does he?' She shielded her mouth to make it sound like she wasn't outdoors. 'And don't tell me you've given him the full confession on everything else, Karin, and that he's fine with that too. Even if you've told him some of it, you won't have told him all of it. Or you've lied. You seem to like doing that.'

'Piss off, Louie. Look, if it's money you want—'

'It is.'

The silence that followed was invaded by a bee buzzing, and then a squirrel hopped onto the fence, which made them both jump. A hedge trimmer somewhere in the distance.

Karin was standing very still, like she had taken root in the garden.

'If you're going to marry granddad, then yes, I absolutely do want your money.'

'How much?' asked Karin, sounding nervous.

'How much is it worth?'

The bee continued to buzz while Karin considered it. 'I'll give you five thousand and then you leave me alone.'

Louie made a hissing noise, causing Karin to hold the phone away from her ear. 'Come on, Karin, you're going to have to do better than that. If you're choosing him over me then I want it all. Every last penny. I have copies of the letters. It's all in there, what you did. The police have only to contact your Swedish mamma and you're done for. She'd be only too happy to fill them in. Wouldn't she?'

Karin slumped down onto the ground, as if someone had deflated her.

'Choose me and we don't have to do any of this.'

Hitting her thigh with her injured hand, Karin swore, taking a few breaths to recover.

'I'm only doing this to protect you,' Louie explained. 'However. Let me make this clear to you. If you relay one word of this conversation – *ever* – to that prick you're intending to marry, I promise I will tell him every last detail. I swear I'll leave nothing out. I do know everything, Karin.'

'I didn't think you were this much of a bitch, Louie. What happened?'

'You left me. And I still don't really know why.'

'I've told you. It was for both our sakes.'

'*All* your money.'

161

'No fucking way, Louie.'

This left her no option then, and Louie cut the call. When Karin realized that, she got up and returned to the bird table, wrenching it out of the ground in her temper. The wood was rotten and it snapped in two towards the bottom. Karin flung it down again but Louie could see that she was holding onto her fingers and maybe she was bleeding.

'Karin. Are you okay?' she shouted, fighting her way through the bushes.

Karin backed off, like she was seeing a ghost rushing towards her. 'What the hell are you doing here?' She checked over both shoulders, to make sure they hadn't attracted the attention of her colleagues, but there was no one in sight even she had wanted them.

Louie gave her a gentle smile. 'Let me look.'

'Get the hell away from me. Why aren't you in Morecambe?' Then she realized she was trapped when she hit against a thick wall of conifer behind her. 'You have to go. Please. I'll sort the money out later, I promise.'

Louie went in closer.

'The Midland gave me unpaid leave for my exhibition. I can take as long as I need,' she said.

Producing the scarf from her pocket, she wrapped it tightly round Karin's hand. It was bleeding, but not too much. Karin looked confused when she saw the scarf but said nothing. When the first aid was done, Louie took a firm grip of Karin's other arm and she immediately began to struggle.

'If you scream or make a fuss, you know what will happen.'

She pushed Karin towards the hedge into the adjoining garden, forcing her through it, bringing her to a standstill alongside the house on the other side.

'Right. Now I want you to call your guy in the yellow hat and tell him that you've had to attend to something urgently. Do it.'

Louie hated having to adopt this tone with her.

162

After Karin had made the call, she guided her out into the next street, where she had parked the rental car earlier. Karin resisted getting in at first and had to be reminded of the consequences if she didn't. Did she really want to end up in jail, her life ruined?

She got in the passenger side without any more fuss after that.

'Where are we going?' she asked when Louie started the engine.

Karin sounded frightened and Louie regretted that also. But she would understand. Eventually.

'We're going to get your passport and your driving licence.'

'What the hell for?'

'Fasten your seatbelt. I don't want you to get hurt, Karin.'

30

Karin

'You can always change your mind,' said Louie. 'You do have a choice. Even at this point.'

Did she? Really?

'How's your hand?'

'As if you care.'

She made Karin stop, wanting to take a look at it, and carefully unwrapped the scarf that she had put round her hand earlier. At first Karin thought she did actually care, but then realized why she had removed it. 'I'm afraid we have to leave that off now or it'll look like something it isn't. Keep that hand out of sight.' Louie stuffed the scarf back into her jeans pocket.

As soon as she spotted the bank's logo on the sign up ahead, Karin knew exactly what was happening. Louie was definitely behind all those notes. And now she was going to steal everything. Why hadn't she closed that stupid joint account? Karin asked herself. Initially it was because she feared that Louie might somehow be able to find her, so had simply left it open and gone back to using her own one. Maybe she could have asked for a confidentiality clause or something.

Too late now.

In any case it didn't seem to matter because Louie announced that the money was to go into her personal account, not the joint one. Which was sort of obvious really, when Karin thought about it.

'Don't worry,' said Louie, as if genuinely trying to reassure her. 'The fact that we have a joint account will make it look like it's a legitimate transfer.' She grinned when she added, 'Which of course it is.'

Louie had certainly done her homework, gone through every potential question they might be asked, found out that Karin would need two forms of ID. Giving her a thorough briefing in the car on their way here, she had instructed Karin on what she would be expected to say once they were inside the bank.

'And no funny business, Karin. You know what'll happen.'

Louie's arm was so tight around her waist she felt glued into Louie's side, forced to fall in line with her step just so she could remain on her feet. A few yards from the bank's entrance Louie brought them to an abrupt stop, pulling Karin into the wall but being careful of her hand.

'One last chance. Choose me and you get to keep the money. But if not, I can't just sit back and let you give it all away to that slime-ball.'

'Listen, Louie.'

Karin was trying to make her voice sound strong, yet she knew she was facing the inevitable now.

'You have to promise me that once this is done you'll leave me alone. I mean forever. I need to hear you say it before we go in there.'

Karin felt a shove in the small of her back, driving her towards the entrance.

Louie held her firm as the doors swished open. Passing through them, she whispered in Karin's ear that she had to remember to smile.

The cashier was overly pleasant, with a rather sickly manner. She thought them *a sweet couple*, saying ridiculous things about *how lovely* they looked together and *how lovely* it was they were getting married. This was made all the more convincing by Louie's adoring gaze on her wife-to-be, kissing her on the cheek at every opportunity, and Karin was even made to flash up her engagement ring. The cashier said *how lovely* it was, and *how delighted* she was for them both. Louie had a tight grip of Karin's uninjured hand throughout the whole charade, squeezing it every now and then to keep Karin on track.

During their exchange Karin smiled and nodded, wishing only to wake up from this terrible dream and be able to walk away from it. It was one of those scenes from her life where she was looking down on herself: at her dad's funeral, and when her stepdad was swinging from the beam; nearly all of the time she was living on the streets. As though this wasn't her life at all, at least not the life she was meant for.

At the same time, Karin clearly heard herself making the request to transfer her entire fortune from her personal account into Louie's, leaving a mere £500 on which to live. That was Louie's idea. Karin also heard herself explaining where the money had come from, and the cashier saying she only wished she had a mother who was that generous.

'Now, are you sure you don't want this to go into your joint account?' she asked them again. It was the only time she raised a flicker of doubt, but when Karin felt Louie's nails digging into her hand, she smiled, and answered: 'No. It's because we're having an art studio built. Also Louie's looking after the wedding side of things, so if we could leave £500 in my account and put the rest into Louie's. It just makes sense for us to do it this way so we can keep track of our expenditure.'

The cashier tapped away on her computer, pushed forms through for Karin to sign, explained there would be a £25 charge and that the transfer would be done by CHAPS. She also informed them that the balance would be unlikely to land in Louie's account today as it was too late in the afternoon, but it should be there in the morning. She then went to double-check with a colleague and came back to say it might not actually appear on Louie's screen until Monday, but that wouldn't mean it hadn't already gone through. She didn't think there would be any problem.

Karin felt nauseous.

When it was over, and they were back out on the street again, it seemed a burden had been lifted, but then came the aftershock as Karin visualized the money being zapped into Louie's account, as if by some high-powered suction device. She returned to feeling angry again. And yet, however unpredictable Louie might be, Karin still struggled to think her capable of this. Until she reconsidered how much she had hurt Louie. How badly she had let her down.

Cars were stacking up at the traffic lights on North Lane, the normality of the day remained uninterrupted, people going about their business as usual. An old man with a walking frame ran out of time on the crossing and a bunch of students dressed as nuns had a private laugh at his expense. Any other day and Karin might have said something. A few years ago Louie would have backed her up. Maybe she would now. It was irrelevant how different the world felt to Karin, because it was carrying on regardless. To think that, only last Friday, on her twenty-second birthday, she had £957,000 to her name, then one week later it had gone. That it had landed there at all had taken some getting used to, but the fact nearly a million pounds had vanished from her account was even harder to accept. And what was she to tell Aaron? She shuddered to think what new set of lies this would generate, having only just cleared a backlog that hadn't been quite so necessary in the first place.

Poor Aaron. She really didn't deserve him.

'Satisfied now?' she said, turning to Louie.

'Not really, no.' It was as if Louie had penetrated her thoughts. 'He's a dick. He doesn't deserve you or your money.'

Louie tried to come near but Karin managed to dodge out of

her way as someone needed to enter the bank. She set off walking in the direction of Ashby Road with a brisk anger in her step. Louie was soon by her side, causing Karin to pick up the pace.

Her longer stride helped Louie stay slightly ahead and she started walking backwards to address Karin face on. 'Look. I'm not going to force you onto the street again or anything, Karin.' Every few steps she had to turn round to check where she was going as Karin refused to slow down. 'That's what *he'd* end up doing to you, though. Are you listening to me? I'm only keeping it safe for you.'

She pulled hard on Karin's arm, forcing her to stop.

'Ow,' said Karin. It was her sore hand.

'I'm sorry, wrong arm. But, like I said, Karin, if you breathe one word of this to him, or to anyone, I am watching you like a hawk. Because you know what happens next. Don't you?'

Louie stood facing her, hands in the pockets of her jeans. She shrugged, elbows out, and said: 'Come back to me any time, Karin, and I'll be waiting for you. I just love you, I can't help it.'

Karin didn't react, not even when Louie gave her a cautious peck on the lips. She waited a few extra seconds, watching Louie's face drop when she rubbed her hand across her mouth and spat her disgust onto the pavement. In almost the same movement, she pushed Louie into the wall causing her shoulder to bounce off it.

After her initial surprise, Louie's smirk returned, and Karin felt a spike in her temper. Not wishing to risk a public scene, she managed to swallow it back down, muting her fury. Stepping closer to Louie's face, she said: 'Don't you ever, *ever*, come near me again. I'll always hate you for this, Louie.'

31

Mel

Mel hadn't seen Karin since last Thursday when they parted company at Swank after the art show. That was three days ago. She wondered what state Karin was in by now, having seen how wound up she was that night. The malicious notes from Louie, Will's disappearance, maybe even her relationship with Aaron must all be weighing heavily on her mind. All this on top of her working flat out for the launch this coming Saturday as well.

As expected, when Karin walked through the door, she looked completely worn out.

Mel was about to make it a whole lot worse.

To soften the blow, she had prepared a lasagne and beckoned Karin into the kitchen to prevent her from disappearing upstairs. Karin kicked off her work boots, yawning, and flopped into a chair. She said she wasn't really hungry and was supposed to be going to the cinema with Aaron tonight, but felt too tired even for that.

'Just text him and then have something to eat,' said Mel, sliding Karin's phone down the table until it was in front of her. 'You look shattered. I'll run you a nice hot bath after you've eaten and then why not just go to bed? Or, I've stocked up on supplies and we can have a girls' night in.'

'That's really sweet of you, Mel, but I'm fit for nothing.'

Karin yawned, and Mel ruffled her hair to say that was okay.

169

Karin gave her a weary smile then picked up her phone and began to type out a message, like it was a huge effort even to do that.

Mel served the lasagne, but Karin could only manage a few forkfuls before declaring herself full. She was almost asleep, her chin collapsing into her hand. Finally she put down her fork in defeat, pushed back her chair and was about to make her excuses.

'Don't go just yet,' said Mel. 'Look, erm. I'm really sorry to have to do this, but there's something you need to see.' She rooted under the growing pile of takeaway leaflets, magazines, junk mail and theatre booklets on the table. 'This came a few days ago. I really think you should open it.'

Karin froze when she saw what it was, sliding back down her chair like she had suddenly melted. The letter *K* stuck onto the front of the envelope was ominous, its style all too familiar. She refused to take it.

'Do you want me to open it then?' Mel offered. 'I mean, we ought to see what she wants.' But then she hesitated, adding, 'Well, *whoever* it is wants.' Because how could they be sure where to point the finger? 'Look Karin. I think you and I both know this isn't going to go away, not unless we deal with it.'

Karin flinched as Mel ran her knife under the gap, slitting the envelope across the top and making a jagged tear. Mel checked again to see whether Karin wished to take over, but she didn't, so Mel proceeded to remove the note, handling it with her fingertips like it was contaminated.

'What does it say?' asked Karin, impatient all of a sudden. She must have seen that Mel's fingers were trembling.

'Shit,' said Mel.

Karin snatched it from her and read it for herself.

I KNOW YOU DID IT
PAY £ 950,000
CALL: 07733 737598
YOU HAVE 48 HOURS

'When did this come? What day? What day, Mel?'

'Okay, okay, just let me think. Might have been Friday. Thursday was the art thing, wasn't it? So yes, Friday. It was there when I got in from work, sitting on the doormat. No stamp on it this time. I didn't know whether to call you, but you've got such a lot going on at the moment, so I just stuffed it under that lot – partly so it wouldn't terrify the life out of me either. Maybe I should have opened it. But what does it mean? What did you do?'

'She's *still* playing games. I don't believe it.'

'This is freaking me out, Karin. It's got to stop.'

'You think I don't want that too?'

Karin began rubbing her forehead.

'Should I call that number, see what happens?'

Mel did it anyway, without giving Karin time to answer. It was a distorted voice recording.

'What's it saying?' asked Karin.

'It gives payment details. Bank account. A name I don't recognize. This is serious shit.'

Karin considered it for a moment.

'Has anyone been to the house while I've been staying over at Aaron's? Think, Mel. Think. Anyone at all.'

'I'm trying to!'

'Sorry.'

'It's okay.' Mel gave her hand a squeeze. 'Well Aaron, obviously. Doing the fence.'

Karin appeared to be rubbing away a thought she didn't want to be having. 'Anyone else?'

'Not that I know of. I mean Will knows where we live obviously. He could still be out there. As well as Louie. I can't take much more of this. It's time to get the police involved.'

'No!'

'We have to.'

Karin screwed up her face, trying to make it go away.

171

'Why not? Stop protecting her, or whatever it is you're doing. Pay up or call the bloody police, Karin. This is killing me! Wait, what are you doing?'

Karin was ripping up the note. 'She'll get tired of her stupid games soon enough.'

A heavy pounding on the front door gave them both a start. They looked at one another.

'You expecting anyone?' asked Mel.

Karin shook her head, gathering up the shreds of paper, sliding them back into the envelope which she shoved into her pocket, tucking it down making sure it wasn't visible.

'Do you think it could be Louie?' whispered Mel, following behind Karin who was tiptoeing into the hallway. 'Or maybe it's Will?'

The letterbox pushed slowly inwards and Karin flattened Mel against the wall. They were motionless, not daring to breathe. Then the letterbox snapped shut, the spring too quick to allow anyone to peer in.

'I don't know,' said Karin, panting as if she had run a marathon in those last few seconds, her hand pressing against her heart.

The banging grew more insistent.

'What if it *is* Louie?' said Mel. 'What if she smashes the door in?'

'She won't.'

Karin was edging along the wall, getting closer to the door. More movement outside meant they could now see a dark outline through the stained glass.

'Bloody hell, Karin. I think it could be the police.'

Karin tried to make a dash for it, but Mel caught her in time, pulling her back.

'Where are you going? We don't even know what this is regarding yet.'

'Please, Mel. Please don't say anything about the notes. Or Louie. I promise I will sort this.' She was forcing her frown lines together so hard it formed a deep gash in her forehead. 'I thought I already had sorted it.'

'Just keep your cool. Let's see what they want first.'

Mel moved towards the front door, holding onto Karin's arm so she couldn't shoot off. Letting go of it slowly, with her other hand on the latch, she turned to Karin and said: 'Ready?'

Karin nodded, and Mel opened the door.

'Ms Rhodes?'

The police officer flashed up her ID, introducing first herself, followed by her male colleague.

'No, I'm Melanie. This is Miss Rhodes.'

Karin looked like she was about to crumple. She gave them a nod that instantly made her look both guilty and terrified. She really needed to pull herself together.

'May we come in?' asked the police officer, already halfway over the threshold.

32

Karin

The female officer took a seat in their kitchen. It was another surreal scene: notebook resting on the table, open and eager. The sight of it made Karin think of her mother's letters upstairs and she wished she had already destroyed them. She still hadn't, because she had decided to read them *all* again first.

What if they searched her room and found them? But then why would they do that? On what grounds? Unless someone had said something. Like Louie. Was she really so set on revenge? Even now, when she had all her money? Had she been to the police and turned Karin in anyway? It seemed so out of character, but then so were a lot of things Louie had done recently.

The only other person who knew what Karin had done was Will.

It couldn't be Will. He wouldn't betray her. Would he?

Or was it her mother? Was she having second thoughts about the money and this was her way of getting it back? Get justice at the same time. She must feel like it was long overdue. Karin's mind wouldn't stop galloping. She was sweating and chewing her nails.

Thankfully Mel was much calmer. She offered the two officers some tea, which they both declined. However the female officer told her to make one for Karin as she had become rather pale. The male officer stood by the window looking out at the garden, generally being observant.

Karin was berating herself now for cancelling on Aaron. The thought of the two of them at the cinema was far preferable to this. Her tiredness hadn't been the only reason she didn't want to see him tonight though. She had been avoiding him as much as possible since transferring the money over to Louie on Friday. Although she had spent the last few nights at his place, she used the excuse of working long hours for going straight to bed after dinner. Aaron hadn't brought up the subject of money again. Maybe he was giving her a cooling off period about buying one of his properties. But Karin knew it would come up again at some point, especially as her initial enthusiasm had been so great.

Karin continued to turn out all sorts of other possibilities as to why there were two police officers sitting in their kitchen. Was it the bank transfer? Had the bank found some irregularity in the payment to Louie?

But it would always come back to her mother. Any moment now they would start firing questions at her: *Did you kill your stepfather, Ms Rhodes? Did you accuse him? Did you or did you not kick the steps from under his feet, making his legs swing and his neck snap? Did you intend to kill your stepfather when you kicked the steps away? I'm afraid it cannot be both, Ms Rhodes. It's either a yes or a no. So which is it?*

'Yes.'

'Miss Rhodes?'

'Yes.'

'I'm afraid we found Will Langham's body in the River Aire this afternoon.'

'What?'

'Did you hear me, Miss Rhodes?'

Karin eyed the police officer but her words were not registering. They were floating around the kitchen in a meaningless dance, random letters bouncing off the walls and popping like bubbles mid-air. Her survival instinct suddenly kicked in, telling her to say *something* at least. All she could manage was: 'Yes.'

'He was living here on the *Room for a Night* scheme, I under-stand. Is that right? Miss Rhodes?'

Karin wanted to give in to the sensation that was making her tilt heavily to one side. She may well have passed out, if she hadn't been sitting down. 'Erm. That's right,' she said, forcing herself to sit upright. 'And then we let him stay on a bit longer, as a friend.' She looked to Mel for back up, relieved to see that Mel was nodding.

'I'm sorry. It must be a terrible shock,' said the officer.

Mel handed Karin some kitchen roll in anticipation that she was going to need it. But tears were a long way off yet. Karin screwed the kitchen roll into a ball and put it to one side, afterwards thinking this might have seemed like a peculiar thing to do. She wrapped her fingers tightly around her wrist, taking some deep breaths. Until, at last, she felt able to say something that might make some sense. 'We've been working on a chari-table housing project on Ashby Road,' she began. 'And Will – Will is, *was*, supposed to be moving in there next weekend. He'd been working so hard on it too, but then suddenly said he'd changed his mind and would find it difficult to fit in. He doesn't have a mobile phone so it's not easy to keep tabs on him. I just don't—'

Mel placed her hand on Karin's shoulder, giving it a squeeze. Tighter than it should have been, as a kind of warning. Karin appreciated the reminder. Her stomach was cramping as she spoke.

'Don't what, Miss Rhodes?'

'I just can't understand it.'

'So when did you last see him?'

'Erm.'

Karin had a flashback of saying goodbye to him on Woodhouse Ridge last Tuesday, late afternoon. She was about to say this. That she had watched him heading into town with his rucksack laden down with hefty books, his sleeping bag dangling off the end, a roll of £20 notes stuffed into his jeans pocket and the rainbow keyring she had given him too.

For friendship.

Some friend.

Suddenly Mel stepped in because Karin wasn't answering. 'Tuesday morning, wasn't it?' she said. 'You *haven't* seen him since then, have you, Karin? I know I haven't.'

Karin shook her head. She wasn't sure what she was meant to say.

'He had his own key though, I take it?' asked the officer.

Mel carried on answering. 'Yes. But he left it behind, I suppose, when he left on Tuesday morning. It was out in the hall, I do remember seeing it now.' Mel paused, waiting for Karin to verify, but when she didn't she carried on. 'He was a lovely guy, never any trouble. Interesting, too. Read a lot of books, clever books. He kept himself to himself pretty much. Do you think it was an accident?'

Karin avoided Mel, absently tearing the piece of kitchen roll into tiny shreds, becoming aware of how insane that must seem. Another silence had descended. Karin stared down at the mess of torn paper on the table in front of her then looked up at the police officer. Wanting, not wanting, to hear the answer to Mel's question.

'Well we have witnesses who say they saw him walking along the river in the centre of Leeds in a very inebriated state on Thursday night.'

'Thursday night?' Karin instantly felt the heat from having repeated that, because in so doing she made it seem significant. Which it was. They were very near to the river on Thursday night. She could have saved him. If only she hadn't been such a coward.

'That's right. Around eleven thirty. It's likely he drowned either later that night or possibly after, but his body wasn't spotted until this afternoon, due to the rucksack he was carrying on his back weighing it down. I'm sorry, Miss Rhodes. Were you close?'

The officer paused for a moment then tried again. 'You were a friend of Will's, you said.'

Karin shifted about in her chair. 'Yes. Yes, we were good friends. I used to be homeless too, you see.'

'And yet you didn't report him missing?'

'Well no. Technically he wasn't. I-I saw him out in the hallway on Tuesday.' She paused because this was her moment to correct Mel and say that she had in fact seen him in the afternoon as well, on the Ridge. But that wasn't what she heard herself say. 'Morning. Tuesday morning.'

She didn't need to look at Mel, could just feel the heat coming off her. Karin had to continue with this now. 'That's when I tried to talk him round,' she went on. 'But Will's a determined guy. I knew I wouldn't be able to stop him, his mind was set on leaving. Well he's very much his own man. I had hoped he would change his mind, turn up for work at some point. I've kept on hoping that, but he hasn't. He erm – he told me to give his room to someone else. Which we haven't done, obviously. I mean everyone would welcome him back with open arms.' Her voice tailed off, clogged with tears.

'And you didn't try to find him yourself, Miss Rhodes?'

Karin shook her head.

'Might you have known where to look, if you had wanted to? You said you lived on the streets, together?'

'Leeds is a pretty massive city,' said Mel. She handed Karin another sheet of kitchen roll when she saw Karin's tears were flowing. Then Mel took it upon herself to pick up where Karin had left off.

Once again, Karin was grateful for the rescue.

'He'd come and go all the time,' she heard Mel explain. 'So I mean it wasn't like he led a regular life or anything, even when he was staying here. And he didn't have a mobile phone, as Karin mentioned, so we could never get hold of him to check where he was. Must have had his troubles, I suppose. Living on the streets can't be easy, can it? Especially when you're deaf.'

'Did you know he had a drink problem?'

Karin hesitated. She ought to have known they would ask that question and could have prepared something.

'Will was known to us, Miss Rhodes. We were aware he was an alcoholic.'

'He never drank while he was here,' said Karin. 'I did know about his drink problem, yes. When we lived on the streets we'd share a bottle of cheap cider or whisky just to keep warm.'

The officer turned to Mel to see if she had anything to add. Mel shrugged. 'So you think he got drunk, stumbled into the river and drowned?'

'The post-mortem will tell us more. But if you think of anything else, either of you, which might be relevant, then please get in touch. Anything at all. This is my contact. So, would it be possible to take a look at his room?'

Karin nodded, letting out a sigh of relief when Mel offered to show them. They were back down again in no time, as there wasn't really anything to see. Will had packed up his belongings and the room was as if he had never been in it at all.

Karin heard them out in the hallway, Mel opening the front door saying goodbye. The sound of the door closing again sent a shockwave through her. Like it was the door to her prison cell. Heavy and echoey.

What had she just done? She knew *so* many things about Will. Relevant things. She knew his friends; his enemies out there on the streets, because they were her enemies too; she knew his haunts, his bedroom down on the towpath. The extent of her betrayal began to weigh heavily and she had no idea why she had failed to tell them that she had said goodbye to him on Woodhouse Ridge. That she had last seen him on Tuesday afternoon. Not morning. Why didn't she correct Mel? And why hadn't she told them that Will had seemed afraid, told her to watch her back too?

The worst thing of all was that Will had said she was a good person. It couldn't be further from the truth.

The news hadn't properly sunk in yet that he was gone. Even now she still half expected him to come bursting through the back door into the kitchen dressed in his decorating overalls, paint-spattered boots stomping across the floor. Or turn up at Ashby Road, tomorrow or the next day, saying that he had changed his mind. Karin couldn't bear the finality of it. In Will she had lost one of her closest friends and it broke her heart that she never got to save him in the end. Will would never get to live that better life she had always promised him, even when it was at his fingertips. It still didn't make any sense that he would throw it all away.

What a waste.

Where was the rainbow keyring now? she wondered. At the bottom of the River Aire? Or maybe displayed on a steel trolley in the morgue, along with his clothing and other belongings from his rucksack. Books. Cheap bottles of whisky. She shuddered at the thought of Will's naked body, white and bloated, laid out on the slab ready for the pathologist's knife.

By the time Mel came back into the kitchen, Karin was on her feet. 'I need to go and tell them I saw Will on the Ridge last Tuesday afternoon,' she said. 'Tell them what he said to me. It could be important.'

Mel shook her head.

'Think about it, Karin.'

'I have and it's the right thing to do.'

'What did that note say? "I know you did it". Did what, Karin?'

Karin almost choked in her hurry to get an answer out. 'I didn't kill him. Not Will.'

'Of course you didn't. Why would you kill one of your best friends? But what if someone saw you on Woodhouse Ridge, like you described it to me? The two of you signing at each other, it might have looked like you were angry with him. You told me you had to stop him from walking off and that you found cheap bottles of whisky stuffed into his pockets. To anyone else it might

180

have seemed like you were *giving* those to him. All I'm saying is, think about it first before you go rushing out there.'

Karin swallowed hard, lowering her body back down into the chair. She could feel her frown deepening, the cramps in her stomach tightening. A bruising headache was not far away.

'*Did* you go down to the river after I left you on Thursday night?' asked Mel. She sat across from her at the table. 'At least be straight with me on that.'

Karin felt her head beginning to pound, like a wrecking ball bashing against it. 'I did go back, yes. To the river.'

'What? Are you serious?'

'But only to stand on the bridge. I didn't go down there, I was too frightened. I just thought about Will for a while and then went home, back to Aaron's. I got myself an Uber, I was so scared.'

In that moment, Karin suddenly had a thought.

'Oh my god. We left the restaurant together, didn't we?'

'What the hell are you implying, Karin?'

'I see what she's doing now. It's Louie. She's playing us off against each other, wants us to fall out, turn against one another. My guess is that she saw us both leaving Swank together, and now she can say that either one of us went down to the river that night. If she wants to.'

'But Louie was at her art exhibition.'

'Not at that time. It was pretty late by then. Aaron could have told her where we'd gone, even shown her where the restaurant was on his way home. She could have hung around until we came out.'

'Spying on us?'

'It's what she's been doing.'

'Blimey. So you think it was Louie who killed Will?'

Karin wanted the pounding to stop but, as yet, was getting very little relief from it. 'I really don't think she pushed him. She can't have done that,' she said, rubbing her temples. 'But she could have got Will so drunk that he ended up in the river. Maybe.'

'Fucking hell. So what are you going to do?'

'Nothing.'

'Nothing?'

'Not yet. I can't yet, Mel. Please, just bear with me on this for a bit longer. I need to get the launch out of the way first. I can't let the charity down, not when so many people's lives and futures are depending on that project. I promise I'll deal with this as soon as that's over. I *promise*.'

'But that's still a week away nearly. *You* might want to wait that long, but will she?'

'She doesn't have any choice. I'm not going to let her get to me.'

Something exploded inside Karin's head.

Louie had already got to Will.

He was dead.

33

Louie

Louie was feeling much brighter since returning to Morecambe. She preferred the sea air to a big polluted city like Leeds any day. But that was not the reason for her overall optimism. The trip had been successful on the whole. Karin had seen her paintings, the two of them had reconnected, and she was sure things would work out the way they were meant to very soon. She just had to be patient and bide her time. Her bank account was bulging, not that she cared about the money, but securing it into her account was also a major triumph.

The pebble bounced into the waves. One. Two. Three. Then disappeared.

In nearby Heysham, windsurfers were slicing through big, salty waves. They looked competent enough to know about the strong riptides or the dangers of the mudflats beneath their feet at low tide. That was a fantastic sight, the sea in its retreat all the way back to the horizon, exposing miles and miles of flat, wet sand. The edge. Louie used to call it that as a child. It was heaven; the point where the sea becomes sky.

Go to the edge, and you never come back.

This bay.

With its quirky tides and currents, where often the sea was nowhere to be seen until suddenly it was everywhere, wrapped around you. Caught out again by those watery tentacles. The edge was where she had first met Karin, a shivering silhouette, sinking into her dark muddy grave. 'Leave me alone,' Karin had shrieked as Louie battled to wrench her out.

'We have literally two minutes to get to safety,' Louie yelled at her. 'You can't stay here.'

And Karin had maintained that she knew what she was doing, that it was none of Louie's business. But as she got considerably more tired, Louie could feel her resisting less and less. Eventually she managed to pull her free and made Karin run as fast as she could before the long sweeping arms of the sea flowed into one, flooding their escape routes. Just a few minutes later and it would have been too late for both of them.

Maybe that wouldn't have been so bad, thought Louie, tossing another pebble into the waves. If they had both got sucked under that night, at least they would still be together now.

Once Louie had got them out of danger, she took Karin back to her place to get warm and give her something to eat. She looked like she hadn't done that in quite a while. 'Then you can tell me everything,' Louie said to her. 'And if you still want to do this tomorrow, I won't stop you. I promise. You can drown in peace.'

It was Karin who had taught her this pebble thing. She threw another one into the sea. There was no shortage on this beach and she began to gather up armfuls. One for each of his eyes, his heart; one for each of his limbs; his neck, eyes, mouth. She would make sure that he never came back. That old bastard, standing in her way.

Wait for *him* to come to her.

Louie had received a text from Karin telling her there was no more money, nor would there ever be, and to leave her alone. That she should stay away from her friends, too. And Aaron. He was withdrawing his offer to help her now. Also her friend Will; she was angry and hurt by his death.

Louie didn't respond to the message.

The repercussions would follow, that was for sure; she just wasn't certain when or what form it might take. But sooner or later that old bastard would pay.

Even if she saw him in the next few days, Louie would be ready.

Back in their bedsit, she ran the blade over the sharpening stone, every so often blowing off tiny metal filings, holding it up to inspect. It had a few nicks and dents taken out of it. Used mostly for forcing limpets off rocks, or cutting through tangled fishing rope, slicing up bits of driftwood.

Until now.

34

Karin

'I'm really sorry about Will,' said Aaron, kissing her forehead. He had come to meet her the following evening after work and Karin was showing him around. He said he wanted to see how they were getting on with only four clear days to go before the launch. Aaron knew how anxious Karin was, said he was feeling nervous on her behalf.

It seemed wrong to ignore Will's room, but Karin was finding that she couldn't be in it for long. The emptiness was too much. Aaron refrained from commenting on the shocking colour scheme Will had chosen. They stood arm in arm looking out of the window, down the garden at Will's bench, almost finished now. She had organized a commemorative seat to be built in his name. She supposed they would have to find a replacement for Will at some point, which wouldn't be difficult given the long waiting list, but for now this was simply Will's room. At least until after his funeral, whenever that might be possible.

'I just can't believe he's not around any more,' said Karin, pulling away from Aaron to indicate this was quite long enough to be in here.

'I can't believe he's gone either,' said Aaron, as she closed the door.

She locked up and set the alarm.

When they were in the car, Aaron continued to say encouraging things about the project, rounding off with: 'You'll be ready for Saturday, I'm sure you will.' She gave him a feeble nod. Karin didn't think there was any doubt they would be ready but there was an awful lot on her mind besides. 'I can put in a few hours, if it helps,' Aaron offered, not understanding.

How could he understand?

He leant across to kiss her cheek, and said: 'Maybe Wednesday, Thursday? There's a bit of slack in the diary now, thanks to you. Got people off my back.'

Karin felt quite sick at that reminder. When was the right moment to tell him there wasn't any money for this now? She had let them get all the way to Chapel Allerton without saying a word. When they pulled up outside an old church that had been converted into offices, she almost choked trying to keep back the tears. This could be her dream home.

'Here we are,' he said, pulling on the handbrake. 'Still want to look around?'

'Erm, no. I don't need to.'

'You know already? That's good.'

'I'm afraid I can't buy it, Aaron.'

'Oh. Well there's still the Headingley house, if you'd prefer to do that. Needs a bit of TLC though.'

'No, it's not – I don't have the money any more. My mother took it all back again, said I didn't deserve it. I told you she isn't a nice person. It's just the sort of thing she'd do. I'm so sorry, Aaron.'

'But – can she even do that?'

'Well it's her money, not mine.'

'Yes but if it landed in your account, then it's yours.'

'Actually, it never got there. It was supposed to arrive on my birthday and when I checked with the accountant he said it was going to be sometime this week. But this morning he said that she's withdrawn the payment altogether. She's a bitch, I told you that.'

187

It had begun to rain. Light spots on the windscreen, becoming watery channels racing down the dusty glass as it got heavier. Karin was feeling that edginess of being trapped in a carwash; she closed her eyes to escape it.

Aaron started the engine again without saying anything.

Their mood was pensive on the way home and the rain not helping matters. This could be the end to the dry spell they had been enjoying, blue-sky days and long summer evenings. Most cars had their headlights on as the light had faded early, turning the traffic into a streaky blur and the buildings on this particular stretch into a dull grey. As they got nearer the town centre, Karin's thoughts were on a young homeless crowd who used to hang out along this route around the Playhouse. She remembered, too, that the rain was a nightmare. Even summer rain. It wasn't cleansing or refreshing. Just wet, stinky clothes; soggy cardboard beds; leaky tents with penknife slashes; rain seeping through holey shoes; and very little charity from passers-by, who scurried along with their heads bowed under hoods and umbrellas, screwed-up faces screening them against the rain with a good excuse to look the other way.

Karin also thought of Will.

Snapping back to the present, she realized the silence had gone on for too long.

'It'll be okay, Aaron. Won't it? I mean, we'll be okay.'

Aaron slammed on the brakes and swerved into the kerb.

'Aaron!'

The handbrake made a scraping sound, clawing up a barrier between them, the engine still running.

'Why can't you just call your mum?'

'What?'

'I don't mean about the money. I just mean there are so many secrets around you, Karin, I don't know who the real Karin is. Not really. I thought I did but I absolutely don't. You're lucky to still have a mum and it just seems wrong that you don't even try to have a relationship with her. I respect the fact you fell out and there's hurt on both sides, but if it were me I'd at least try. You have to start opening up to me, Karin. Otherwise, no, we definitely won't be okay.'

He pulled away again.

'Sorry,' he whispered almost immediately after, and rested his hand on her leg. 'A good day just turned into a bad one. Not your fault. Don't worry, I'll find another solution.'

'It's me who's sorry, Aaron.'

When they arrived back at his place, Karin was racking her brain as to what more she could safely tell him. Perhaps there were things, small things: a few more anecdotes about Birgitta, her dad, even a bit more detail on Louie and what their relationship was actually like. However it only seemed to highlight a situation that was worsening by the day, the list of forbidden topics increasing, with the added uncertainty that Aaron might at some point be the recipient of one of Louie's notes.

Would they ever be able to discuss anything without Karin worrying that she was about to let something slip? Her only hope was that once this had all blown over, things would gradually improve. For now it was hard to see when that could possibly be.

Karin was about to sit down next to Aaron, a bottle of wine and two glasses in her hand, when something made her check her phone first.

COME HOME NOW.
MEL

She made some feeble excuse about Mel not being well, which only deepened the atmosphere already hanging over them.

Aaron kindly offered to drive her back to Headingley, but Karin insisted on getting a taxi.

189

35

Mel

Mel heard another car pull up outside and her body tensed. She had been waiting in the lounge for over an hour, endless cups of tea to keep her going until Karin got here.

'Is that you?' Mel shouted, nervously. She sprang up as soon as she heard the key turn in the lock and hurried into the hallway.

'Put the bolts on,' she instructed, once Karin was inside.

'Mel, what's up?'

'Just put the bolts on. Top and bottom.'

'Okay, okay.'

After Karin had done that, she rushed over to Mel and put her arms round her.

'She says she's coming for me,' said Mel, wiping away her tears.

'What?'

'She was here. That fruitcake ex-girlfriend of yours.'

'Louie? Was here?'

Karin held onto Mel's shoulders, trying to keep her steady, desperate to get more information out of her. Mel caught a glimpse of herself in the hall mirror; her cheeks were streaked with mascara and she was shaking.

'Calm down and explain what happened,' said Karin, guiding her to the stairs.

She perched on the bottom step, leaving room for Karin.

When Mel still didn't speak, Karin tried to coax it out of her. 'Are you sure it was her? Are you sure it was Louie?'

'Of course I'm bloody sure,' Mel shrieked. Then, more calmly, 'I thought it was you, that you'd lost your key or something. So I opened the door, and she forced her way in.'

'What did she want?'

'She said she wants a million pounds, even if you have to ask your mother for it.' Mel handed her another note, letters and numbers cut out from newspapers, similar wording to the last one that had been sent. 'She-she bloody threatened me, told me all the terrible things she'd do to me. Then when I said I'd call the police, she said *she* can go to the police any time she likes and say that either one of us killed that homeless freak.'

'That's what she called him?'

'Fuck's sake, Karin. Political correctness isn't the issue here. She threatened to kill me if you don't pay her the money. Tonight. As much as you're allowed to transfer electronically, and the rest via the bank tomorrow.'

Karin stared at her, blankly.

It was worrying that she didn't seem to be getting the urgency of this. 'She's backed us into a corner, Karin. Wake up, will you?'

'I'm-I'm just trying to make sense of—'

'Well from where I'm looking it seems she's more in love with your money than with you. Psycho bitch, she terrifies the life out of me. So what're you going to do?'

Karin looked down at the note in her hand. After a few seconds she tore it up, in as symbolic a fashion as she had the previous one, screwing the remnants into a tightly packed ball and throwing it at the wall. It exploded on impact, and what was left of it rolled onto the floor like some benign cat toy.

'What the hell did you do that for?' shouted Mel.

'Because I've already done it.'

'Done what?'

'Louie pretty much kidnapped me on Friday afternoon. Made

me go to the bank, forced me to transfer the money into her account.' Karin let out a groaning sound. 'I just can't believe she's doing this.'

'What? So-so how much did you give her?'

'She promised to leave me alone. She *promised*.' Karin was digging her nails into her head. 'How can she possibly want more when she knows damn well I can't ask my mum for *anything*. It's already nearly a million pounds, surely that's enough.'

'What? You fucking gave her *all* your money? Are you serious, Karin?'

'She left me with five hundred.' Karin hesitated. 'Pounds, that is.'

'Well why didn't you say something?'

'I just don't get—'

'Crap!' Mel was on her feet now, pacing up and down in the hallway. 'Did you honestly think someone like Louie would go away that easily? I thought we were meant to be handling this together.'

'What difference would that have made?'

'She's trying to *kill* me! Got rid of Will and now it's my turn.'

Mel noticed that Karin was pulling her phone from her pocket. 'What're you doing?'

'I'm calling Louie.'

'Wait! We need to think about this first. If you tell her there's no more money, well then she might do what she says she's going to do. To me. Or to Aaron. What about him? He's not safe either. Why can't you just ask your mother for some more? We're screwed otherwise, and she terrifies the fucking life out of me.'

'You know I can't, Mel. Look I'm sorry you're involved, but I don't think Louie really means this. It's still just a game she's playing. I've been thinking about Will too, and she would *never* do that. He must have drunk those bottles of whisky and then bought some more with the money I gave him. Later he just stumbled into the river. A tragic accident.'

Mel was laughing. Shaking her head at Karin as she continued to protest Louie's innocence.

'She wouldn't kill him, Mel. I know she wouldn't.'

Mel produced the evidence from her pocket, dangling it from her fingers. 'She told me to give you this.'

Karin stared at the rainbow keyring in Mel's hand.

'That crazy bitch said she knew it was yours and thought you might like it back.'

Karin refused to take it. The look on her face was somewhere between horror and revulsion. Mel put it down next to her on the bottom step, where they were still sitting.

'But I just don't see how,' Karin began, swallowing her tears as she contemplated it, 'how would she know that? I only got this keyring a few months ago and it's only ever been on Will's set of keys.'

Mel studied her. 'Well maybe she's been spying on you more than you think. She's completely insane.' She tapped her phone against her chin and then checked the time on it. 'I really have to go,' she announced, getting to her feet.

'Go? Go where?'

Karin stood up as Mel was looking in the mirror trying to tidy her appearance.

'To work. Even with this shit happening, life has to carry on. Ugh, God.' She drew breath. 'It's okay, I-I've calmed down now.'

'But Louie might still be out there,' said Karin, speaking to Mel's reflection.

'I'll be in the car.' Mel was unbolting the door now. 'If I'm not back in a few hours, then I've been murdered. I'll leave it up to you to decide what happens after that.'

'Mel!'

36

Karin

Karin opened her hand to look at the rainbow keyring again.

For friendship.

Some friend.

It was twenty past midnight. She had been lying on her bed for nearly three hours, sweating, waiting, praying for Mel to come back, trying to convince herself that Louie had nothing to do with Will's death. But how to explain the keyring? None of it made sense. She wrote countless messages to Louie, but didn't send any of them. They helped to make the time pass quicker, that was all.

Hearing the front door slam, Karin raced downstairs.

'Mel? Mel, is that you?'

She didn't answer. Not even when Karin landed in the hallway.

'Oh, thank goodness you're safe. I've been so worried about you.' She could tell that Mel was still angry. 'Look, I'll sort it, Mel, I promise. But after the launch, okay? Just a few more days. A lot of people are depending on me for that. I can't let them down.'

Mel pushed past to get upstairs, shedding clothes and removing earrings as she went. She stormed into her bedroom where she changed into her pyjamas. Karin had been following her and stood waiting for Mel to speak.

Finally, she did.

'So, are you going to tell Aaron, or what? He needs to know what's going on. Don't you think?'

'Yeah, I will,' Karin replied softly, hoping to take the edge off Mel's tone. 'But only after the launch.'

She had already considered this. Telling Aaron would inevitably lead to more trouble, which, for the time being, she simply couldn't deal with. In all honesty, Karin was now of the opinion that she would rather take the hit on the money. So far it had caused her no end of problems, and what was stopping her making her own way in life? She didn't even need Birgitta's money. Persuade Louie to leave her alone and the status quo could be restored. They could all carry on their lives in peace. In reality, though, she knew Aaron would have to know at some point and he was bound to say it was inconceivable to allow Louie just to walk off with nearly a million pounds.

And what about Will's death?

Karin returned to her own room, got into bed, her mind still churning things over. Suddenly Mel burst in and started climbing in on the other side.

'I'm sleeping with you tonight,' she announced. 'Crapping it, on my own.'

'Oh! Okay,' said Karin, making room. 'But I really don't think Louie will show her face again.' She was glad of Mel's company all the same.

'How can you know that?' said Mel, bouncing onto her side, with her back to Karin.

'I know Louie.'

'Well I just hope you're right. Will's *dead*, remember. I just wonder what she'll do next.'

Karin put the pillow over her ears to block out her mother's screams. His legs swinging. Side to side. Like a human pendulum.

Except this time, the face is not her stepdad's.

It's Will's.

37

Karin

It surprised her how hard it was to let go of these letters, despite the pain they still caused. But they were the only things Karin had left of herself, and of her dad. Birgitta, too. Her entire past. As Leeds Parish Church came into view, she pulled over and put on her hazards. It was quiet here at this time in the morning, pre-rush hour, but traffic wardens might already be on the prowl and Karin still wanted to re-read a few of the letters before disposing of them in some random bin.

It was important to face up to what she had done, one final time. Before destroying the evidence.

Dear Mamma

I know what I'm about to say will make you upset and angry, but I have to tell you the truth. (We both know we've never got on, but that's not really the point.)

So here goes.

The thing is, I allowed you to misinterpret what I'd said because it was suddenly an easy way to get back at HIM. But there was nothing going on and he really wasn't coming on to me. Only trying to comfort me when I was upset about my dad. I let you think the worst and I'm sorry for that now. Not that I don't still resent him being in our house and taking Dad's place. He isn't my dad and never will be. So all of those things still apply, and I can never forgive you for marrying him so soon after Dad died. A complete stranger! Behind my back too. Or that you were seeing him when my dad was still alive. I know it's been going on for years and you're just too ashamed to admit it.

I once asked my dad if he was happy. He told me that he was your worker bee, but that he couldn't compete with all the other butterflies. I didn't understand what he meant at the time. I think I do now.

None of this takes away from the fact that I allowed you to think the worst and I admit it was stupid and immature of me. I'm seventeen, not a child, as you keep on reminding me. So I take full responsibility for my actions. He's probably told you that I told him to 'Go hang', but he knows I didn't mean that! I can't believe I said that now. I was angry.

I'm sorry, Mamma. I'm crying as I write this letter. Are you okay? I'm going to come home at the weekend to put things right and say sorry to both of you. You will have read this by then.

Karin.

P.S. I hope you can both find it in you to forgive me.

Suddenly she was back there again. The day she returned home to try and put things right. But it was already too late when she arrived. The letter had never got there in time. For once her mother had believed Karin and challenged her stepfather about the so-called allegations.

There was a hush about Birgitta, like she was in some kind of free-fall.

'You didn't get my letter?' Karin asked, frantic, dumping her bag in the great hallway, striding after her. But if she had got the letter then she would know that she was intending to come home for the weekend.

To put things right.

Finally Birgitta stopped, turned round.

'What exactly did it say in this letter?'

Her voice was a Swedish winter with its brittle clarity; her words hung off branches like pointed icicles. She beckoned Karin with her finger, the naughty child again, into the vast kitchen. Shiny and sleek in its design, silver and grey; too perfect and unrealistically clean. As uninviting as the rest of the house. She stood over Karin with her arms folded and Karin knew the drill by now. Her chair scraped on the herringbone tiles, polished to spotlight precision, and she waited for the interrogation to begin.

Her mother's face was so close she could feel her breath against her cheek. 'Did he *ever* lay a finger on you, Karin? Did he? I want the truth now.' She spaced out her words like she was speaking to a foreigner. Yet Karin always regarded Birgitta as the foreigner. When she spoke to her in Swedish, Karin would only ever respond in English, just to annoy her.

'I never said he did in the first place. You just took it that way.'

'Pardon?'

'All I said was that he gave me the creeps and I wasn't comfortable around him.'

'We both know what you were implying, Karin, and I believed you.'

'Well that's a first.'

Her mother slapped her face so hard she knocked her to the floor.

'What have you done?' she yelled. Her words sliced through the air, spinning towards their target.

Karin stood up, holding onto her cheek. The inside of her mouth was sore where her teeth had cut into the flesh and she could taste blood. She whipped round to her mother and lashed out like she had never dared to before.

'Well why didn't *you* comfort me then? Why?' Tears rolled down her cheeks, dripping off her chin. She swiped them away as fast as they came. 'I just wanted *you* to hold me. I wanted *you* to tell me it was going to be okay. I just wanted you. Not HIM. YOU!'

'You disgust me. You are not my daughter. My daughter would never make such accusations.'

'I didn't accuse him of anything. You did.'

'You're not a child, Karin. You're seventeen. You know how the world works.'

'You still don't get it, do you? I *am* your fucking daughter and that's the problem. I *am*. *You* made me into this.' The sobs punctured her chest, her throat was raw from yelling. 'I just wanted my dad back.'

'How do you think he feels after what you accused him of? What else did you say to him?'

What was the point of holding back when Karin had already told her the truth in a letter and apologized? It would arrive at some point; she had put a stamp on it and posted it through the slot.

'I told him I wanted him dead and that he could "go fucking hang!"'

Birgitta ran into the hallway calling his name. Her voice filled the whole house, flooding corridors, staircases, through doors never opened, into rooms never used. Karin ran into the garden. She thought she had a better idea of where to find him.

The log cabin was hers really. Built for Karin, designed by Birgitta. It was her childhood hideaway, her teenage hangout. Karin made it very clear to *him* that it belonged to *her*, but she knew he still used it when she wasn't there. Things were always out of place, cushions arranged differently, a chair at an odd angle. But maybe he sought the same peace in it as they all had? She couldn't really blame him for that. It had been her dad's sanctuary too.

Karin pushed open the heavy wooden door, expecting to find him sitting there. She was intending to go in and apologize. Make friends. Tell him it was fine for him to use her log cabin whenever he liked, because she actually didn't mind.

But it was a different scene altogether. She hadn't anticipated that she would be walking in on his execution.

In all probability he would have done it anyway. His legs would have swung loose from those steps, even if she hadn't done what she did. And the truth was, she *did* think about saving him, holding his legs while she called for her mother to come. That *did* cross her mind. It was just that, within that split second, he deserved only one thing.

To die.

'Stay right there, Karin!' he yelled, as soon as she had begun to enter the cabin.

His fingers were tucked into the rope around his neck and Karin knew that the second he took his feet off those steps it would suck all the air out of him, tying a knot in his lungs.

'Look I didn't mean for you to—'

'This isn't about you, Karin. I don't blame you and I deserved it. You should know the truth.'

He told her details of the affair, confirmed that it had gone on for years. That her dad was aware of it and had just tolerated it. He said they built up a friendship, became like brothers. He also told Karin how much he regretted that his own family had suffered because of it, his daughter especially. 'But the thing I'm ashamed of most of all, Karin,' he continued, 'is watching your dad have a heart attack right in front of me, and doing nothing to save him. Nothing. I watched him die. Selfishly all I could see was the day I could finally marry your mother. It was too late to save him when the ambulance arrived. I'd already let him die. I'm so sorry.'

A volcano erupts inside her.

She hears her mother shouting as the door opens behind her. But still she races towards him and kicks those steps away with such force they fly across the cabin floor and bounce off the wall, clattering onto their side. Karin watches them go, as if some magic spell has transported them that has nothing to do with her.

The metallic clanking sounds continue long after the steps have landed. Karin stares at them, mesmerized, as they lie perfectly still again.

Meanwhile his legs are swinging.

Side to side.

A human pendulum.

There is poetry in the movement and the sway of him holds her hypnotized. Until she is aware of her mother screaming to get him down.

By then it's all too late. And her mother has seen.

Everything.

They attempt to get him down but fail, and no amount of pleading is going to get Karin out of this. '*But what he said to me was*—'; '*What he told me was*—'; '*The reason I got so angry was*—'

Birgitta refuses to listen.

'Don't you dare come up with any more of your made-up stories, Karin. That man is dead because you accused him of something he didn't do. And I just witnessed what you did with my own eyes.'

'No, Mamma. But that's not *why* he did it. He told me that—'

'Get out, Karin. GET. OUT.'

It was thanks to her mother, however, that his death was recorded as suicide. She never said a word about Karin kicking the steps away. Not a word.

The letter arrived eventually. Too late. Obviously. But Karin knew Birgitta had read it because it was returned to her, stuck down with Sellotape. All the others Karin had written before and after this event came back too. The ones written after were unopened:

Return to Sender.

She stopped writing altogether after Birgitta said she would call the police if she ever tried to contact her again.

Karin's fingers trembled as she fanned through these letters now, picking out words, sentences. Most of which her mother had never actually read.

Dear Mamma

I don't know what to say. You must know I didn't mean to ruin your life; but I realize this doesn't change anything and I can't bring him back.

I'm so grateful that you are not going to say anything about kicking the steps away. I can't expect you to believe me; but I wish you would reconsider your decision because your words: "You are no longer my daughter" are incredibly hurtful.

It must have been awful to see him hanging there like that. All I'm trying to say is that I've always found it difficult to make you listen, to make you love me, when I know you work really hard and I've wasted your money at that school getting drunk and skipping lessons. But me and Dad never got any say in anything. Not ever. You trampled over his feelings as much as you trampled over mine and it's screwed me up.

The counsellor says I have to learn to accept so I have to accept that you are no longer my mamma. You never were a mother to me. That's the problem.

From Karin

P.S. Elliott the accountant has been in touch about when I turn twenty-two. Or before, if I go to university. Thank you for being so generous, I'm sure it will last a lifetime but honestly I would rather come home and be with you than take this money. I hope one day you can forgive me. Somehow I know you won't. It makes me sad to think that you probably won't even read this letter and it will come straight back to me like all the others. I won't write again if that's what you really want.

P.P.S. This could be the last time I call you mamma. That makes me sad. Does it you? No I didn't think it would.

Karin tore up the pages, as many as she could get through at once. There were so many of them it made her fingers sore. She got out of the car, hunching over to the litter bin outside the parish church clutching the remnants of her past in her T-shirt. A half-empty can of Coke was spilling its guts into the rest of the rubbish. She watched the words waterfall into it, soaked up by the Coke, turning them to pulp.

She got back in the car and drove to work. With the letters destroyed she could remember the past however she liked now.

Or forget it completely.

As Karin neared Ashby Road, however, she heard Louie's words again: *I have copies of the letters, Karin. It's all in there, what you did. The police have only to contact your Swedish mamma and you're done for...*

But had Louie really done that? It was yet another thing she wouldn't have thought her capable of.

And then she hears Birgitta saying: *Yes, that IS the truth Your Honour. My daughter DID kill her stepfather. She accused him of TERRIBLE things, told him to GO HANG and then KICKED the steps from under him.*

38

Louie

Louie wasn't afraid of that old bastard. He hadn't got the measure of her at all. As ever, the old underestimate the wisdom of the young. They think they know it all just because they're old.

She was sitting by the window, keeping a lookout down at street level three floors below. At the same time, flicking through photos of Karin taken on her phone in Leeds, wanting to get the best possible light in which to view them. The one taken from the café window was her particular favourite, because Karin had been coming towards her and looked natural. She was frowning, but Louie liked that. It showed her vulnerability as well as her strength, and was also the first expression she had seen on Karin's face the night she had saved her from drowning.

Later, Louie would turn these images into paintings. It made her sad to think this was all she had to work from.

For now.

Suddenly a burst of Karin's laughter filled the room. She was dancing across the floor. Badly. Karin had no sense of rhythm but she liked to dance because she knew it amused Louie. They were so happy together. Why did she go?

One day, soon, Karin would understand that she hadn't betrayed her. And never would. How could she betray the one she loved? But when she did come back, Louie wanted her complete trust again and for Karin to be *sure* that she loved her, that she had always truly loved Louie. Otherwise it was not worth having at all.

When she saw a car she didn't recognize pull up outside their building, she reached for the belt that was on the kitchen unit, constantly within grabbing distance, and put it round her waist. The knife was still in its horizontal sheath that was attached to the belt.

Louie took it out and examined the blade.

The car pulled away again.

39

Karin

'Right. I need everyone to pull their weight today and work as a team,' said Karin. It was the morning of the launch and she had gathered everyone together to run through a few final things. 'Remember we're under scrutiny from the press and TV cameras, so we absolutely have to get this right.'

Morale had taken a knock this week with the news of Will. Not least her own. But Karin had managed to turn this into a positive, by encouraging everyone to work hard for Will's sake. 'Today has to be perfect,' she added, concluding her team talk. 'We're doing this for Will.'

So far the police had not been back asking any more questions. As far as she knew, they still thought his death was accidental. *By misadventure.* Nevertheless, it still felt like a torrent of water was only moments away from rampaging through her life, sweeping everything along with it.

It was simply a matter of time.

Certainly all the pressures of the launch had helped take her mind off other matters. The last thing Karin wanted was for anything to kick off, either in the run-up, or on the day itself, and she was relieved that both Mel and Aaron were respecting her wishes to deal with these *other matters* once today was over.

Aaron was now aware of the situation with Louie. Or rather, he knew as much as Karin dared tell him. He found her yesterday morning, head in hands, slumped over the side of the bath and it just didn't seem fair to keep him in the dark any longer. So Aaron knew that Louie had blackmailed Karin out of her mother's money, even if he didn't fully understand why. Karin just told him that the reason for not mentioning it sooner was out of embarrassment for having allowed it to happen in the first place. In turn, this had led to the lie about her mother withdrawing the payment altogether, for which she apologized. Aaron was furious, naturally, and wanted to take action immediately. But Karin had made him promise not to do anything until they could both sit down and work out a plan together. She never even mentioned the connection with Will's death, and that Louie possibly had something to with that.

Karin just wished this would all go away quietly. But it wasn't going to.

Her only hope was that Louie would see sense quickly and they could reach some kind of compromise. What Karin hadn't yet worked out was how much more to reveal to Aaron about why Louie had the power to blackmail her to begin with. Rather ironically, although she had no intention of telling him, Karin now felt that Aaron could *possibly* forgive her for what she did to her stepdad, as long as she explained absolutely everything to him. Whereas having sex with Louie in the toilets just before he proposed to her was still something he would never be able to deal with. Karin didn't doubt for a minute that Louie would use the latter to her advantage if pushed.

She still wasn't convinced that Louie would be vindictive enough to send her to prison. After all, what would that achieve? Besides, Louie could be done for blackmail herself presumably. Mel had kept hold of those earlier intimidation notes. And then there was Will's death too. At the same time, Karin did wonder how things could conceivably work out with both her secrets and her relationship with Aaron intact. They were supposed to be getting married. Sometimes she had to remind herself of that.

For now, though, she had to concentrate on the launch. None of these *other matters* could occupy her mind today.

'The BBC are coming. We'll make the evening news,' said the site manager, flying at her as she came out of Will's room.

'It's just the local news,' she replied. 'Don't get too excited, Ron.'

'Nope, it's the national! The Government's supposedly rolling out some half-baked initiatives to try and tackle this problem. We're in the spotlight and so are they.'

It was only after celebrating this incredible news with him that Karin considered its implications. This was as high-profile as it could get, which meant that even her mother might see it.

She began to reflect on the person she used to be:

Karin the useless daughter
Karin the hopeless student
Karin the basket case
Karin the suicide victim

Today simply *had* to go well. Not only for her sake, but for the sakes of all the people on the scheme, and many more besides who would benefit if this one was deemed a success. She didn't think for a minute that anyone would jeopardize things from within the project. Even if some still needed help to adjust, everyone had put their heart and soul into it. There had however been a few murmurings in the local and wider community, the minority voice claiming this was nothing more than a glorified hostel or halfway house.

In the end, trouble came in another form which Karin hadn't expected.

It was the same two police officers as before. They were shown into the site office flashing their ID, addressing her as Miss Rhodes, wanting to ask her a few more questions about Will.

'We've spoken again to ... your housemate ...' The police officer stopped to consult her notebook. 'Melanie Pritchard.'

Karin felt her body freeze. 'Okay. Yes, Mel.'

'We've found some items of jewellery near to the scene of the incident. We wondered if you'd ever had any go missing, Miss Rhodes?'

Karin tried to swallow. Anything she said could potentially contradict what Mel had already told them. They were waiting for her answer, weighing up every second's delay. It was like being on some quiz show against the clock where the answers had to completely match.

But Mel was a loyal friend. She had tried to 'cover Karin's arse'. Her words. So she felt sure of her answer.

'Erm no. We trusted Will, totally. Like I told you, he and I were good friends.'

Apart from anything else, Karin really couldn't bear the idea of anyone thinking Will was a thief, and especially not today. He was dead. The least she could do now was defend his honour. A flash of inspiration suddenly came to her. Another lie, but what difference would one more make?

'He did say once that he had a few bits of his mother's jewellery. She died. I never saw it or anything but that's possibly what you found.'

Her answer seemed to satisfy them but they weren't ready to leave just yet.

'Would you mind showing us round, Miss Rhodes?'

Karin had to disguise her unwillingness. She began with Will's room, in the hope this might be enough and then they would go.

'We're still calling it "Will's Room",' she explained as they walked down the hallway to the last door on this level. 'For the time being anyway. There's nothing of Will's in here though. He didn't actually move in. Just decorated it, ready for when he did.' As she turned the handle, she wondered whether to warn them about the colour scheme they were about to encounter, but stopped herself.

209

It still smelt of paint.

'Gosh,' said the female officer as she stepped into the room.

Royal blue with flame red woodwork.

'Will always said that he liked to *hear* colours,' Karin found herself explaining. 'To make up for not hearing sounds.' The memory of Will's eagerness to show her the finished result came flooding back. It just made her sad whenever she came in here now, especially as she knew that the next occupant would probably find it too noisy and stressful and want to change it.

Karin sniffed, wiping away a tear.

'Was there anyone who might have wanted this room, enough to want Will out of the way, do you think?'

'Erm. I wouldn't think so. It doesn't really work like that. People have to earn their place, work hard, train up to get the necessary skills.'

They wanted to see the garden after that. Karin had foolishly pointed out the commemorative bench they had been able to see from the window.

'A couple of the other project workers made it,' she informed them. 'This was Will's favourite tree, and we're going to have a plaque too.' The bench wrapped around the trunk of an ancient oak at the bottom of the garden. For now, it just had *R.I.P. WILL* carved into the bark.

Although it was a relief when they said they were going, Karin felt their visit was rather cursory. Insulting to think they were only paying lip service to investigating Will's death. In the scheme of things, his life didn't really matter. A deaf homeless man. Will was only too aware of that himself.

Karin stood in the porch and watched them go. In her mind she was running after them, shouting, as they climbed into the police car: *I have more information for you. Wait!*

Will deserved so much better than this. From Karin. From everyone.

But she waited until they had disappeared down Ashby Road

and then returned to his room. On her way there, people were coming at her from all angles trying to speak to her. She told them she needed a moment on her own.

Sitting on Will's bed she felt the emptiness and loss all the more. She pictured him at his desk, his head in one of those Russian novels, stroking his beard. She must have stayed like this for at least a quarter of an hour, in quiet contemplation. It was the hideous colour scheme which revived her in the end, and becoming aware of it again made her laugh out loud. 'What the hell were you thinking, Will?' she said, getting up off the bed.

She had to get back. There were things to be done, to oversee. People were relying on her. As she was about to open the door she noticed there was a missed call from Mel on her phone, so she listened to her voicemail before going out.

'*Karin. Just had those two sniffer dogs back asking about Will. They've found some jewellery and were asking if we'd ever had anything go missing. I said we hadn't. Hope that was what you'd want me to say. Am guessing the sniffer dogs will probably be on their way over to you now. I wanted to warn you, so hope you listen to this before they get there. Hope it goes really well today. So sorry I'm working but I will look out for you on the TV. Bye for now.*'

Karin kissed her phone and went back out again.

40

Louie

The news had just finished when the knock came. The item on the city of Leeds leading the way in tackling solutions to the homelessness problem had caught Louie's attention. When she heard the Ashby Road Housing Project in Headingley being mentioned, she looked up from the painting that she was working on and increased the volume. There was Karin, wearing her bottle green dress, instantly recognizable. It was the one she had worn for Louie's art show, which she was most flattered by because it showed Karin had regarded that as a special occasion.

Some local celebrity was ceremoniously cutting through the ribbon strung across the doorway, having to catch it first as it dodged his oversized scissors in the flickering breeze. Louie thought she must have walked through that doorway herself, the day she volunteered there. When she was helping Karin out – in more ways than she actually realized.

A round of applause erupted as the camera pulled back to the presenter. Standing next to her was Karin. 'You must be absolutely delighted today,' the presenter said, indicating behind them, as if to say *with all of this*.

Karin waited for the microphone to arrive under her chin. 'Totally. Yes. I'm just so thrilled we can offer so many people new homes and new skills with this project. We need lots more schemes like this though. Not just in Leeds, but countrywide.'

Hearing her speak so confidently and with such passion gave Louie a sense of pride. 'Go tell 'em, girl,' she shouted at the TV.

Karin was still speaking: 'At the moment these initiatives are just too small and too few, and this really has to be the way forwards. I'm sick of tripping over people sleeping rough on our streets. I think we all are. Leeds has realized it has to clean up its act. And I don't mean by bulldozing these people out of the way. When will we wake up to the fact that homeless does not mean helpless? These people are in this position for all sorts of reasons, young or old, from all walks of life, and with a bit of assistance they *can* help themselves. I implore all councils in this country, and our Government, to get properly on board with this. Give solid incentives to landlords and the private sector to turn these empty spaces into affordable, habitable homes. It needs proper funding.'

'You used to live on the streets yourself, didn't you, Karin?'

The question made Louie anxious. Would she really want to be labelled that way? But Karin responded as confidently as before.

'Yes, I did,' she said. 'It's tough and degrading. Dangerous too.'

'Especially for a woman,' the presenter cut in.

'Well yes. Luckily I made a very good friend who always looked out for me. And then, also, I was fortunate enough to be helped by someone who actually took me off the streets. Helped me get back on my feet. She wouldn't want to be named but she knows who she is.'

She meant Louie. Of course she meant Louie. It made her shed a tear, and Louie *never* cried. She was so overcome with emotion she had to text Karin immediately to say how proud she was of her.

The reporter was about to ask another question, but Karin grabbed the microphone, saying: 'I just want to ask this.' She had that spark in her eye and was pointing her finger at the camera. Karin was so sexy all fired up like that. 'Why are there a million people in this country – and that figure is rising by the way –

using food banks, when we are still the fifth or sixth largest economy in the world?'

'Okay,' said the presenter, making sure she got the microphone back this time. 'You certainly have a lot to say on the subject. Maybe the Government ought to take notice of this young woman. The voice of a generation perhaps.'

There was another round of applause. Then the mood shifted.

'But tell me, Karin. You were good friends with Will Langham, I believe. The homeless man who died in tragic circumstances, drowned in the River Aire about a week ago. He would have been living here now, wouldn't he, having worked very hard on this project. Is that right?'

Louie could see the dread in her eyes. She obviously hadn't been expecting to be asked this question and therefore wasn't prepared for it. When she became too emotional, the presenter took her by the arm, the camera following them down the garden to a bench dedicated to Will Langham.

The knock on the door had startled Louie, even though she was half-expecting it, having been on the alert for days now. When the banging grew more insistent she turned the TV off, firing out a series of energizing breaths – a reminder that she was ready for this. Louie felt underneath her T-shirt for the knife, still in its horizontal sheath attached to her belt. She practised drawing it quickly a few times then put it back.

It was necessary to pick her way carefully across the room, walking round the easel, avoiding the propped-up canvases leaning against any available wall space. On reaching the door, she put her ear to it, listening out for any warning sounds. In case he was trying to shove a firework through her letterbox, or gas, or petrol.

Another knock.

Keep him waiting a bit longer. Let him get angrier.

She waited until his knuckles turned into a fist and he was braying at the door. Her hand hesitated over the handle.

One, two, three.

'Aaron,' she said as he tumbled into the room. 'Shouldn't you be in Leeds? I just saw your fiancée on the TV. Couldn't you be bothered or something?'

He grabbed the neck of Louie's T-shirt and thrust her against the wall. 'Listen you thieving little bitch, you pay that money back into Karin's account because I am not leaving until you do.'

'Well that could be a long wait then.' Louie was finding it difficult to speak as the neckline of her T-shirt cut into her windpipe. She could smell alcohol on his breath. 'Would you like some tea?' she sputtered, surprised when he let go of her, tossing her backwards.

Rubbing the soreness out of her neck, she tried to pre-empt his next move. It was sudden when it came. He lashed out at a chair with his foot. The leg came off and then it toppled over. Louie touched her belt through her T-shirt for reassurance, feeling the bulge of the knife in its sheath. She didn't want to draw attention to it though, and pretended she was adjusting her T-shirt, pulling it down over her thighs.

Aaron wiped the sweat from his top lip. His other finger was raised, hovering in that position, until he shouted: 'Put that money back into her account. It belongs to Karin, not you.'

'Oh. Is that why you're marrying her?' Louie put her hands up to protect herself as Aaron came towards her again, but then realized he was looking for something else to break, not her. Not yet. Deciding upon another chair, he smashed that to pieces too, afterwards standing with his legs apart, hands on hips, demonstrating the hierarchy in their strength. It seemed like he had had quite a lot to drink and Louie wondered how he had got himself over from Leeds.

Her hand was poised, ready to whip underneath her T-shirt. She had practised the move many times.

'To think I went out of my way for you, as well,' he said, wiping his lip again. 'I could have opened doors for you in the art world. It could have been the making of you. Too bad.'

'Well I did consider it, I must admit. But I can open my own doors, thank you. Got some good contacts from that exhibition in Leeds, as well as quite a few sales. So how do you like your painting, the one I gave you? *Meet Me at the Edge.* Did Karin tell you the story about it? I saved her life, you know.'

Aaron kicked out at the easel. The canvas she was currently working on wobbled but didn't fall. Louie had no intention of stopping and continued to bait him. 'Do you even love her? Or just love having her draped over your arm? Old boy like you, it must give you such a confidence boost. I'm guessing her money helps too, of course.'

There was no room to manoeuvre in this tiny bedsit, and even less now with all the broken wood strewn everywhere, but she began to circle him as best she could, stepping over the debris in her way.

'I didn't even know about the money,' he said, following Louie with his eyes, switching direction quickly when he lost sight of her. She carried on circling and the pattern repeated itself.

'So why are you here in that case?' she asked.

'Because you've stolen her money, you evil bitch.'

'Karin hasn't explained it to you then, obviously. You see she was worried that vultures like you would be trying to get their talons into it, so she gave it to me for safekeeping. You can ask her. She knows she can completely trust me; I'm the only one she can.'

Aaron picked up a stray piece of wood and smashed it against the wall, leaving a jagged edge, holding it like a baseball bat. 'Do you seriously want me to go to the police and tell them you've robbed someone of nearly a million pounds? Do you?'

'Oh come on, I think we're all going down if you do that. I doubt your property portfolio is as squeaky clean as it ought to be. And doesn't it bother you that Karin is still in love with *me*? She always will be; you need to know that.'

'So why is she marrying me then?'

Louie forced out a burst of laughter. She was used to not showing her fear in these situations, even though it had been a while since she had found herself in one.

She could outrun most people, yet here she felt trapped.

'I do have a theory on that one,' she said, digging her nails into her palms.

But that was all she said.

Let him beg.

He threw his arms out, coming towards her with the piece of wood. 'Well?'

'You'll have to play nicely.' Her hand was resting on her belt, ready to draw the knife if she had to. But he backed off, and Louie began circling him again. There was even more debris on the floor than before. 'Karin's had a pretty rough time of it, I'm sure you know that much at least. And looking for stability in her life. Sadly I think she's confused that with plain old boring.' Louie could see he was twitching, keen to retaliate, but his curiosity was stronger than his pride and he was letting her carry on. 'She clearly views you as a father figure, wouldn't you say? Which I can quite understand, given her own father died and you probably remind her of him.' Louie gave him an extra-wide grin when she added: 'Well you are a bit of a corpse yourself, Aaron.'

He made an attempt to grab her, but she was quicker, taking a step backwards out of his reach.

'Hold on,' she said, raising her hands to stop him advancing any further. 'You may want to hear this next part too.'

Aaron squared his shoulders, trying to look intimidating but also preparing himself for what might be coming next.

'I take it you don't know that me and Karin had sex in the toilet at The Midland? Hot, desperate sex. Deep and dirty, the way she likes it. Did she tell you that? Then you asked her to marry you just after. Basically she panicked and said yes. It's true, you should ask her. Why d'you think she was behaving so weird that night? Disappearing the whole time, coming back flustered

217

from the toilet, cheeks all flushed, lost an earring. My god, she was hot. And at the art show, she wanted it then too, but we didn't.' Louie dared to move closer, jabbing her finger in his face like he had done to her. 'I'm no expert, Aaron, but I'd say that's not a good start for a marriage. Would you?'

He was mortally wounded; words could do that to a person. She thought he might lash out again, but he didn't.

'Is *that* why she paid you the money?' he asked, desperately trying to make sense of it. Poor sod. 'So that I wouldn't find out?'

'No. I think she was more worried that you were going to steal it from her.'

'You're a lying cow. I don't believe a word.'

He was scanning the bedsit, a look of destruction in his eyes once more, and returned to the recently started painting resting on the easel. It was the latest one of Karin, although he probably couldn't see that yet. It was Karin sawing up a tree in the garden in Ashby Road. The easel toppled over this time; he kicked it hard. Then stamping on the canvas, he put a hole through the middle of Karin's face.

Louie didn't try to stop him.

Wiping his forehead with his shirt sleeve, he pointed his finger at her again. 'If you don't return that money, I swear I will make sure you *never* paint another picture. Do you understand me?'

His eyes flickered, still seeking to lash out. They landed on the mannequin in the corner of the room.

'Don't touch that!' Louie shouted, lunging at him.

He gave her a shove, sending her to the floor with a crack. The mannequin went over too. Louie dabbed her lip: there was blood on her hand. He followed up with a disdainful nudge to her stomach, using the end of his shoe.

'You'll just have to kill me,' she said, licking the blood off her lip.

He grabbed her, suddenly, manhandling her over to the window.

She was being dragged across the floor, mostly on her knees as she was struggling to stand, and only just managed to avoid crashing her head into the window ledge as it came speeding towards her. The wood was rotten all around the frame, flaking paintwork, and a shade of mouldy green growing in the gaps, which Louie had used for a colour match in *Ophelia*. The sash mechanism didn't work any more.

Aaron hoisted the window upwards. It rattled and fell down again, reminding Louie of the idiosyncrasies that she had simply grown used to in their bedsit.

Their love nest. Hers and Karin's.

Did he realize that yet?

She thought about making the suggestion of using the broken broom handle to prop the window open, currently at eye level due to the fact that he was forcing her head down, holding her by the hair. Louie could feel a tightening in her scalp which made her eyes water.

He must have figured out a way of keeping the window open with his other hand, because she felt herself being shoved outside, her stomach ending up in a painful V-shape over the ledge. At least the knife was easy to reach in this position. Staring down at the street three floors below, she got a whiff of someone's cooking in the flat directly beneath theirs. Stewed vegetables. A man out walking his dog was forced to stop when the dog cocked its leg against the lamp post. Cars parked either side of the road. In the breath of air above the cooking fumes she could also detect the sea, familiar and fresh-smelling.

Then she got a flash of her own crumpled body, lying broken on the pavement. A bloody stain, seeping from her head. Neighbours screaming.

Louie breathed hard.

Don't show him your fear.

'Could I just point out that you can't kill me *until* you have the money?' she shouted, trying to direct her voice up and back without alerting the rest of the neighbourhood.

Louie waited for him to react. One way or the other.

Moments later she was being hauled inside again.

Once her feet were firmly on the floor, she grinned at him, saying: 'Well that was exhilarating.' Her head was still tingling, glitter shapes floating across her eyes. She shook them away and waited for her heart rate to come down and her head to clear.

'Right,' she said, almost recovered, 'let's sit down, shall we, and try and be civilized about this? Have to be the sofa though, as you've smashed up all the chairs. I'm assuming you won't want to sit on the bed, given that's where Karin and I used to sleep. Well, we did one or two other things in there besides. Obviously. You sure about that tea?'

He was struggling to deal with the intimacy of this room now. Wasn't quite prepared for that. He reminded Louie of a wild animal, suddenly tamed by a tranquilizer shot into its backside.

Eventually he opted for the sofa. She could tell by the way he reluctantly sank his weight into the cushions that he was wondering if they had had sex on there too. Which, of course they had. Many times. But she would spare him the details.

Louie took a seat next to him, as close as she needed to be. Despite having the upper hand, his pride was wounded, and he could still lash out at any point. She felt her heart begin to pound at that thought.

'So,' she said, trying to ignore it, 'do you still wish the money to be paid into Karin's account? You really didn't seem too impressed by the toilet sex.'

He was oscillating between anger and confusion, running his fingers through his hair and then smearing them across his face. The look he gave her was full of hatred and contempt. She knew that he wanted to kill her. Her hand was just underneath her T-shirt, ready.

'Karin loves *me*, Aaron.'

'How do you know that?'

'Because I know Karin. Better than you or anyone else will ever know her. And I can prove it.'

The bedsit was in a state, as if some drunken brawl had gone on. She picked up the mannequin, inspecting it for damage but there didn't seem to be any as far as she could tell. It was a shame about the canvas that he had destroyed, although she hadn't got very far with it and could easily start again from scratch.

Putting the broom handle in place at the window, she watched for Aaron to emerge at street level. He came out, started walking towards the sea. There appeared to be somebody waiting for him at the end of the road, standing beside a car. Louie strained her neck to get a better view, but it was too far away to take in any detail and the car door was obscuring most of the person in any case. It was probably a female outline, although she couldn't say for sure.

She saw Aaron getting into the passenger side. After a short while the car drove off.

221

41

Mel

'You okay?' said Mel, waiting for him to get nearer before she asked the question.

He didn't answer.

They both got into the car at the same time. Aaron slammed his door and she could feel the tension coming off him immediately. There was blood on his sleeve, but she didn't say anything.

'There *has* been something going on, even at The Midland. I can't fucking believe it.' He hit out at the door, rubbing his fist afterwards.

Mel sighed. She wasn't sure how to respond. 'Well you don't know for sure if that's the truth, Aaron. Speak to Karin first.'

He was like an unexploded bomb, and the bottle of whisky he had finished off on the way over hadn't helped either. That was on top of what he had drunk at the launch.

Mel had received the phone call towards the end of her shift. Aaron was insisting on driving over to Morecambe this evening. 'I have to confront the bitch, Mel. I can't leave it any longer. Just me and her, have this out.' He said that if Mel wouldn't give him a lift then he would drive himself anyway. It was plain from his voice that he had been drinking, even at that point, and so she really didn't have any choice. But it was fine.

Mel faced the steering wheel, gripping it tightly, and then let go of it again. Maybe she ought to try and calm him before they set off.

'You can't trust anything that comes out of her mouth, you know,' she said.

'Whose? Karin's?'

'I meant Louie. Well of course she'd say something's been going on. Because she wants you out of the picture, doesn't she?'

Aaron fired an angry jet of air from his mouth, tipping his head backwards and pressing his fingers into his eyes. With an extended groan, his chin flopped down onto his chest again. 'Can we just go please, Mel? I really want to be in Leeds now.'

Mel started the engine and pulled away, watching his reaction as they drove past The Midland. She was about to remark on how impressive it looked, curving into the bay as if it belonged to the landscape. Instead she put her hand on Aaron's shoulder to acknowledge his pain, leaving things until they were well clear of Morecambe before asking him any more questions.

'So did she say anything about Will?'

Aaron still seemed distracted. She repeated the question, this time adding: 'Poor Will.'

He was staring out of the window, lost in his turmoil. 'What?' he said, turning to her. 'No. No, she didn't say anything, and I didn't ask.'

'And so what about Karin's money? Can we get it back for her, do you think?'

Aaron said that he just wanted to sleep now. Or maybe he closed his eyes so that he didn't have to answer any more of her questions.

The roads were quiet. Mel put the radio on low to keep herself awake. As they approached Leeds a couple of hours later, queuing to come off the roundabout, she applied the brakes harder than she needed to in order to wake him, as by that time he clearly was asleep.

'Almost home,' she said. 'Do I drop you at yours?'

'I wish you'd told me, Mel.'

'Told you what? I knew no more than you did.'

'You knew about Louie, that they were once an-an item. Jeez. You could have said something about that at least.'

'I was hoping Karin would do that herself. Look, it wasn't my place to say anything. Come on, Aaron, you still love Karin and she loves you. Am I right?'

He didn't answer.

Mel dropped him in front of his apartment building and told him to go straight to bed. 'And if you need me, either of you, I'm right here. Okay? You take care.'

He stumbled out of the car.

'Hey,' Mel shouted, forcing him to come back again. She hadn't quite finished but didn't want to broadcast what more she had to say. Aaron staggered over, stuck his head through the window, hanging onto the roof like he might fall over otherwise.

'What I *can* tell you about Louie is she's pretty unpredictable. Unhinged, even. I'm just warning you. Goodnight, Aaron. Try and get some sleep, you look shattered.'

42

Karin

Aaron had mentioned to her that he would have to shoot off straight after the launch and therefore couldn't stay for the celebrations. At the time, Karin had done her best to conceal her disappointment. It sounded like it was important, whatever it was, a meeting or something, but even so it was rather short notice. In the end he left without saying goodbye because Karin was in the middle of an interview, which was a shame as she had hardly seen him all day.

The launch was over now, and had been a success. Everyone said so. Why wasn't she feeling a little more elated then? But really, she knew why. Because she had desperately wanted Aaron to say that he was proud of her. In fact the only person to actually tell her this was Louie, who texted to let her know that she was watching her on the news, glowing with pride. Even coming from Louie this still meant something. Without really knowing why she did it, Karin texted back to say thank you for caring.

She had the same mixed reaction when she read Louie's next message about Will. It said how sorry she was to hear that he had drowned. Karin shuddered to remember that Louie may have been responsible for Will's death.

Two days on from the launch, she still hadn't seen very much of Aaron. He had come back late on Saturday night, drunk, and been working ever since. But this morning, before he left for the office, they agreed to sit down over dinner and make a plan. The way Aaron kissed her goodbye as he went out the door gave Karin some reassurance that there might actually be a way out of this and a glimmer of hope for the future.

Their future. Together.

She was still prepared to write off the money, being the easiest solution of all, but Aaron was in no mood to let Louie get away with it and had made that very clear. Karin did wonder at what point the bank would raise concerns if this money was to yo-yo once more out of Louie's account and back into her own, where it had landed in the first place from her mother. Might it look like there was some money laundering going on, switching it about like that? Then again, the bank knew her and Louie as a couple now. In any case, Aaron dealt with large sums all the time with his property deals, so he must know ways around it, if indeed this was a problem.

They could discuss the details later.

In preparation for this evening, Karin had walked into town to buy some ingredients from M&S. She wanted it to be special, in spite of the inevitable challenges their dinner table discussion would create. As she stepped into the lift, trying to get her bags of shopping under control so she could press the button for the tenth floor, the sparkle of her engagement ring caught her eye. Karin had to admit that something had changed whenever she looked at it now. The initial euphoria of – *Which part of Leeds would they live in? In what sort of house? How many children would they have? When would be a good time to start a family?* – had turned into *How will this end?*

But if they could devise a good plan this evening then maybe there was a chance.

The possibility of a fresh start.

Karin had already suggested that as soon as the money landed back in her account, they could get on a plane and build a new life for themselves. Somewhere. Anywhere in the world, in fact. And even though she had no idea how to reach this next phase, she was beginning to feel excited by it, believing it might actually be possible.

Karin had never imagined leaving Leeds since making it her home just over a year ago. She would be sad to abandon the charity, the projects and the people associated with it, but other than Mel she had no real ties here. She had even worked out a plan for Mel too, if she could be persuaded to come and join them once they were established. She could get a job, maybe meet someone over there. Mel was always talking about wanting a change of scene.

Aaron seemed to be in favour of this plan.

The lift came to a jolting halt on the fifth floor, reminding Karin that there was a whole mountain to climb before they got to that point. She noticed her fingers had turned white where they wound through the handles of the carrier bags, and she was just swapping them over when a family with a pushchair entered the lift. Karin shuffled up to make room, smiling an apology for her bags. She looked at their happy little unit and it made her want to cry.

Stumbling into the hallway, she closed the door with her foot and went into the kitchen with the provisions. Tomato and mozzarella salad followed by a fat, juicy steak, cooked rare, just the way Aaron liked it, with sweet potato fries and homemade relish. For dessert, her special chocolate pudding loaded with Grand Marnier. Cooking wasn't really her thing but she knew that Aaron's ex-wife had some flare in this department, so she was keen to make an effort, and especially tonight.

While unpacking the bags her phone started to ring. Karin thought it might be Aaron and, in her hurry to answer it, it flew out of her hands like a bar of soap. 'Sorry. You still there?' she shouted, retrieving it from the kitchen floor. 'Hello? Aaron?'

It wasn't Aaron.

'Hey, Karin. How're you doing?'

'Lou.'

Karin sank to the floor.

'What do you want?'

'I was just wondering what you're cooking tonight.'

'What? How do you know I'm—? Where the hell are you?'

'Don't worry, I won't be late. Aaron said around eight o'clock.'

'What?'

'Hasn't he told you? He wants to talk to me about my artwork and thought it might be nice if the three of us discuss it over dinner. As we're all such good friends now, I mean why not? So I'm not in breach of our agreement, Karin. It's all above board. And you really were sensational on Saturday on the news. Dead-dead proud of you.'

It sounded like she was driving. Why would Aaron do that without informing her? Was Louie even telling the truth?

Once the call had ended, the only thing she felt she could do was to get on with dinner. Aaron would be home shortly; she would keep herself busy until then. Maybe this was all part of his plan? If it was, then, ideally, she would have liked to have run through it with him before putting it into action. Alternatively. If Louie was bluffing and turned up here uninvited, at least they could deal with her together.

All would be fine.

Karin chopped the tomatoes and mozzarella, narrowly missing her fingers several times due to her nerves. Her next problem was: did she serve this on three plates or two? Did it even matter? She moved onto the steaks. They were large enough to go three ways if necessary; however she doubted she would be able to eat a thing if Louie was here in any case.

Louie was bluffing. She must be.

Karin didn't hear the door opening. Closing again. Or the footsteps on the kitchen tiles. He must have slipped his shoes off in the hallway, so when Karin suddenly saw someone behind her

228

she screamed; immediately after, throwing her arms around his neck when she realized it was Aaron.

Aaron freed himself, holding onto her hands. 'Has she called you?'

'Louie? Yes! What on earth is going on?'

He let go of her but, before answering, poured out two glasses of wine. Watching the liquid fall from the bottle so freely, Karin felt the tautness in her stomach all the more. Every part of her was tight. There was so little time for discussion now, not if Louie was already on her way.

'It's going to be okay,' said Aaron, taking a mouthful, clinking his glass against hers afterwards.

Karin put it down again, without drinking. 'Please Aaron. I need to know what's happening.'

He nodded, but still took his time to reply. Finally he put down his glass, and said: 'Well the main thing is to let her think she still has all the power.'

'She's the one with the money!'

'*Your* money. Don't forget that. Louie thinks she's coming over to discuss some deals that I've got lined up for her artwork. But, we are going to get your money back.'

At least that tallied with what Louie had said on the phone; she hadn't been making it up then.

'When she gets here at eight o'clock, you need to tell her that I'm running late and I'm not going to be back until at least nine. You with me so far?'

'I think so,' Karin replied, hearing the doubt in her own voice.

'And then – this is the important bit, Karin – you tell her that you've had a change of heart. You want to be with *her*, not me.'

'What? Are you sure?'

She needed a moment with that, and Aaron allowed her some breathing space. Realizing she was still struggling to understand, he added: 'She'll never give you the money back otherwise, Karin.'

'I really don't—'

'Trust me,' said Aaron.

'Well. So then what?'

'That's all you need to know. Believe me, the more natural you are the more believable this will be.'

'Aaron. I don't think I can do this.'

What if Louie were to say something that would compromise her even further? Could she risk that? But what choice did she have? She was squeezed every which way. By Louie. By her past. And ultimately, by her own mother.

One step at a time, Karin told herself, breaking into a sweat. She took an ice cube from the freezer and ran it over her forehead, which was now beginning to throb. If Louie started accusing her of anything, anything at all, she would deny it. Louie had proved herself to be untrustworthy, a blackmailer and a thief no less. Maybe even a murderer. If it came to it, Aaron couldn't possibly believe Louie's word over hers.

Could he?

She had detected a change of atmosphere between them lately. And maybe it had been creeping up on them for a while, although she couldn't say exactly when it had started. Things had been pretty stressful of late, so it could just be that.

They waited in silence for Louie to arrive. Aaron topped up Karin's glass and poured out more for himself, to calm their nerves.

Thirty minutes later the doorbell rang.

Aaron put his finger to his lips. 'I'm right here,' he whispered, tiptoeing into the other room.

The doorbell rang again.

Louie was not going to go away.

43

Louie

As soon as Karin opened the door, Louie made sure she was through it like a current of air. This was what she had been waiting for. Nudging Karin out of the way, she closed it again quickly, then immediately planted a kiss on Karin's mouth before Karin had a moment to think. She held it there, pressing firmly against her lips and it turned into something amazing, like biting into a juicy, fleshy fruit. Karin let it go on far longer than she needed to, which told Louie all she needed to know.

Eventually Karin pulled away again, leading Louie by the hand into the kitchen.

'Is he here yet?' asked Louie, checking around for signs of someone else's presence in the apartment. She knew they wouldn't be alone.

Karin looked down at the floor, unprepared and awkward. Louie felt sorry for her, having to put her through this, but she would thank her for the final outcome.

'Aaron's going to be late,' she replied. 'Stuck on the motorway and he won't make it back until about nine-ish. But it gives me a chance to tell you something actually. Because, I've been thinking about what you said. A lot. And you were right all along. I don't love him because – well because I do still love you.'

Karin's words were like honey poured into her ears. She moved in to kiss her again and Karin didn't protest. 'So how about you show me that you really mean that? Mm?' said Louie, pushing herself against her. She found Karin's bra strap and released it, delighted to be able to roam under her T-shirt as much as she liked and hear Karin inhale one long ecstatic breath as she closed her eyes.

Aaron would be watching from somewhere in the apartment, so why not put on a good show? See how long he could stand it for. Maybe his jealousy had subsided now, and this wouldn't bother him so much? But it reminded Louie of the old days, stealing their moment, unguarded and dangerous. Maybe they could get all the way?

'Wait,' said Karin, forcing her backwards, 'I need you to prove it to *me* first.'

Louie threw her arms out. 'What more can *I* possibly do? You know I've always been here for you, no matter what happens. Always.'

'Transfer the money back into my account then, if you really love me. I have to know that you trust me.'

'Hm.' Louie considered it carefully, lingering. 'So how do I know this isn't some kind of ambush?' A burst of adrenalin shot through her veins as she wiped the sweat from her top lip. 'How do I know he's not here, Karin?'

'Because he isn't,' she replied, knowing that sounded weak. She flushed, and Louie felt sorry for her again. 'But when he does get here, I'm going to tell him about us, Lou. I really am, I promise.'

The idea of their having dinner together to discuss this particular matter amused Louie. At the same time there was an element of risk, which, although exhilarating, actually scared her. None of this was rehearsed and all three were improvising in some way.

'You're going to have to prove to me that he's not here right now though,' said Louie, forcing her hands inside Karin's T-shirt again. 'Let's do it in the kitchen, the hall …' She ran a line of kisses up and down her neck. 'The lounge. All over his fancy apartment.'

It was a joy to feel Karin moving in time to her rhythm as she pressed against her. Louie was even allowed to kiss her breasts, at which point she really did think Aaron would spring from his hiding place. But he could take all night over this, as far as she was concerned. Once or twice Louie did think she could detect a slight struggle in Karin, as her conscience fought against her desire, but she knew Karin was feeling this just as much as she was whenever their lips came together, tongues intertwined.

Poor Karin. Having sex with that old fart must be like having sex with a worn-out sofa. Static and solid, grappling with a load of old stuffing and springs. No one knew Karin's body like Louie did. Not when she had painted every bit of it and made love to every part of it.

'I think we can stop there now.'

Aaron's voice came from somewhere behind them.

Louie backed off, feigning surprise, and Karin began rearranging her clothes.

'How could you do this to me, Karin?' said Louie.

'How could I do this to *you*? You're the one who's stolen every last penny from my account.' Karin was trying to make her voice sound strong, but it wasn't.

'Not *stealing*,' said Louie, determined to make her properly understand this now. 'Keeping it safe for you.'

Karin still wasn't believing it.

Not yet.

'That's just as well,' said Aaron, stepping between them, 'because you're going to transfer it back again.' He reached over for the laptop that was on the unit. 'Right. Now.'

'Erm, I don't think it's possible for her to transfer the whole lot in one go, Aaron,' said Karin. 'We'll have to go into the bank, like we did before.' Her voice tailed off.

Louie couldn't help smiling at that but she kept it from Karin.

It was time for the next phase. She had already spotted the array of knives on the magnetic strip, but decided not to risk it.

Louie had come prepared in any case and removed the knife from her belt. The long blade caught the light when she began to wave it around and she found herself captivated by its spot-dancing along the walls. She even wondered if she could capture this in a painting, cutting the light into glittery pieces. Realizing her distraction, Louie ran her fingers down the edge of the blade, feeling a slight nick, and then began sucking her finger.

Karin had to see that she meant this.

'For God's sake put that down,' said Karin, anxiously. 'Let's talk about this.'

'He's only after your money, Karin. Do you really think he'll stick around once he's got his hands on it?'

Aaron moved towards her. 'Put the knife down, you stupid bitch.'

Louie lifted the blade again, keeping him away with short pulsing stabs. Aaron raised his hands in submission and stepped back.

'You can keep the money,' said Karin. 'I don't want it. Just go.' She sounded breathless, her eyes glistening with tears.

'This isn't about the money,' said Louie. 'It's about *us*. Did you know he came to see me on Saturday night?'

Karin shot Aaron a glance. It was his turn to look awkward this time.

'Did he tell you he was proud of you, like I did? I bet he didn't. Too busy getting rough with me, smashing *our* place up. Yours and mine.'

'What do you mean *came to see you*?' Karin's eyes moved in confusion, going from one to the other.

'How else was I supposed to get the money back, Karin?' said Aaron.

'He asked for it to be paid into his own account. Not yours.'

'That was only when she told me about you two at The Midland,' he responded. 'In the bloody toilet. So is that true?'

Karin directed an accusing glare at Louie.

'I had to tell him,' said Louie. 'I thought he was going to kill me, shove me out of the window.'

She looked like she needed time to digest these things. Poor Karin. The truth was in there somewhere, struggling to get out.

'There's nothing going on, Aaron. I swear there isn't,' she said. 'It didn't mean anything that night. I was just in shock at seeing her again. I'm really sorry.'

Karin was looking to both of them when she said these words. The same amount of guilt and the same amount of sorrow for each.

Louie resented that.

'You lied about the money too,' said Aaron. 'Never told me you had it in the first place and then said your mother took it all back. I tried to love you, Karin, but it all makes sense now. Were you two *at it* at the art show as well? Is that why you freaked out at the painting? Well, let me tell you, I may have been duped by my ex-wife but I'm not going to be duped by you.'

'Aaron. Please.'

He ignored her, opening up his laptop as he carried it to the table. After tapping a few keys he sprung round, in one rapid movement, and pounced on Louie, dragging her to the table with her arm twisted up her back. The one that was holding the knife.

He swiped it from her and held it to her throat.

'Aaron, no,' shouted Karin, darting forwards. She pulled up again, shocked when he turned the knife on her.

Satisfied that Karin had got the message, Aaron returned the blade to Louie's neck, twisting her body round and forcing her to sit down. 'Do it,' he said, giving her head a shove into the laptop.

'Louie, just do as he says!' said Karin. 'It's absolutely fine, I won't let him hurt you even after you've done it. Please.'

Louie shoved the laptop to one side and stood up. Slowly. She was aware that the blade was following her throat. Shunting the chair behind her with her foot, she waited to hear it clatter to the floor. In the distraction this created she twisted under the knife, like a cat curling under a tripwire.

'Louie!'

'It's okay. He can't kill me unless he's got the money, can he?' As she said these words, Louie side-kicked the knife into the air and as soon as it landed she was onto it. So now it was Louie's turn to dance and swirl with the knife, keeping her focus on Aaron while addressing Karin. 'I need to hear you say that you want to be with *me*, Karin. That you still love me and that you've always loved me. Say it like you really mean it.'

'I can't. I don't.'

'Say it!'

'Okay. If you put down the knife.'

Louie turned the blade on herself, pointing it at her stomach. Karin screamed.

Louie could almost feel the pressure in Karin's lungs, see her breath suspended. 'If you don't love me. If you really don't want to be with me...'

Karin was shaking her head. 'No, Lou. Please don't.'

'Meet me at the edge. Remember that?'

'No!'

'If you go to the edge you never come back. You always wanted us to go together, Karin. You were forever saying it. So what are you afraid of now?'

'It was a stupid thing. I wasn't well. You know I want us both to live.'

'Together?'

'No.'

Louie plunged the knife into her stomach, staggering backwards. She held onto the table, aware of the blood creeping across her shirt. White. Turning red. It was beautiful. Poetic. She wanted to paint that too.

The knife fell, Aaron picked it up and wiped the bloody handle on his shirt. When Louie lurched forwards suddenly, he held the knife with his sleeve, keeping her back, then passed it to Karin. She held it in her trembling fingers not knowing what to do with it.

Louie smiled at Karin as she sank, slowly.

Down.

Please understand, Karin.

'Louie, no! What've you done?'

The knife clanked onto the tiles. Karin must have dropped it. And Louie saw her rushing towards her in those final twists of her body before she thumped to the floor. Louie felt a trickle of blood down the side of her mouth. Then Karin was on her knees, beside her, cradling her head into her chest.

'Say that you love me,' Louie whispered.

Something was pressing into her stomach. Aaron, on the other side, was trying to stop the blood flowing out of her.

Louie closed her eyes.

'Call an ambulance,' she heard Karin say between desperate sobs. 'Louie. Stay with us. Louie.'

Aaron: 'I think we're losing her.'

Then Karin: 'Just call a fucking ambulance!'

An eerie silence floated above her as Karin's words began to fade. It was peaceful: how she imagined it would be. Serene. Like a calm Morecambe sea.

'We can't just let her die, Aaron.'

It was unexpected, the pulsing sensation on her chest. And then his lips on hers, blowing air into her mouth. The taste of his aftershave. Revolting. She wanted it to be Karin, the one closest to her now.

Aaron stopped when Louie moved her head. She turned to Karin one final time, and whispered: 'Say that you love me.'

Admit it, Karin. Just admit.

Only silence.

Aaron was checking for a pulse in her wrist. 'I think it's too late,' he said. His voice was faint and matter-of-fact. 'I think she's gone.'

Her head was in Karin's arms again. Louie heard her wail, felt the tears dripping onto her face like rain, in between her sobs, as Karin rocked her back and forth.

At last.

'I do love you, Louie. I always have and always will.' Louie could feel the heaving in Karin's chest as she was struggling to speak. 'But it's a crazy love and it scares me. I was scared of loving you too much. Scared of losing you and-and scared of what we had because I was terrified of loving someone that much. That's why I got jealous and paranoid. Kept us in our own little world so no one else could get in. I suffocated us both and I know it was me who ruined it all. I felt I didn't deserve such happiness, I didn't deserve you. Saw death as a way of keeping you. And then I blamed *you* for what that was doing to us, but I know it was me. I'm sorry. I'm so sorry I ran away from you, but I just didn't know what to do. I didn't know how to fix it and I didn't want to take you down with me. But I do still love you, Louie. I do.'

Finally.

Knowing this, Louie could happily slip away.

44

Karin

Karin pushed herself back in horror, sliding across the tiles until she slammed into the wall.

The implications now beginning to sink in.

So where was Aaron? How long had she been sitting here in this daze of confusion? Clambering to her feet again she asked herself: *why would Aaron stick around anyway?* As soon as the police and paramedics arrived, he wouldn't want to be implicated in any of this, and Karin couldn't blame him for that.

He shouldn't have to clean up her mess.

Aaron didn't deserve this.

A sudden banging from the next room caused her to freeze. It stopped, followed by a swishing sound, like something being pulled across the floor. Karin felt her lungs would burst if she didn't start breathing again soon and discover what it was. A few moments later, Aaron appeared, dragging in the rug from the bedroom.

'Aaron!' She rushed over to help him. 'What're you doing?' Her words were full of joy and relief, but she knew that couldn't last.

'What does it look like I'm doing?' Aaron snapped, barging his way through. Karin was forced to one side as he hauled the rug into the centre of the room, slapping it down next to Louie.

'So you didn't-didn't call anyone then?' Karin asked. What she really meant was: did he call 999?

He ran his arm across his forehead, saying: 'This is *my* apartment, Karin. Your money is sitting in *her* bank account, and, although it might not seem like it, *we* are engaged. How do you think that looks, hm? We have to get rid of her.'

'But how?' Karin inched closer. 'Let me help you, Aaron. Please.'

'Don't – you come near me!' he yelled, putting his hand out to stop her.

Karin immediately shushed him, a finger to her lips as a reminder of people in the adjoining apartments.

He was calmer when he next spoke.

'The thing is, Karin, I would *still* have given you a chance. Right up to that point, I really thought—'

He pressed his hand against his mouth, as if it was too much to bear. After a few moments, he managed to continue. 'I thought that maybe we *could* start again. Somewhere new, just like you said. I wanted to believe you were sincere. But then you said those things.'

'I only said them because she was dying, Aaron. Because Louie needed to hear them.'

'And so did I!' he yelled. Then, calmer: 'And so did I.'

He bent down for the rug again, changing his mind and throwing it back in disgust. 'Did you *ever* love me? Or was I always just the safe bet?'

'I loved you – I do love you – in a different way. You don't make me feel out of control.'

He laughed, scoffing. 'Is that a good thing?'

'The truth is I loved you both,' Karin said, her voice quietening.

Instinct told her to throw her arms round Aaron's neck, but she couldn't read him any more. Their relationship had never been fully tested.

Not like this.

'Listen,' she continued, 'I know we didn't get the money back from Louie, but I have about five hundred left in my account. Pounds, I mean. Not thousands.' She felt herself blush. 'I'm really sorry, Aaron. Aaron? Are you listening? I'm saying that I still think we can make a fresh start somewhere with what we've got. Between us. We really don't need that much to be happy. You've got property to sell, we'll be okay.'

Her voice faded.

Aaron glanced at his watch, spinning round as if uncertain of his next move.

Karin was surprised when he suddenly landed at her feet, kneeling down. He took hold of her wrists, stretching them out, and began rubbing his thumbs over the milky white part of her skin. 'I did love you,' he said, winding the engagement ring round her finger. 'If I hadn't stepped in when I did, how far would you have let things go with that – *girl*?'

'You said I had to make her think I wanted her.'

'But you did. Want her, I mean. Didn't you?'

'No! I didn't know what I was supposed to do.'

Aaron slid the engagement ring up her finger. It caught on her knuckle and she winced. He pulled harder, angry that it was resisting him. Once it came loose he held it to the light, admiring it; white gold set with tiny diamonds.

Karin rubbed her finger to ease the soreness, wondering what was coming next.

'Call me old-fashioned, Karin. But the least you could have done was to have the decency to let me know we were a sham.'

'What? No, it wasn't like that. We weren't a sham at all.'

'I'm sick of being lied to, cheated on. You know that.'

Karin nodded; her guilt and his pain made something very toxic taste in her mouth.

'Do you honestly think I'm going to let you do the same to me as my ex-wife? And with another *woman*? How could I ever trust you now? You might be able to live a lie, but I certainly can't.' He looked at his watch again, handing the ring back to Karin as he stood up. 'Keep it. You might need it.'

'Why are you looking at your watch, Aaron?' He rubbed his neck.

'Have you called the police?' When he didn't answer, Karin felt her stomach lurch as he took hold of the end of the rug again. 'Wait. Please,' she shouted, but he wasn't going to be halted this time.

She watched him slide Louie's legs across it. Until now she had blotted out the fact that Louie was lying dead on the kitchen floor. When Aaron went round to the other side of her body, Karin made sure she was there first, and blocked him. She wanted to hold Louie one last time.

Still warm. Her eyes closed.

Karin ran her finger over the seahorse tattoo on the inside of Louie's wrist. She kissed it.

'That's enough,' said Aaron, prising her away. 'We need to get the job done.'

Her eyes. Sea blue. Like shiny glass marbles. To think they would never paint another picture. Never trek across Morecambe Bay on the lookout for driftwood or shells. Never see the sun or rain or fresh falling snow. Never see Karin.

Not ever.

She missed Louie.

She had always missed Louie.

The problem was that everyone else before her had let her down. Including her dad. Karin had learned that the only person she should rely on was herself. Running away from Louie ensured that she couldn't be let down by her as well.

Then Mel's take on things had always been that Louie was some kind of crazed, possessive stalker. She did behave that way at times, but maybe Karin drove her to it. For leaving in the way that she had, without saying a word, not even a goodbye. And really her own possessiveness had been far worse, during the relationship. Their dangerous obsession with death, that was all Karin too. It was true that Louie liked to explore it in her artwork, but only so she could work through her own demons. It was Karin who saw death as a way of hanging onto Louie. Not the other way around.

Meet me at the edge.

That was too much to ask of anyone. Karin should never have made them say it, knowing Louie would do absolutely anything for her. The moment she felt herself spinning out of control, she had decided not to take Louie down with her. It gave her another reason to leave.

Yet now, here was Louie lying dead. It had come to that anyway.

Aaron rolled up her body in the rug, leaving a pool of blood on the floor where she had been lying. He was still refusing Karin's help, but secretly Karin was glad about that, recoiling at the thought of Louie's body having to be dumped in some dark, lonely place.

'What will you do with her?' she asked, feeling her stomach heave, needing to look away. Maybe one day, though, when she could face it, she could go and say goodbye to Louie properly.

Like she should have done before.

Karin realized she had asked the wrong question. What she meant was: *where will her final resting place be?* And not: *how will you dispose of the body?*

His answer was cruel. 'Burn her,' he said. 'There's a disused quarry I know.' Aaron looked at his watch, wiping his brow with his forearm. 'Petrol and an oil drum should do the trick. We should have enough time.'

Time for what, Karin didn't dare ask. Nor any of the other questions she had. *Won't it smell? Won't people be able to see it burning?* Cremating Louie's body in an oil drum seemed like a terrible send off. Somehow so much worse than burying her deep in the ground where the worms could get at her. And that was bad enough. The sea would be Louie's preferred resting place. Always the sea.

Karin bit down on her lip, fighting back the tears.

Aaron gave her a scowl. The way he was looking at her, standing over the rolled-up bundle, Karin found reminiscent of her mother. Before calling the police, she had given Karin's face the fiercest slap but then afterwards was calm as falling snow. While reporting that her husband had just committed suicide, she glowered at Karin, never took her eyes off her for a second. And Karin stood by, waiting for her to add that it was her daughter who had kicked the steps from under him.

But Birgitta had another punishment in mind. It was Birgitta who gave her the life sentence.

Karin was jolted back to the present when her stomach heaved so uncontrollably she had to divert to the bathroom. It seemed her body needed to turn itself inside out, get rid of everything that was rotten inside it. Expel the badness that kept coming in violent thrusting waves, in between all her sobbing and wailing. Until finally. The storm passed. Leaving her stomach washed up on the shore and her head banging against the rocks.

When Karin completely trusted that it was over, she leant back against the wall exhausted.

Two of her best friends dead.

Will.

And now Louie.

Karin wasn't sure how long she had been gone but, when she returned to the kitchen, she found herself completely alone. If it hadn't been for the blood streaked across the floor it would have seemed like a perfectly normal kitchen. Utensils and pans hanging from shiny S-shaped hooks; china mugs, white, evenly spaced and all facing the same way; the knives arranged in order of size on the magnetic strip.

Then suddenly, her thoughts turned to Aaron. He must surely need help getting Louie into the lift.

Karin rushed to the door.

It was eerily quiet on the landing, well after ten thirty by now. She pictured Aaron's route out to the car park. It was always lonely down there, so with any luck, he probably wouldn't have to encounter anyone. Plus it was dark. Even during the day Karin hated it, and at night she avoided it whenever possible. The area directly outside the apartment block was also inhospitable, old Leeds industrial desolation awaiting development, and the River Aire.

These things were positives right now. But there was still a lot that could go wrong.

She heard the lift doors closing on a floor above or below. It made her think about CCTV, if there was any; she hadn't noticed before, never had a reason to, but there was bound to be some. What would be captured on it tonight? She fled back inside the apartment and shut the door again quickly, panting heavily. It made her sickness return, despite her hollow stomach.

She was emptied, inside and out.

Come on, Karin. You can do this. Go into the kitchen and get cleaned up. Get things back to normal.

Normal? Would there ever be a normal again? She stared at the bloody streaks across the floor and wept. Except there were no more tears left to come out of her either.

Karin reached for her phone. She needed to talk to someone.

45
Mel

Mel was busy packing, bagging and boxing up her possessions, repeatedly asking herself how on earth she had managed to accumulate so much stuff over the years. Radio 6 Music was on in the background and every so often she would turn up the volume and dance across the bedroom floor, returning to her task when the track had ended.

The things she wasn't taking were going into bin liners: books, CDs, old clothes and jewellery, general bric-a-brac. At least she could do her bit for the homeless charity. Whenever she heard a car pull up outside she stopped what she was doing and peered out of the window. It was hard to see very much now, as the streetlamp directly in front of the house wasn't working – another late-night student prank probably – and darkness had already swallowed up the last part of the day. She hadn't quite got used to seeing the 'For Sale' sign over by the fence. It tricked her every time into thinking it was a person standing in the garden, giving her a scare until she remembered.

It was after ten thirty by the time she had finished packing. Feeling like she had earned herself a glass of wine, she went downstairs to the kitchen, noticing the open blinds. As she went to close them, she saw a shadowy mass just beyond the path in front of the window. A figure. Then a light, shining across the garden, made her retreat quickly out of sight.

Aaron had his own key and would use the front door. So too did Karin, and she didn't expect to see her here tonight.

Hovering by the kitchen door, trying to decide what to do, she held her breath and reached her hand towards the cutlery drawer, opening it as silently as she could. Her fingers wrapped around the rolling pin. It was at that point she realized that her phone was still lying on the bed upstairs. She couldn't go back up to get it now, in case whoever was out there suddenly burst through the back door.

It was locked, but she still went to check, fumbling with the latch and bolts. Her reluctance to part with the rolling pin made the task more awkward.

All secure.

Mel edged closer to the blinds again, the hairs on her arms rising with each tiny shuffle. She reached out and managed to create a larger gap in the slats by pushing down on them with the end of the rolling pin. In so doing, she saw next door's dog scampering round the garden, the neighbour attempting to catch it. The dog squatted down and for once Mel didn't mind. It was no longer her problem. She would be out of here soon.

Returning to the lounge, armed only with a bottle of wine and a large glass, she flopped onto the sofa and heaved a sigh of relief. She had only been there a moment or two when she remembered that her phone was still upstairs and went to get it.

That's when she got the call.

'Karin? Are you okay?' All she could hear was Karin sniffling. 'You don't sound okay. Where are you? Is Aaron with you?'

After a long delay, she managed to say something. 'Yes, I'm fine. It's okay, Mel. I'm sorry to bother you.'

'Hey, don't worry. Do you want me to come over? Are you at Aaron's? I'm in the middle of packing, but I can come. It's not Louie, is it? Shit. Is it Louie?'

'No, I, erm, I haven't heard from her. We're still working out what to do about that actually. Aaron had a late meeting, but he'll be back soon. I just got upset thinking about everything, that's all. My mind's been whirring, you know, about Will and things. I'll be okay. So have you found somewhere to live then if you're packing? Already?'

'I have. It's an amazing place, you're going to love it. You need to make a start on your stuff, Karin. Not that you've got anywhere near the amount I have.'

'Yes, I suppose I should,' she replied.

'You are still into it, aren't you?'

'Yes, of course I am.'

'Are you sure everything's okay, Karin? Have you and Aaron had a row or something?'

'No. Nothing like that.'

'Well are you certain you don't want me to come over? Because I can drop everything. You know I would.'

'It's not necessary, honest. I feel loads better just for chatting. Thanks, Mel.'

Karin ended the call. Mel tapped the phone against her chin as she headed back downstairs. After a few more sips of wine she convinced herself that everything was okay and not to worry.

There was nothing more she could do.

46

Karin

The smell of bleach was overpowering. Karin had tipped almost a full container of the stuff into a bucket of boiling water and was regretting being so liberal with it now. Dipping the mop into the bucket only encouraged swirls of steam to drift upwards, delivering stinging fumes to her eyes and nostrils. At least the swaying motion of the wet strands across the floor had a more calming effect. It couldn't stop the maelstrom of thoughts from spinning through her mind though. Nothing could stop those.

Luckily the pool of blood was contained to a single area, with just one wider streak where Aaron had pulled Louie's body onto the rug. Karin tried not to pay too much attention to it, turning the mop blindly in all directions, keeping her eyes half-closed. But each time she dipped it back into the bucket she was forced to take note of the deepening shade to the water. Red. Redder. Redder still.

Thicker than water itself. That's what they say.

Suddenly another thought crash landed into her head. Where was the knife? She remembered letting go of it as Louie was falling, but hadn't seen it since. Maybe Aaron had retrieved it and would dispose of that too. The only slight worry was that her fingerprints were all over it. What might that mean if it was found? But then, did it really matter in the scheme of things? If she was going down for one murder, why not go down for all three? Her stepdad's, Will's, and now Louie's. Even if Karin herself hadn't put the knife into Louie, she was responsible for her death regardless. If she had stayed in Morecambe and tried to sort things out then perhaps they would still be together, still living their happily ever after.

Karin dropped onto her hands and knees in case the knife had shot under the fridge, or got wedged in some other small gap beneath the units. Behind the fridge maybe? She couldn't shift its glossy designer bulk on her own. Hot and frantic, she resorted to going round the kitchen opening cupboards, drawers, pulling cookbooks off the shelves. It was hopeless. The best she could hope for was that Aaron had scooped the knife up and disposed of it in the disused quarry.

Along with Louie.

Karin shuddered at such an appalling thought.

Forcing herself to put everything back in its proper place, she collapsed onto the floor and began weeping all over again. The tiles were still wet, and the bleach filled her lungs with toxic breaths, making her cough and choke.

She deserved it.

An insistent ringing of the doorbell forced her to get up again. Surely not Aaron, back so soon. He couldn't have burned a body in that time, it wasn't possible. And besides, he had a key to his own apartment; she had seen him take it.

Unless there was a problem? Maybe it was the police.

A thick, bleachy-red liquid sloshed over the side of the bucket when she dropped the mop too carelessly into it. Grabbing a tea towel she wiped up the mess, wafting the air with it to get rid of the smell. Without thinking, Karin also used it to rub the sting out of her eyes, making it worse, yelling in silent agony and cursing her own stupidity. Tossing the tea towel into the bucket, trying to blink away the caustic sting as she carried it into the hallway, she was careful not to slosh any more of the red liquid over the side and shoved the bucket into the cupboard, reminding herself to empty it later.

The doorbell went again.

'I'm coming,' she shouted.

Her voice sounded different under pressure, like a train passing through a tunnel. As she scurried to the door she noticed damp patches under her armpits and suddenly got a whiff of herself. Which prompted her to check for more tell-tale signs on her clothing. Blood stains. It was blood that would give her away.

She couldn't see any.

Karin peered through the spyhole, not recognizing the man standing there. He didn't look like a policeman but could be in plain clothes. Perhaps it was a neighbour, heard noises earlier, come to ask if everything was okay.

She opened the door, and the man asked for Aaron.

Karin swallowed her fear as best she could, trying to exude calm. 'I'm sorry, he's not here just now. Can I pass on a message? Or have you tried his mobile?' She hoped that he hadn't, or wouldn't, in fact, and instantly regretted that suggestion.

'It's okay, I've already left him a message,' he replied.

Who the hell are you anyway? she wanted to scream.

'I was just in town and thought I might be able to drop a few things off. I know I'm not supposed to be here yet.'

'Oh. Erm. Sorry, your name is—?'

'Russell. I'm the new tenant. Are you the old one? Or maybe the cleaner?' He sniffed the air, getting the bleach smell.

Get the fuck out of here.

'I see,' she said, confused and still in shock.

He must have registered her uncertainty because he reached into his pocket and pulled out a folded piece of paper. It was a rental contract with Aaron's signature on it. Karin had had one of those herself, so she knew it was genuine.

'Right. Well I suppose you can leave stuff in the hallway then,' she said, blocking him from coming in too far.

251

'If you're sure.'

Karin stood guard as he brought in four large storage boxes. He felt the need to make polite conversation in between each one, which set her even more on edge. Asked if she was intending to leave Leeds. She said she wasn't sure yet. When he was finally done, he wished her well at her next place, wherever she ended up, and left.

It prompted Karin to question whether she ought to be making plans of her own, instead of waiting for Aaron to come back. Was he even *going* to come back? Like ever?

Why should he?

They hadn't recovered the money from Louie; it was still sitting in her account like sunken treasure under the sea.

Karin decided to take a hot shower. Put on clean clothes.

Fresh clothes, fresh start.

Who was she kidding?

But it did help to wash away at least some trace of what had happened here tonight. Afterwards, she swept her hands over the rest of her things hanging in the wardrobe – a row of multiple Karins – dragging them down until they were a frenzied heap on the floor. Then began stuffing everything into the extra-large suitcase that she had brought over when Aaron suggested she should spend more time here.

Karin looked round for the remainder of her possessions: jewellery, books, toiletries. If the new tenant was moving in soon then she had to be out. With or without Aaron.

You're a survivor, Karin. You've lived on the streets. You're a fighter. Rely on yourself. Everyone lets you down in the end.

Think.

Without Will, without Louie, her world was shrinking rapidly. Even so, she refused to write Aaron off completely. She told herself that she was just getting prepared. For anything.

And she wasn't alone in any of this.

Call Mel.

'Please come over, Mel. Something terrible *has* happened.'

'Okay. Calm down, Karin. I'll have to get a cab because I've had a drink now, but I'm on my way.'

47

Karin

Karin lay on the bed waiting for Mel to arrive. She was seriously beginning to wonder now if Aaron was ever coming back, although his things were still here and she had even checked that his passport was in its usual place, which it was.

Why was Mel taking so long?

Waiting. Karin was used to this. Waiting for someone to find out, waiting for something to happen. First her stepdad: rope around his neck, head loose, tongue lolling to one side. Then Will: blue face, hollow eyes, clothes dripping from the River Aire. And now Louie: knife in the stomach, leaving pools of blood wherever she went.

All three, passing through the walls, day and night.

The apartment was in darkness, seeping into every room, but Karin didn't want any light to get in. It wasn't yet midnight and already she feared the sun coming up, bullying her into a new day. Suddenly she remembered Louie's painting under the bed. It was shoved there out of the way because neither of them had wanted to look at it and they hadn't decided what to do with it yet.

Karin switched on the bedside light and pulled out the canvas, blowing off a thin layer of dust that had already settled. She managed to lever it onto its side, noticing the tiny seahorse that Louie had drawn on the back in one corner. Running her fingers over it made the sadness wash over her again. She managed to twist the frame around, and with a good deal of huffing and panting, rocked it onto the bed. Then she climbed on top of it and lay down.

The hard canvas dug into her spine. She must have been on the edge of sleep though, because when she heard a key turn in the door, it seemed to wake her.

Karin sprang up and ran out into the hallway.

It was Aaron. He reeked of smoke.

'Thank God you're okay,' she said, pulling up before she quite got to him. The boxes were in the way but that wasn't the reason she had stopped.

Aaron was staring at his hands. They looked like he had tried to wash them, but the dirt-filled scratches and blackened finger-nails were a giveaway.

'I've been worried sick about you. Did it go – all right?'

'That's something I never want to have to do again,' he said. He was holding a tin out for her. 'Your souvenir,' he added.

It rattled when she took it from him and she had to swallow hard because she had asked for Louie's ashes. Nevertheless, this needed some kind of acknowledgement.

'I erm – I never doubted you, Aaron,' she said, after a deep silence had set in.

He looked at her, as if to say: *if only that were true.*

'Right, well, I'm going for a shower,' he announced.

Karin had no time to process anything because, just as Aaron was disappearing into the bedroom, Mel suddenly arrived in the hallway, pulling a large suitcase that she left by the door. The hall was getting cluttered with all the stuff that was being dumped in it.

'Oh you poor thing,' said Mel, rushing to Karin. 'Don't worry, I'm up to speed. I bumped into Aaron in the lift. Should we go and sit down? You look terrible.'

Karin allowed Mel to steer her into the kitchen, resting her head on Mel's shoulder as they went.

'Wow,' said Mel, wafting the air. 'Strong smell of bleach in here.'

They sat down at the table, and Mel took a bottle of whisky out of her bag, tossing her head back to drink some. She offered the bottle to Karin, wiping drips off her chin, but Karin declined.

Karin was too busy staring at the tin. It was on the table in front of her. She pushed it away and it rattled again.

She noticed Mel smirking.

'Is that the crazy lesbian in there?'

'Don't call her that, Mel. She's dead!'

Karin detected a strangeness to Mel's mood. She was pretty drunk.

'You think I give a shit?' said Mel. 'Stupid bitch won't be bothering *me* again, that's all I care about.'

Mel grabbed the tin, and before Karin could stop her she had removed the lid. Karin pressed her hands to her mouth in horror.

'Hm. I guess these don't burn.' Mel shook the bones against the sides.

One brief glance was enough for Karin. To see that they were brittle, crumbly and charred was more than enough and she grabbed the lid back off Mel, replacing it with her eyes half-closed, needing several attempts until it slotted into place. As she did so, she pictured Louie's contorted body, burning and shrivelling in an oil drum somewhere, under a charcoal sky.

Karin felt like she was inside that tin. And wanted to be. She wanted to be with Louie.

'Listen,' said Mel, giving herself another swig of whisky, 'you have to know something, Karin.'

'Oh-kaay.' Karin took her eyes off the tin, slowly, and looked up at Mel, sensing that she wanted her full attention. 'What is it I need to know?'

'Well.' She wiped her hand across her lips then licked them thoroughly before continuing. 'My dad committed suicide too.'

'Oh.'

Karin had assumed it would be something about Louie. This seemed too much of a leap and she heard herself jabbering out a reply. 'God. Did he? I didn't know that. I'm really sorry.' She remembered Mel telling her that both her parents had died but didn't think she had ever said how. She switched seats to be next to her, to offer some comfort, but Mel didn't seem to want it and batted her away.

'Well why didn't you say?' asked Karin. 'It would've been okay to tell me, you know. Obviously, I know what that's like.'

Mel gave her a strange sort of a look, which Karin wasn't able to interpret. The silence between them began to ice over. Until Mel shattered it again, her tone of voice at odds with the words she was delivering.

'Well anyway,' she said, 'he hanged himself. Just like your stepdad.'

Karin was getting a bad feeling about this now. 'God, that's truly awful. So what happened? Have you any idea why?'

She really didn't think she wanted to know.

48

Mel

Mel took another gulp of whisky, offering the bottle to Karin again, but she still declined.

'Oh I didn't care about my dad at all,' said Mel, enjoying the look of impending dread on Karin's face. 'I hated him. He'd been seeing another woman for years and my mum always covered for him, making excuses. Ever since I can remember in fact. My dad worked away a lot, gone for months on end sometimes. I knew they weren't married, he and my mum, but turns out he was leading a double life.'

'What a bastard.'

'This woman was rich apparently, Swedish.' She gave Karin a leer. 'So I suppose that was the attraction. We never saw a penny of what she gave him though, and hardly anything from what he earned either. My mum wasn't able to work, so it was pretty grim. I had to look after her. We couldn't even afford to put the heating on for more than an hour in the winter, and I remember feeling constantly hungry. You know that gnarling you get in your stomach? 'Course you do, you went hobo for a while. Well anyway, when this woman's husband died, my dad just abandoned us completely. He couldn't get out of the door quick enough. As soon as the bloke's body was in the ground, they got married. I've no idea why he hanged himself though, Karin.' She leaned closer. 'Have you?'

Karin made out that she needed to dislodge something in her

chest. It was probably the truth that had got stuck there. Mel let her finish coughing before she carried on. She didn't really expect Karin to answer.

Not just yet.

'So maybe he thought his life would be hell with her after all,' Mel continued. 'I mean, your dad wasn't happy, was he? Or maybe the bitch decided she didn't want him any more? Whatever. He just didn't seem the hanging type to me though, somehow. What do you think?'

Karin was rubbing her temples. Mel hoped the pain was the worst it had ever been.

'I hardly even knew my stepdad,' she replied. 'You know that, Mel.'

It seemed like she was pleading with her to stop, but Mel had nowhere near finished.

'Your mother never offered us a penny in compensation. She stole our lives for all of those years and not a shred of compassion. I asked her at *my dad's* funeral for some help. Pretty much begged her. Where were you by the way?'

She could see that Karin was still trying to catch up. Mel gave her a moment or two; it was a lot to take in. But this was all part of the fun to see Karin struggle. In the past Mel had always had to conceal her enjoyment. Now she could revel in it.

'Well we'd already fallen out by then,' said Karin, mumbling. 'I'd left home. My mother wasn't interested in where I'd gone.'

'Hm. Well she told me you were back at school. Anyway, I went to your house a few days after the funeral to see her. Couldn't believe my eyes when I saw the place. I told her my mum was sick, that she wasn't able to work – gave her the full sob story. Every word of it was true, of course, but she still wouldn't hear of it. So then I thought about going to the newspapers, expose and shame her that way, but my own mum didn't want the humiliation. She said that would finish her off. That's why she'd tolerated it for all those years, I suppose.'

Karin looked broken.

Mel gave her a smile.

'But how did you know where to find me?' she asked. 'I was living rough.'

'First I went to your school. Fuck me, that's posh as well. But nobody claimed to know where you'd gone, and then one girl remembered you once mentioned Morecambe. Some connection with your dad. So I went there, but couldn't find you.'

She could see Karin frantically trying to slot this piece of the jigsaw into place.

'No, I didn't go there right away. I'd-I'd already quit school, but my bereavement counsellor let me sleep on her couch for a few months. I had to lie low so that she didn't get the sack. It was only later I actually decided on Morecambe. My dad was born there, so it just seemed right. For what I had to do.'

Her voice was thin and petered out at the end. Karin had got completely sunk in her memory. Mel ignored that and carried on.

'Well I gave up looking for you at that point. I always knew I'd figure out a way of finding you one day though. And then, hey, there you are, right under my nose in the creepy Dark Arches of Leeds, of all places. There was something about you, I knew immediately it was you. I'd seen a photo at your mother's place, spotted your red hair hiding under that stupid hood of your parka.'

Mel recognized the longing in Karin's eyes. A pitiful sight. She wanted to ask about that photo. Where did her mother keep it? Which photo was it? Did she throw darts at it? Or was it on display somewhere prominent?

The photo wasn't the only thing Mel had seen that day. When Birgitta's phone started to ring, she said that she had to take it and began parading up and down her huge kitchen, barking out orders to whoever was on the end of the call. In the meantime, Mel looked around, her eyes immediately drawn to an email that was open on Birgitta's laptop. She even had time to read some of it. It was to her accountant, stating that her daughter was to receive £957,000 when she turned twenty-two.

At that point, Mel made up her mind. She would find that spoilt little bitch and take the money from her. Somehow. Get revenge on the family that had completely destroyed hers. She would find a way.

Karin was staring at her. It brought Mel back into the present moment. *This moment*. That she had waited so long to relish.

And Karin looked like she was seeing Mel for the very first time.

Mel grinned back, nodding.

'So we're-we're stepsisters then?'

'Yup. Afraid so.' Mel took another large gulp of whisky, swilling it round her mouth, waiting for the burn when she swallowed it. 'But don't get any ideas. I've been doing nicey-nicey for far too long now and it was a fuck of a wait till you turned twenty-two, so if you think I'm going to see that money go to waste after all of that—'

Mel broke off to enjoy the hurt spreading across Karin's face. She deserved it. Every bit of it.

'You had everything I didn't, growing up,' Mel went on. 'Yet you were such an ungrateful cow. Weren't you?'

'No! You know how unhappy I was. You know my mother sent me away when I was only eight years old, and there was no love in my childhood. Not ever. She was always in complete control and I was miserable. I missed my dad, and then he died. I ended up on the streets. You know all of this.'

'Oh my poor heart bleeds. You had the chance of a good life, Karin, and you threw it away. You wasted it. While you were tossing it off at some ridiculously posh boarding school, I had *nothing*. I hardly ever went to school, and you had everything. You even had *my* dad.'

'But that was nothing to do with me. And money isn't every-thing, Mel. I can vouch for that.'

Mel pushed her face into Karin's. 'Go live off nothing again then, if you enjoyed it so much.'

You will anyway, she thought. Mel kept that to herself for now.

Karin was completely cornered; she knew she was. Yet she still persisted with her bleating. 'You should be punishing my mother, not me,' she whined. 'She's the one who had the affair with your dad. I didn't.'

'Except I can't get at her though. Your mother's too strong and powerful. But I can get at you.'

'What about all that money I gave you on my birthday? Five thousand pounds.'

'Oh big deal! You owed me nearly three for all the rent and bills I'd forked out for. Do you seriously think that's enough for what we went through, me and my mum? We had shit lives, Karin. Because of you. Shit. Lives.'

'Then why didn't you just ask me for a bit more money?'

'A bit more?'

'I tried to offer it to you, I'm sure I did, and you declined. I thought you'd be embarrassed. But if you'd told me all this stuff I would have shared *all* the money with you. Gladly. If I'd known you were my stepsister, Mel, of course I would. Why didn't you just do that?'

Mel took a long inhale. It was good to make her wait.

'You know, you're right,' she said, eventually. 'Money isn't everything. It's really not. That's why I want *everything* you have, Karin.'

'What do you mean *everything*?'

49

Karin

Karin realized this slow process of asphyxiation had been going on for some time. How hadn't she noticed? She was going over the key moments, repeatedly: the signs she had missed, the doubts she had simply brushed aside. Why hadn't she spotted the vultures circling above her head, waiting to pick over her rotting carcass?

Both Will and Louie had tried to warn her that something wasn't right. She knew all along that neither of them was behind those notes, yet had allowed Mel to convince her otherwise. Karin didn't think for a minute that Louie had been round to threaten Mel that night either. That too was a lie.

So Louie really had been trying to protect her, after all, to keep her money safe. Too late now, it was lost forever.

But at least Mel couldn't get to it.

Mel was still next to her, gloating. Karin could feel the resentment coming off her like static. To think of all those times when she had crumpled in her arms, allowing Mel to console and guide her, the friend in whom she had complete trust. Best friend. Surrogate sister.

Worst enemy.

Showing weakness was the last thing Karin wanted to do in front of her now. All those years of being belittled and berated by her mother had taught her to turn her tears into ice when she really needed to.

'So these past months, you've just been waiting to punish me,' said Karin. 'Those notes were from you, weren't they?' The hate in Mel's eyes suggested something darker. It led Karin to wonder about Will, and a terrible thought crossed her mind. 'He never stole anything, did he? Will. You set him up.'

Mel's face was crawling with spite. How could such a kind face – a face Karin thought she knew well, a face that once came to her rescue on the streets of Leeds – suddenly look so detestable?

'So did-did you kill him, Mel?'

She was silent.

'*I said*, did you kill him?'

'Well let's just say we had a bit of a party down by the river. He could knock back the whisky that one, for someone who didn't drink. Very grateful for the extra supplies, he was, too.'

'You took him more?'

'He was so drunk that when I squeezed his balls, he just – fell in. It's your fault, Karin. If you weren't going to tell me why you were so afraid of going to the police, then I had to give you a good reason myself. And that weirdo mute was getting on my nerves. Plus he was beginning to suspect something, always following me around, watching my every move. He was a waste of space.'

Karin struck Mel hard on the cheek. Mel put her hand to her face, but the grin was still there. Karin couldn't believe the extent of her ugliness; any shred of pity she may have had for her was now well and truly gone.

And yet.

In spite of herself, Karin still found it tragic that Mel had not seen the value in what she had gained.

'Doesn't it mean *anything* to you that we're stepsisters?' she asked.

Mel thrust her face into Karin's again. 'Do you honestly think I give a shit about you when your family ruined mine?'

Karin pulled away. Not because she was intimidated, but because it was time for Mel to have the full picture.

Just as Mel had filled in the gaps for Karin, she could do the same for her now. Karin didn't expect it to change anything; Mel's bitterness had rotted her down to the core. She was a decomposing carcass, putrefying in her own decay.

'I know why your dad did what he did,' said Karin.

'And how would you know that?'

'Because I was there. I was there when he had the rope around his neck.'

Karin gave her a moment, assessing whether Mel actually wished her to continue, then carried on anyway because she needed to hear it.

'I'd never set eyes on him until he was suddenly married to my mother. I guess he must have been around all the years I was growing up, especially in view of what you've said.'

'So why did he do it then?' Mel snapped.

'Our fathers had become friends, apparently. Good friends, according to your dad. Even though *my* dad knew all about the affair.'

'A doormat. That figures. Anyone could wipe their shit all over him.'

Karin told herself to ignore the swiping because Mel was a victim too. 'I guess he just loved my mum. Too much. Look I know you're angry, Mel, and I don't blame you. I'm angry too.'

'Just tell me why he topped himself, will you?'

Karin paused. How far should she go with this?

'Okay. So erm. So he told me that the reason he couldn't live with himself any more was because he'd witnessed my dad having a heart attack. And I mean like right in front of him.' Karin felt her voice falter. She cleared her throat, trying to focus on the facts rather than how they made her feel. 'And he just watched my dad die. He did absolutely nothing until it was too late. Deliberately called the ambulance once he knew my dad was already dead. This is what he told me, Mel. You can believe me

265

or not but it's the truth. Your dad told me he was really ashamed for what he'd done. Or rather, not done.'

She paused.

'And there's something else too.'

'What?' Mel said, tersely.

'He said that he was also ashamed because he'd deceived his wife and family for all those years. Especially his daughter. Said he couldn't live with himself any more, carrying round so much guilt.'

At that point, Karin felt the full force of her own guilt; it punched her in the stomach. She wished she could tell Mel the complete truth. If she did that, though, she would certainly end up in jail.

The words came out as if they had been pre-recorded:

'And then he kicked the steps from under his own feet and hanged himself. It was very quick, Mel.'

Karin allowed her another pause.

It was Mel's turn to look anguished. Unlike Mel, Karin got no pleasure in saying any of this.

'I wish I'd known it was you he was talking about. I could have loved you as my sister, Mel, I really could. That would have made me so happy.'

'Sod that. Your happiness is no concern of mine.'

Clearly Mel had made up her mind a long time ago only to hate Karin. Revenge, money, they were the only things that would sweeten her bitterness now.

'There's something else you should know, about what happened,' Karin heard herself say. She could feel the blinding pain between her eyes.

Legs swinging.

Side to side. A human pendulum.

'We tried to save him. Me and my mother. Both of us tried really hard. But we couldn't get to him in time. He'd already kicked the steps away before we could reach him.'

Karin's heart was racing so fast she could hardly manage to breathe. Her fingers tightened round her wrist, cutting off the blood supply to her other hand.

'I really couldn't care less,' said Mel.

At that moment Aaron appeared, fresh out of the shower. A fragrance of shampoo trailed behind him into the kitchen, but it was soon choked by the bleach.

'I'm going to pack,' he announced, filling a glass of water from the tap, drinking it in one go. He filled it up again and took it with him, heading back out.

'Aaron,' shouted Karin.

She shot up and followed him into the bedroom.

He was reaching for his suitcase from the top shelf of the wardrobe. Karin wondered if he had noticed the one she had already packed for herself. He was ignoring it if he had.

'I'm sorry, Karin. I'll let Mel explain.'

50

Mel

'Oh, well, I had to give him the odd nudge along the way, a gentle steer every now and then. But honestly, Karin, you tied the noose around your own neck. I didn't have to do much in the end.'

Mel lowered her voice even more to make sure Aaron wouldn't hear her from the bedroom.

'You're lucky I didn't kill you. I considered it enough times. I could have gone about things in a very different way: revealing my true identity, make you love me as your sister, persuade you to give me all your money and then strangle the life out of you. Make it look like a tragic suicide. The number of times I've stared at your pretty little neck, imagined my fingers around it, squeezing the life from you as I watch your eyes bulge out of your privileged fucking head.'

Aaron came back into the kitchen. 'We should get going,' he said. There was an urgency about him, pulling on his jacket, looking around for things he may have forgotten.

'Where are we going?' Karin asked.

Mel sniggered, waiting for Aaron to put her out of her misery. She found his silence unmanly, looking more apologetic than triumphant, and Mel hoped he wasn't faltering. But she was determined to enjoy this moment whatever. It was the icing on the cake and she had worked hard for this, waited years, and wanted it to be as perfect as she had always dreamed it would be.

'Not you, Karin,' said Mel. 'You're not going anywhere.'

'One of you! Please tell me what the hell is happening here.'

Mel gave her a *what does it look like* sort of a smile. It was such a relief not to have to go through any more of that best-friend stuff and what-would-she-do-without-her nonsense.

'We have a plane to catch. That's what's going on,' said Mel.

'Are you two—?'

Karin's voice disappeared into nothing. She was directing her question at Aaron, but as he still refused to make eye contact with either of them, Mel had to step in again with the answer.

She stood directly in front of Karin.

'I said *everything*, didn't I? Aaron deserves better than a liar and a murderer as his wife.'

'You're accusing *me*?' said Karin, bursting into laughter.

She dodged round Mel and marched up to Aaron, waiting for him to look at her. He did, eventually, but not in a way that worried Mel particularly. He didn't seem like a man who was going to change his mind. Sick and tired of all Karin's secrets and lies.

Besides, they had slept together twice now and made solid plans for the future.

Aaron belonged to her.

'You know she got rid of Will, don't you?' said Karin, pointing the finger at Mel. 'She thinks she can pin it on me, but the truth is she got him drunk and pushed him into the river.'

Karin folded her arms, flicking out her chin at Mel.

Mel hoped she would persist in this playground behaviour, because it showed her to be the immature fool that she was. 'You brought it on yourself, Karin,' she replied. 'All of this. And, quite frankly, we don't believe a word you say any more. Will clearly wanted a sniff of your money, because you very foolishly told him about it. The same with your lesbian friend. I told you not to brag, Karin.'

'I did no such thing.'

269

'Am I right in thinking Will stole some of your jewellery?' Mel continued. 'You wanted rid of him, so you plied him with whisky, knowing he was an alcoholic, threatened him on Woodhouse Ridge and later that evening pushed him into the river.'

'I did not.'

'Whatever other little secrets you hold, Karin, I dare say you're not going to want the police getting any closer now. Are you?'

When Mel had finished her speech, Karin came towards her but chose to stop in the middle of the room. She seemed to want centre stage, arms folded. Mel thought she might have an idea of what Karin was about to say.

'Terribly sorry to burst your bubble, Mel. But the money is still sitting in Louie's account. That feels like a certain kind of justice to me.'

Mel pretended to consider that carefully as she circled round Karin. Wanting to make her punishment last even longer. After a couple of rotations, she positioned herself shoulder to shoulder with Aaron.

'Are you going to break the news, or shall I?' she asked him.

Aaron flickered slightly, indicating it should be Mel. She would have liked more from him at this point, but it was enough to show his solidarity.

'Okay. Well, I think we can safely say that we got to Louie before you did. We struck a deal with the crazy bitch.'

'What sort of a deal?' said Karin.

Mel took her time, refusing to be hurried, even though Aaron kept checking his watch.

'Lover girl was desperate to come and see you one last time. Wanted to see if you really loved her, wanted to die in front of you. Isn't that sweet? We weren't going to stand in her way, as long as she didn't get in ours. Right then, Aaron. Are we all set?'

He seemed keen to make a quick exit, which Mel took to be a good sign. Aaron tossed his backpack over his shoulder, making for the hallway where their suitcases were waiting.

Mel followed, knowing Karin wouldn't be far behind.

'Oh. Now there is just one more thing,' said Mel, stopping abruptly so Karin's shins bashed against her suitcase. 'You do need to be out of here by the end of today. And, strictly speaking, you should have been out of the Headingley place by now, but you've Aaron to thank for that. I was all for giving your stuff away to charity. The new tenants moved in this morning, so I'm afraid your things are downstairs in the hallway. The locks have been changed though, so you'll have to knock. We know what you're like for putting homeless people in other people's houses. So, Karin. I'm afraid it could be back to your old address again. The Dark Arches, Leeds. You never know, someone might randomly stop and buy you a cup of coffee and a cheeseburger.'

Mel reached up to Aaron and planted a kiss on his mouth, stroking the back of his neck.

Poor, stupid Karin.

'Aaron,' Karin called to him in desperation.

'I'm sorry,' he said.

51

Karin

It was winter time. They were out in Stockholm for a few months. Snowy buildings and clear blue skies, ice skating at Kungsträdgården with her dad. They always split their time between Scotland and Sweden. Karin had various tutors travelling with them back and forth. It was a strange isolated upbringing. She never went to school, not even *förskola*, or nursery in the UK. Her dad had wanted her to go, and Karin felt that she might like to try it, but it was her mother's decision. Always her mother's decision. Karin never had any friends. Then aged eight it was straight to boarding school.

A sense of shame raced through her conscience as she considered these things. Tears burning the backs of her eyes when she thought of her mother. Karin had punished her, for sure, but it never felt quite as good as it ought to have. Because it was never meant to end the way it did. At the same time, where were all the ice creams, the bedtime stories, the hugs and reassurances as a child when she was troubled or afraid? Where were the treats and trips to the park? On the face of it, Karin had everything most girls could ever dream of. Mel, for example. And yet she had nothing. She couldn't recall ever being in her mother's arms. Not once. Not even when her dad died.

Frozen as the ice on Lake Mälaren.

Karin was brought out of her trance by a duck quacking and

splashing at a boat coming past, disturbing its peace. She watched the boat go by, the duck bobbing up and down on the waves it left behind. This was Will's spot. She had come here to reflect. Sitting on the bench that was nearest 'his bedroom', she had forgotten how peaceful it was here during the day. Cyclists and dog walkers, people strolling by. But she could never forget how threatening a place it was at night.

Another boat was approaching. Karin could make out a dog standing on deck as if in charge. When the boat drew level, she noticed the dog staring at her. Did it know what she was thinking? Had it seen things? Was it thinking the same as her now?

That Will did not deserve to die. Not here, not like that. In this river.

Will's death was the one that bothered her the most. She missed Louie with the same amount of sadness and sorrow, but what Louie did was ultimately her choice. That wasn't the case with Will. He had been relying on Karin to keep him safe.

Safe.

In this new world, to which she had introduced him. She had given Will assurances and guarantees.

And she had failed him.

So now it was up to Karin to put things right. That was the least she could do. For Will.

Whatever the implications.

Going to the police would inevitably mean prison at some point. As well as her stepdad's murder, there was a strong possibility that she could be charged for Will's too when it came to it. Thanks to Mel. Without any hard evidence to prove it was Mel who had plied him with drink and pushed him into the river, there was very little hope. They might also accuse her of killing Louie. She still didn't know the whereabouts of that knife.

The Midland had told her that Louie was on unpaid leave for another five days when she had called them. She knew they would be the ones to raise the alarm when Louie didn't show up for work. At least this gave Karin some time to think about how to go about things. Ultimately, though, she had made her decision. She just wanted the truth to be out there now. It was up to the police and the justice system to decide what to do with it.

Will deserved better. Will had always deserved better.

Karin caught the bus back to Ashby Road to prepare. The charity was allowing her to stay there temporarily, in Will's room. They had very kindly said that she could stay for as long as she needed, until she found somewhere to rent. There seemed little point in telling them that she wasn't even bothering to look because her next home would be in Her Majesty's prison.

She packed a bag for her trip.

It was time to say a final goodbye to her mother.

274

52

Karin

She took the train to Fort William and then a bus to somewhere nearby. It was four and a half miles from civilization when she got off at the other end, but the walk would do her good. There would be no lift. Her mother wasn't aware that she was coming.

The day was warm, despite evidence of rainfall.

As well as a desire to say goodbye one final time, if her mother would allow that, Karin also wanted to give her some warning that the police would soon be on their way. Although she couldn't say when, they would be coming to ask questions about her daughter.

It wasn't Karin's intention to try to change her mind. She knew Birgitta well enough to know that would be pointless in any case. But there was an additional purpose to her visit nonetheless. She wanted her to be aware that something positive had eventually come of her life, however brief it was in the end. Inevitably, once the scandal hit the tabloids, the headlines would change from good to bad but this still didn't take away from Karin's success. Not only had she got the Ashby Road project off the ground, with more schemes to follow, she had also become *the voice of her generation*. And if her mother needed proof she could show her the clip from the launch.

Afterwards, Birgitta could do whatever was necessary.

She could turn Karin in, there and then, if she wanted to;

Karin wouldn't blame her for that. In fact a part of her *wanted* punishment now. Not so much for her stepdad, although she certainly wouldn't deny kicking the steps from under him, but it wasn't quite as simple as that, and she lived her punishment every day for this crime. It was punishment for Will that she was really seeking.

Because she could have saved him.

Karin knew that Will didn't really care for Mel, just like she knew Mel didn't care for Will either. Yet she had chosen to ignore that because it suited her. She was having too good a time with Aaron. Letting Will down was one of the worst things she had ever done.

That, and running away from Louie.

Most people were surprised when they saw it. They expected the Swedish queen of design to have an ultra-modern self-build of never-ending glass and wide-open spaces, devoid of interior walls, minimalist décor. Instead they found a seventeenth-century Scottish castle, crawling with old ivy over three floors, a labyrinth of corridors, sweeping staircases and grand hallways; rooms with ornate ceilings and decorative plasterwork. All lovingly restored, but the only thing to say 'modern design' was the kitchen, a vast and bold statement for the Svendsen brand.

This was not home. Karin never once felt that she belonged here.

Birgitta was out in the garden. Karin detected movement around the pergola, and then caught a glimpse. Keeping herself concealed, hardly daring to breathe, the first thing she noticed about her mother was how much she had aged in such a relatively short time. Her hair was still long, but almost white now instead of her trademark blonde. The way she was reaching up to trim the roses wasn't quite as agile either, not as Karin remembered her movements to be, and she kept rubbing her lower back in between snips, probably not even aware she was doing it.

What stood out most was her loneliness.

And that was Karin's fault.

Hiding away behind this lofty hedge gave Karin the opportunity to get used to seeing her again, familiarize herself with her surroundings.

The log cabin, *her* log cabin, was still standing. Positioned down at the bottom nearest the stream in a perfectly peaceful spot. It looked much the same, on the outside at least. It had been unveiled to Karin on her sixth birthday, and she wondered if Birgitta still went in it these days. She had half expected it would have been torn down as soon as the police had finished in there, the body stretchered out covered in a white sheet. So perhaps it was kept as a sort of shrine to him, with flowers and photographs. Or was it the crime scene that Birgitta wanted to preserve, his execution site left undisturbed after all this time? The dusty stepladders lying on their side; the rope curled up on the floor like an empty snakeskin, noosed at the end; the beam, splintered and grooved.

'Mamma,' she said softly, daring to get a bit closer. Then, 'Mamma,' louder that time because she hadn't heard her over the clicking of the secateurs.

Her mother turned. Stern as ever. Lips tightening.

There were more lines on her face, which Karin thought actually suited her.

'I've, er – I've come to tell you something.'

When her mother's expression turned to shock, Karin realized that she may have misinterpreted.

'Oh, I'm not pregnant or anything. It's not that.' But this wasn't part of her script and now she was thrown. Disarmed. The underdog again. For a moment it did get Karin wondering what her mother's reaction would have been, if this had been the news she was bringing her.

Silence.

The big freeze had begun. The power of ice, from the top

down. Karin shivered, rubbing her arms. It was a feeling she had experienced all through her childhood, and the last time she felt it was that last time they had seen each other. When Karin was seventeen. The terrible incident. Legs swinging. Her mother's screams.

'Erm.' Karin was left hanging.

Hanging, don't say that.

'Do we go inside, or should I just tell you here?'

She didn't want to go against protocol. Not now, not ever.

Birgitta pointed to the house, waving the secateurs. Karin was wishing she hadn't given her the option now because it was always better to be outdoors. She remembered that too late. Despite its size, the house felt like a prison. Cold, even in summer.

They removed their shoes in the entrance hall in the continuing silence. Karin followed her through to the kitchen where Birgitta began pouring a glass of elderflower lemonade from the fridge. Homemade *fläderblomssaft*. Tears pooled in Karin's eyes when she took it from her mother's hand, not daring to blink in case the watery film should burst into a tear and betray her. She couldn't remember the last time she had tasted this. It used to be a frequent daydream of hers at boarding school, craving this one small act of kindness, the taste of the lemonade representing a kind of sweet normality.

'How have you been, Mamma?' she asked, not wanting to dwell on that childhood memory, for fear of it knocking her even further off course. She immediately qualified that with, 'Am I allowed to ask?'

The frown line on her mother's face was carved deeper into her forehead. Karin's was the same, a genetic thing.

'I work. I sleep. I do the garden,' she replied.

So she *was* lonely.

Do you ever think of me, Mamma?

Despite this being their last ever goodbye, Karin still didn't dare ask that question, and even though she detected a certain fragility in Birgitta now, she still remained wary of her.

'I'm sorry,' she said. 'About what happened.'

'Is that what you came here to tell me?'

'No.'

Couldn't they just exchange a few pleasantries first? *How have you been? What have you been up to?* Enjoy sipping elderflower lemonade again, swapping stories about the past five years. That was never the way her mother did things though. Everything was dealt with in a businesslike fashion. Even life. Even a child's life.

'I already said I was sorry,' said Karin.

How many more times could she apologize for her mistake? Not that *sorry* would ever bring him back.

'No, I actually came to warn you about something. You er – you might be getting a visit from the police. Fairly soon. I'm in trouble, but it wasn't my fault—'

'It never is, is it?'

Karin rolled her eyes. She was on the verge of spilling out the whole story. Being blackmailed by someone who ended up being her stepsister, who claimed to have met her mother, who went to her stepdad's funeral, who had actually set foot in this very house, who came to ask Birgitta for money.

But this wasn't what Karin had come to say. She wanted to take responsibility, and Mel was irrelevant to that.

'It's a long story but someone close to me got killed. Now I want to put things right. He was my friend and I owe it to him.' Her mother raised an eyebrow but Karin wasn't going to be discouraged. 'Ever since I turned twenty-two and got that money, well it's seemed like my life – which had been going really well just before that – started to fall apart. I'm grateful for the money, Mamma, I truly am. But I think it changed the way people saw me.'

Karin spoke quickly, expecting to be interrupted at any moment. 'Get to the point or keep quiet,' her mother would always say. Not just to Karin, she said it to her dad too, and maybe others, people who worked for her. Maybe even her stepdad. When Karin was really young she was afraid to open her mouth at all.

Eyes like two ball bearings. Hard, shiny steel. Beautiful, though. Almost silver. Did her mother really want to listen to her now? It seemed like she did.

She told her about leaving school early, that she was sorry for wasting the fees and never getting her International Baccalaureate like she was meant to. She told her about going to live in Morecambe, although missed out the bit that she had actually gone there to end it all. Then recounted meeting someone in Morecambe, who helped her find work at The Midland hotel, who then became a good friend. No mention of them living together, but she told her about fleeing to Leeds when Morecambe didn't quite work out, including the fact that she had lived on the streets and then was rescued. The name *Mel* wasn't used, in case it rang any bells. Karin didn't want her mother to know that she no longer had the money, even though she would find out soon enough. She would read it in the papers probably. But for now that wasn't what this was about.

'You lived on the streets, Karin?'

'Oh. Erm yes, I had to.' She couldn't decide whether her mother was concerned or merely horrified. 'I didn't have any money. But that's where I met Will, my friend who got killed. Anyway look, Mamma. The reason I'm here now is to warn you that when the police come it's likely they'll accuse me of crimes I haven't committed. And no matter what happens, I want you to know that I am innocent.'

Birgitta threw her head to one side with her steely stare. Karin held up her hands. 'And before you say it, I'm not referring to my stepdad. I fully accept that what I did there was wrong, and I wish I hadn't kicked those steps away. However, I did, and I hate myself for it every single day. Just like you said I would in that letter you sent me.'

They needed a moment to deal with the pain this still caused them both.

Karin couldn't let the pause go on for too long though, or she would be thrown off course again, interrupted or silenced completely. She was also crying and about to rupture, but she managed to pick up her thread. 'I *could* let the person who killed my friend get away with it, because it would make my life so much easier. But Will was homeless and he didn't deserve to die. Plus the reason he was killed was down to me.'

Karin found a tissue buried in the pocket of her jeans. Her sobs were so violent it felt like her chest was trying to strangle her. She had to get the last part out before she lost the power of speech altogether. 'I just wanted to warn you and to-to say goodbye properly. Because we never did say goodbye. And I've missed you, Mamma.'

Those words came from a dark, neglected place and there would never be a chance to say them again.

No reaction from her mother.

Karin managed to compose herself. 'Before I go, though, I'd like to prove to you that I actually managed to achieve something good in my life.'

They moved across to the table to use Birgitta's laptop.

The table curved out of the wall like a river. Karin had never liked it, she was forever being told not to spill anything on it. She found the link to the news clip and set it playing, standing back to observe her mother's face. As usual, it gave nothing away. Then maybe a slight flicker at the point where Karin was ranting about the Government's ignoring the issue of homelessness, the tragedy of food banks, and the presenter saying that she was *the voice of a generation*. It finished on a blurry freeze-frame of Karin. She got rid of the link to stop it playing again.

'I was in all the newspapers too, and everywhere on the internet. People actually listened to what I had to say for once.'

It wasn't meant to sound like a dig but Karin immediately realized that's how it sounded.

'I listened to you, Karin. And a man took his life because of it.'

'That's not true. *I* never said he did anything.'

'You implied it, and that was enough. You were not a child, you were seventeen. We've been through this.'

'Exactly. I was a depressed, suicidal teenager who'd just lost her dad.'

'That's no excuse.'

'No, it isn't. But my loneliness was like a black hole, Mamma,' she wailed. 'Especially after my dad died. And you never once reached inside to pull me out. Did you? If only you'd bothered to read my letter, the one with the truth in it. You see, he told me something before he – before I – when he had the rope around his neck. He told me that he was ashamed for neglecting *his* family for all of those years. He told me he was ashamed because- because *my* dad had had a heart attack right in front of him and he just let him *die*.'

Karin swiped the tears away with her fingers but no sooner had she done that when more were dripping off her chin. She leaned into her mother's chest because all she needed, then and now, was a memory to take with her. Back to school. To prison. As she sobbed inconsolably, a hand was brushing wet strands off her cheek, a swaying motion gently pulling her in closer.

The smell of Birgitta. Avocado. Lavender.

'All this charity stuff is for your conscience, isn't it?'

She straightened up again because her mother's body was rigid. As a glacier. She hadn't melted, not one bit, not even a trickle. There was no memory for Karin to take away with her. Only this memory, frosted over and cruel.

'I swear that's what he said to me. He admitted it. I know you thought it was because of me accusing him of some inappropriate behaviour. But it wasn't that at all. He knew I was a confused teenager grieving for my dad, and he said that he forgave me for saying those things. I could never forgive *him* though, not after what he'd just told me. How could he watch my dad die and do nothing to help him? How could he do that? That's why I kicked the steps away, Mamma. Because I was angry. Maybe he even wanted me to do it. Maybe he was too afraid to do it himself. I don't know, but *that* is the truth.'

Karin stood up, reaching for Birgitta's sketchpad at the end of the table. She scribbled something on it.

If you ever need me, Mamma, here's my number. Goodbye. And I am truly sorry. You can tell the police everything when they contact you. I don't think it will be long now.

On her way out, in the hallway, there was a photograph in a silver frame. Karin, in her school uniform, probably about twelve years old, with bushy red hair. Maybe it was the same photograph that Mel had seen.

She turned it face down and left.

53

Karin

The morning air was cool due to the thick blanket of cloud hanging over the day. Karin hadn't seen the forecast but it was of no consequence whether the sun was going to burn through later or not. Or turn to snow for that matter. From now on the subtleties of the British weather were irrelevant. Take an umbrella, don't take an umbrella. Coat or no coat. Sandals or shoes. Shades or no shades. None of it mattered because sooner or later she was going to prison.

She had decided to walk to Weetwood rather than taking the bus. The police station was probably a good three miles up Otley Road but she had no idea what she would say when she got there, so needed the time to think.

Tell them what exactly? Where to start?

The money that had landed in her account this morning was also a distraction. It was clearly from her mother, but quite why she had put it there was baffling. It wasn't as though Karin hadn't told her that the money she got for her birthday was all gone. So why transfer more? A hundred thousand pounds was a considerable amount to give her, on top of what she had already received. But should she thank her for it? Would Birgitta want that?

Or leave it and do nothing.

The dilemma was making Karin's head pound, and if this was to be her last walk of freedom she ought to at least try and enjoy it. So she turned her attention to the summer blooms straining their colourful necks above stone walls in neat gardens as she passed by. She felt sorry for those poking through weeds in the untidy ones, at the unfairness of their neglect. Birds fluttered in trees that she had never noticed before, and a dog wagged its tail up ahead, allowing a child to stroke it because there was a treat to be had if it did. Children playing out in the school playground, squealing and larking about, like Karin had never experienced.

Once across Lawnswood roundabout, dodging the ring road traffic, her mood changed. This was starting to feel like the walk of shame the nearer she got to her destination. Karin wasn't afraid of prison: she could handle that. It was all the things leading up to prison – the questions, the guilt, the shame, newspaper allegations, social media revelling in the scandal – all of that terrified her the most. Then even more questions. The arrest. The trial.

Humiliation.

She imagined the headlines: *Voice of a generation on killing spree. Charity worker kills homeless man. Svendsen daughter brings shame on the brand. Svendsen daughter hangs stepdad. Kills former girlfriend.*

Despite the inevitable backlash, however, the truth was the only thing left for Karin and she fully intended to get it out there. Her mother could tell them about her stepdad; it might even bring her some closure. But the rest was for Karin. She would inform them that she last saw Will on that Tuesday afternoon on Woodhouse Ridge. *Not* Tuesday morning, as Mel had said. She would tell them that Will was scared, that he had bottles of whisky stuffed into his pockets when he didn't even drink, and that he had told Karin to watch her back. She would tell them that Mel had falsely accused Will of stealing, planted some of Karin's jewellery at the scene. And she would suggest that they look at the CCTV footage from Tesco Express in town on the Thursday night, just before it shut at eleven, the night Will was drowned. Mel had said she was going to pop in there on her way to the taxi rank. And they might also like to check the CCTV footage in their local off-licence in Headingley. It was likely that the bottles of whisky Mel had purchased would match those found on Will at the scene.

Karin intended to tell them about the blackmail notes too, even though they were probably destroyed by now. She would have to tell them about Louie, that she was dead. But Karin would emphasize that Louie had only been trying to keep the money safe, until they finally got to her as well and then she took her own life. They would accuse Karin of killing her, because there was a knife somewhere with her prints all over it. But she would tell them how Aaron had prevented her from calling an ambulance, and how he got rid of the body by burning it. Karin still had the tin of bones to prove it, much to her horror and revulsion.

There was also the rainbow keyring which Karin had given to Will on the Ridge on that Tuesday afternoon. The rainbow keyring which then ended up in Mel's possession, proving she had seen him again when she said that she hadn't.

Sadly, not much of this amounted to anything in the way of *solid* evidence and the keyring was no proof whatsoever, only for Karin. Unless they could get CCTV footage to match the whisky bottles, really the only thing Karin could prove was that the money had gone from her account into Louie's, and then from there into Mel's and Aaron's.

The pair ought to be relatively easy to track down though. Karin very much doubted they would have gone to the trouble of false names and passports, because they were not expecting her to go to the police. Once they were caught and brought back for questioning, then the spotlight would be turned on her. But that was okay. Justice for Will was her main concern, or at least to clear his name.

If she went down, then Mel and Aaron would too. She would make sure of that, even if it was only blackmail they could be charged with.

Karin had been so busy working these things through in her mind that she hadn't noticed she was already at the long driveway leading down to the police station. She came to an abrupt stop, before turning into it.

Come on, Karin. This is for Will. Do this for Will.

Inhaling her last breath of freedom, puffing it out again in one long exhalation, she *was* ready to do this.

It was rapid, the hand over her mouth, feeling engulfed. She tried to scream but couldn't breathe. Birds were tweeting, too loudly, in her ears. Clouds swirled above her head, morphing into terrifying shapes. The crack in the pavement widened as she was falling into it.

The last thing she remembered was being bundled into a car.

54

Louie

It was going to come as a shock for Karin to see her return from the dead. She had been lying low for a couple of days, to allow the full effect of her death to sink in. But Louie was keeping a watchful eye on her all the same, making sure she didn't do anything stupid.

Two days ago, she was stabbed on Aaron's kitchen floor, carried out in a rolled-up rug, her body then disposed of by incineration in some rusted oil drum on a remote building site under cover of darkness. And now here she was.

Alive.

Louie hadn't wanted to add the stress of Karin's fingerprints being on the knife. It was Aaron insisting on that, but she later discovered that he was taking orders from a woman called Mel, Karin's housemate, who had been behind the blackmail all along.

Karin's pain would soon be over. And Louie's too. As from today, there was nothing stopping them from being together.

The moment she saw Karin step out of Ashby Road that morning, her stomach had spun with excitement. She thought of the two of them setting up home together, a sweet little place by the sea, where Louie could paint – she got an offer of an exhibition from a gallery in Manchester yesterday – and Karin could do her campaigning and lobbying, if she wanted to keep on with that. Maybe they would have a dog, take it for walks on the beach. The kids would love that too.

Karin had set off with a firm purpose in mind, head down, walking briskly, and Louie thought she may have an idea where she was heading. The appearance of £100,000 in her account this morning was bound to make her curious. Her first thought would be that it was from her mother, however unlikely that might seem, although Louie was aware that she had been up to Scotland to pay her a visit in the last couple of days. Alternatively, if Karin had already seen that the deposit was from Seahorse Studio then she would be heading to the bank to clarify how on earth this deposit could have got there when Louie was dead.

Louie slowed down, indicating to pull in, not wanting to get too far ahead. Seeing Karin pass the cricket ground, Louie had to stop herself from lowering the window and calling out to her. She had to choose her moment carefully to come back from the dead. Maybe wait until after Karin had been to the bank.

Karin went straight past it, however, and was now crossing the road, dodging the cars decelerating for the traffic lights. At one point she stopped completely, turning round, and Louie ducked down quickly, thinking she may have been seen. Thankfully Karin carried on walking. So her next assumption was that Karin was going to Sainsbury's, as she was heading along the Arndale. Assuming this to be the case, Louie almost turned into the car park, but Karin continued up Otley Road, passing The New Inn, The Three Horseshoes, St Chad's Church, the BP garage, Lawnswood School.

She kept on going.

Louie was growing more and more concerned, and when Karin crossed over the roundabout, she knew for certain where she was heading.

She had to be stopped.

55

Karin

Karin opened her eyes, sensitive to the light streaming into her face. From somewhere. She tried to work out where it was coming from, but it was too bright even with her arm across her face. Slowly, feeling herself returning to some kind of normality, she realized that she was sitting in the back of a car. There was an outline of a person in front of her. Karin tried to focus but the light was still too bright for her to distinguish anything clearly.

Was it Louie?

Her eyes darted side to side. Frantically trying to make sense of what they *could* be seeing.

Karin screamed, struggling to unlock the door.

'You fainted,' said Louie. 'I'm sorry I shocked you.'

They were parked outside the crematorium, down a quiet side street. Was this really happening? How on earth could it be Louie when she was already dead? Was she haunting her so soon?

'Hey, hey. It's okay. It's me. It's me, don't be scared.'

'No,' Karin whimpered, trying the other door, kicking it when it wouldn't open. Eventually she gave up and stared at Louie's ghost. 'What's going ON?' she shrieked, bashing on the window with her fist.

'Calm down. I didn't really die, Karin. Look, I'm fine. See. All intact.'

'What the hell are you talking about?'

Karin felt her lungs shrinking as she was gasping for air. She really had to get out of this car. 'But you were dead,' she wailed, pulling at the door handle in further desperation. 'I saw you lying on the floor. The knife, you stabbed yourself. You were bleeding. There was blood all over the place. Please, just let me out.'

'Fake knife, fake blood,' said Louie. 'Easy.'

Karin was shaking her head, refusing to accept. 'The bones. In the tin. They were all black and burned, it was horrible.'

'I know, I'm sorry. I think he must have got some animal ones. God knows why he thought he had to do that. I'm really, really sorry for making you think I was dead, Karin, but I had to save you from those bastards somehow. I negotiated a hundred grand for you though.'

'What?'

Karin blinked. It really did seem like Louie, nodding and smiling at her in the front of this car.

'I'd have kept the lot if I thought they'd leave you alone,' she said. 'But that was never going to happen.'

Karin reached out to touch her arm. It felt solid enough.

'It is me, Karin. Honest.'

This was all too disturbing.

'Why-why did you have to kill yourself though? Or pretend to kill yourself? I don't get it, I just don't get it. I need to get out; please let me out.' Karin was struggling to breathe again, and scraped her fingers down the window. Louie must have lowered it because it started to go down. Karin stuck her head out to gulp some fresher air.

'I needed you to tell me that you loved me, Karin. I needed to hear it, and you had to admit it to yourself. It was the only way. You ran out on me, and I never got to know why, not until I was lying there dead to you on the floor. And of course *he* needed to hear it too, slimy old bastard. It was the moment of truth for both of us. Me or him.'

Karin felt dizzy. Maybe *she* was the one dead? This wasn't happening. Maybe she was the one who died on the kitchen floor?

'I realize now that he wasn't the one blackmailing you,' said Louie, carrying on regardless. 'But to be honest, it didn't take him long to want the money paid into his account and not yours. He couldn't bear the thought of us ever being together.' She laughed. 'Hey you're safe now though, Karin. You're rid of them both, and we're free to live our lives in the way that we want to. We can go anywhere. Together. You and me, fresh start. Get a place by the sea. I know you'd like that too.'

'What?'

'Maybe you need a brandy. You look like you do. Or a coffee?'

'No!' Karin banged on the door with her fists, then kicking it. 'Just let me out. I'm going to the police. Open the door, Louie. I have to do this.'

'You know I can't let you do that.'

'She *killed* Will. She confessed. Mel did it. Please, Louie, I have it all worked out and I'm going to say that you tried to protect me, which you did. You'll be fine, I promise.'

Louie jumped into the back seat to be alongside her. 'It's okay. Shush,' she said, pulling Karin into her chest.

Karin watched her tears soak into Louie's jacket, like snow melting.

'They won't believe you,' Louie continued. 'And then your mother will say terrible things about you killing your stepdad. It will all come out.'

Karin sat up again.

'Exactly. I'm going to prison for a long time, whatever happens. Even if I don't turn myself in, my mother will do it for me. I went to see her. She's still angry with me, and I hated seeing her like that, she's so lonely. So you can't stop this, Louie. But I'm going to get justice for Will.'

Louie punched the back seat. Then sprang into the front again and started up the engine. As she drove off, the smell of burning rubber filled the car.

'Where are we going?' asked Karin. '*I said*, where are we going? *Louie.*'

56

Louie

Morecambe felt different somehow, but in a good way. She was bringing Karin home, restoring the natural order of things.

It already felt perfect.

Karin's phone started to ring. It sounded muffled because it was in the storage box under Louie's arm where she had confiscated it.

'Home sweet home,' said Louie, pulling on the handbrake outside their bedsit off Albert Road. 'You might find it untidier than when you left, I'm afraid. We'll soon get it back to how it was.'

'Lou, please. I need to be in Leeds. I have to speak to the policewoman who's dealing with Will's case.'

'Don't waste your life going to jail for that lot. They were complete shits, and that's including your stepdad. Your place is here with me.'

'Will wasn't a complete shit. He was my friend.'

'I've got an offer of an exhibition in Manchester. Good news, hey?'

Give her time. It's a lot to take in.

She flipped up the armrest and took out Karin's phone. One missed call from the charity that she worked for. 'Tell them you won't be in today,' said Louie, handing it back to her. 'And don't say anything stupid.'

Louie had been looking forward to this moment for such a long time, picturing them racing upstairs hand-in-hand, both of them yearning to get inside so they could just tumble into bed together.

Not like this.

Not with Karin dragging herself up three flights of stairs, saying how much she didn't want to be in Morecambe. That she would rather be in a prison cell because that was where she belonged.

Was it really going to end here?

57

Karin

It still felt the same. The same smell in the stairwell. The same cooking fumes from the flat below theirs. The same voices on the same TV – still on too loud – escaping from under the same door on the second floor. The same baby crying, except it must be a different one by now, and the same person putting rubbish outside the same flat, instead of taking it down to the same bin in the same bin store out in the same back yard.

It surprised her, but as she climbed the stairs it was slowly starting to feel okay. Then as Louie was opening the door, she felt her nerves scratching away at the lining of her stomach. But it was a good nervous.

Maybe.

'Oh wow. You've still got her,' Karin said, laughing.

The mannequin was dressed in some of her clothes that she had left behind. Karin remembered carrying it all the way home that day, having spotted it in a skip outside a shop that was closing down, and had struggled with it through town, people staring. But it was worth it because she knew Louie would love it. They dressed her in outfits and stood her at the window. Or lay her down on the sofa. One time, Louie had put her in bed under the duvet and scared the life out of Karin. Louie liked to paint her, and it became a special theme in her work. They would go on days out, just so they could create a particular scene with it.

Karin removed the hat from the mannequin, straightening up the wig, and put the hat on her own head. 'Hey, that's my silk scarf I lost on the beach,' she said, tugging it free. 'I thought I recognized it when you wrapped it round my hand that day. When you kidnapped me the first time.'

Louie gave her a guilty grin. 'Yes, but I've washed it now,' she replied, choosing to ignore the kidnapping reference. 'I wanted to hold onto it, hoping you'd be back here one day and I could return it to you. But if that didn't happen, well at least I had that, didn't I?'

Karin returned it to the mannequin. 'You hang onto it then. Until I get out.'

'Out of where?'

'Prison.'

Louie stomped across the floor and flopped down onto the sofa. Karin noticed there were no chairs in here now. The table was still in its rightful place but with nothing to sit on. Not much seemed to have changed apart from that. It was untidy, like Louie said, and the studio part seemed to have spilled out into the rest of the space. That old screen she had made wasn't anywhere visible. The bed was messy, the duvet not straightened and things piled on top of it. Karin had always kept that tidy too; she liked a neat bed. 'It's a bed, not a desk,' she would say.

'I can't let you do it, Karin. I'd rather die than see you go to prison.'

Karin sat down beside her. 'You've already done that once,' she said. 'Died, I mean. I don't want that to happen again. Look Lou, you're a brilliant artist and you need to focus on that. And maybe you should move away from here. Maybe there are too many memories for you in Morecambe.'

'For me or for you?'

'I have to take what's coming to me and let the courts decide. That is what *I* need to do. And when I come out, we can decide if we want to be together. Things might have changed by then. But if not—'

Louie was crying. She never cried. She would rather inflict physical pain on herself than shed tears. Karin held onto her, rocking her back and forth. It was tender and sweet. Despite there being plenty of joy and laughter in the relationship at one time, their love was underpinned by a rawness. There was a kind of rough fragility to it. The passion that burned between them, driven by their own separate rage. They were two damaged pebbles washed up on Morecambe beach.

But this felt different.

Maybe they had grown up.

They sat for a whole hour in each other's arms. Afterwards, they took a stroll along the promenade. Karin said she didn't want to go onto the beach. Not this one. Too many memories on Morecambe beach. So they sat on the end of the pier with a cheap bottle of wine, huddled under a blanket.

'Meet me in *Morecambe*,' said Karin, holding the bottle up before tipping it to her mouth.

She handed it to Louie.

'To Morecambe,' Louie replied. 'And growing old together.'

A thought suddenly struck Karin. 'Tell me one thing, Lou. Did you really take copies of my mother's letters?'

'What do you think?' said Louie, laughing. 'I *would* have let you go, if that's what you'd really wanted. If I'd thought you really loved that guy, or just didn't want me. I would. I'd have returned the money and let you go.'

Karin gave her hand a squeeze.

'But not without a fight, and not until I understood what went wrong.'

'*I* was wrong,' said Karin. 'I should never have left you.'

They began pushing each other towards the edge of the promenade, their laughter and screams going all the way out to sea.

Later on, Louie drove Karin to the station to get a train back to Leeds.

58

Karin

The police station was full of activity. A number of uniformed officers were going back and forth without taking much notice of her. She hovered around the desk behind a woman with cuts to her face. Karin noticed a row of seats to her left and sat down next to a man who had something to do with the woman, maybe her boyfriend, in a worse state than she was. The smell of alcohol was overpowering. Soon the officer dealing with Karin returned from behind the desk carrying some papers and escorted her to an interview room, asking a colleague to get them both a cup of tea.

The hot liquid warmed her insides. She was told to take her time. Karin had no idea where to start but she supposed it should be with living rough on the streets of Leeds, where she first met Will. And where Mel had found her under the Dark Arches and afterwards took her home. She didn't mention anything about being stepsisters, as that would lead back to her mother. Karin wanted them to concentrate on finding Will's killer first.

It all sounded so complicated. She felt judged, immediately under suspicion, with no real evidence other than a confession that she claimed to have heard from Mel, and a keyring she said Mel had stolen from Will. They seemed interested in the CCTV footage idea though, and Karin just prayed this would provide a solid link to Mel.

The most important thing was that *she* had told them the truth. That was about all Karin could do for Will now. They said she was free to go and would be paying her another visit at Ashby Road.

Stepping out into the fresh air again, Karin felt lighter, more at ease with herself and the world. She raised her face up to the sky, feeling the warmth from the sun just beginning to poke through the clouds.

'I did it, Will,' she said. 'I did it.'

Back at Ashby Road, in Will's room, the elation soon evaporated. The consequences of her actions were beginning to sink in, and she felt Will's absence even more. Sitting on his bed; her clothes hanging in his wardrobe; brushing her teeth in his sink; seated at his desk looking out at his bench around his special tree. He was gone, and nothing she could do would ever bring him back.

For now, though, her life was continuing and she had a meeting to go to regarding another housing project which they wanted her to manage. She slipped a cardigan over her shoulders, deciding it was too scruffy and opened the drawer next to the wardrobe to find another one more suitable. That's when she noticed a patch of wallpaper coming away from the wall where it joined with the next piece. A frayed edge poked out from behind the wardrobe. On closer inspection it looked like it had been deliberately torn away, and as Will had only just finished decorating this room a few days before he was killed, it seemed strange there would be any damage to it already.

She shifted the drawers to one side and managed to pull the wardrobe forwards, enough to see some words written in heavy black ink on the wall itself. Peeling the wallpaper back further, she realized it was a message from Will:

CAN'T STAY HERE NO MORE
THREATENED ME
NAME IS M – E – L

The letters of her name were spelled out using British Sign
Language signs.

59

Karin

A fortnight had gone by since making her statement to the police. They had seen Will's message on the wall and carried out a handwriting match against the forms he had filled in on his arrival at the charity. Karin was told it would take a while to investigate all the other leads she had given them. They were fairly hopeful, however, that they had tracked down a couple, likely to be Aaron and Mel, to an address in Greece. As Karin suspected, they hadn't used false names or attempted to cover their tracks. The other good news was that CCTV *had* shown Mel purchasing three bottles of whisky at the Tesco Express, after leaving Karin on the night of the art exhibition. Karin had proof that she wasn't with Mel at that point because she had an Uber receipt for the taxi she got back to Aaron's.

Sooner or later the police would want to speak to her mother. The money had initiated from her and they would want to check it was legitimate in the first place.

Karin wasn't afraid of the truth coming out any more, but was determined to make the most of the time she had left. She had met up with Louie a few times, on the understanding that, at least for now, they were rebuilding a friendship so that neither of them would be hurt when it came to being separated. In the end Louie had given her full support for Karin going to the police. Between them, they agreed to say that the fake death was all part of the blackmailing pressure Louie had been put under in order to protect Karin. Which it was, in effect.

Karin intended to carry on working for as long as she could. She was campaigning for the next housing project, while also making sure that someone else could pick up smoothly from where she left off. She had been asked to do a succession of radio interviews and give talks at local schools on being *the voice of a generation.* It seemed that people really did want to listen to what she had to say. Karin had to decline these, however. It wasn't sending the right sort of message out if she was then arrested. The case would be huge when it finally hit the news. Her mother was well known; two people dead, one fake death, and a juicy blackmail trail.

Karin never expected to get that call. Even though she had dreamed of it many times. It happened in the middle of a meeting. Although she didn't recognize the number she felt she ought to take it, due to everything that was going on. Karin excused herself and stepped outside.

'Mamma? Are you okay?' She was shocked to hear her mother's voice.

'Did you go to the police, Karin?'

'Erm yes. Yes, I did.'

Karin closed her eyes, her body slowly sinking.

So this was it then.

'Have they – have they been to see you already, Mamma?'

Her chest felt as though it was being crushed between two giant slabs of ice.

'No, not yet. But am I still to assume that they will be coming?'

'Yes, for sure. And look, I don't blame you.' Karin had to whisper into her phone, not wishing to be heard by people passing in the corridor. She turned to face the wall. 'I didn't mean to make you sad, Mamma. I really didn't mean to do it. I didn't mean to kick the steps away. I really didn't mean—'

'You didn't.'

Karin stared at the wall.

'What?' She thought she must have missed something.

'You didn't kick the steps away, Karin. Okay?'

'No, I did. I really did. But I didn't mean it, Mamma. I'm sorry, I truly am. He told me those things I told you, about my dad, which made me *so* angry and I just—'

'Shush, Karin. Listen to me.' Her voice was stern, sharp-edged. '*I* know what I saw.'

'Well, so what did you see?'

'It's what I told them in the first place. *He* kicked the steps away and hanged himself. *That's* what happened. Because *that's* what I saw.'

Karin lowered the phone, letting her forehead fall onto the wall.

'Thanks, Mamma,' she whispered. 'Thank you.'

Karin wasn't sure what to do with the silence that followed. But Birgitta was still there; she hadn't hung up.

'Does that mean, do you think, I can come and see you? Some time? Up in Scotland?'

She waited but nothing came back.

'There's someone I'd really love you to meet. She's an artist. I think you'll like her. Remember what you said, Mamma? *You said*, when that person enters your life you just know. And that you should hang onto them no matter what. Well it's her. She's called Louie.'

The next pause was worrying. A forever pause.

'I'd like that too, Karin. You should come. Bring your friend.'

Acknowledgements

Thanks to:

Finn Cotton, for your patience and insight. A tremendously good editor with a sharp eye, and a pleasure to work with. And the Killer Reads team in general.

Shelley Instone, a massive influence and brilliant editor.

All the people I can "talk writing" to … fellow Killer Reads authors. Script Yorkshire folks and other members of the Board. Also Maria Malone, Gemma Head, the 'Js', and our recently formed writers group. The ones on social media too.

Those who keep the book scene buoyant in Leeds – Fiona Gell of Leeds Big Bookend. The Hyde Park Book Club. The gorgeous Leeds Library. Your support is so much appreciated.

Lisa and Adrian Burch, the creative duo who produced an excellent book trailer for the last one, *Losing Juliet*.

All my Leeds friends, you really are the best, including those who've moved away. And other friends, you know who you are, I hope we see each other very soon. (I like to keep my friends close and have no time for enemies!)

Walt and Art, for making me laugh and being so smart. Grandma Sal and Nana Boo, you are greatly missed.

The McMahons and the Taylors, who've always been there for me, family is everything. Mrs Joon, with your relentless energy and encouragement, your enormous sense of fun, you keep us all afloat. Tim, I'm sorry I have this writing disease but so many thanks for your support! Pearl, my big sister, whom I miss and adore, I still look up to you even now. Dad, I hope I made you proud.

Helen Cadbury, my friend and fellow writer. You had my back

on the first book and I'll always remember that. I miss your wit and wisdom, your kindness, and all the daft email banter. You were a special human being.

The locations in this book around Leeds are a mixture of reality and fiction. The Midland hotel in Morecambe does exist and is a wonderful place. I have tried to give an accurate portrayal of Morecambe, too, and all the other locations, but bear in mind this is a work of fiction.

The characters are totally made up, I promise.

Finally, if you enjoyed *Keep Your Friends Close*, I'd be grateful if you could leave a review. It's a big ask, I know, but every one of them helps the writer. (e.g. on Amazon, Goodreads, etc.)